HERE'S WH
ARE SAYIN(
ACCIDENTAL DEMON SLAYER SERIES.

"With its sharp, witty writing and a unique characters, Angie Fox's contemporary paranormal debut is fabulously fun."
—*Chicago Tribune*

"This rollicking paranormal comedy will appeal to fans of Dakota Cassidy, MaryJanice Davidson, and Tate Hallaway."
—*Booklist*

"A new talent just hit the urban fantasy genre, and she has a genuine gift for creating dangerously hilarious drama."
—*RT Book Reviews*

If you're looking for a funny paranormal romp with a little heat and lots of action, this book is for you.
—*Fresh Fiction*

"Filled with humor, fans will enjoy Angie Fox's lighthearted frolic."
—*Midwest Book Review*

"This book is a pleasure to read. It is fun, humorous, and reminiscent of Charlaine Harris or Kim Harrison's books."
—*Sacramento Book Review*

The Last of the
DEMON SLAYERS

NEW YORK TIMES BESTSELLING AUTHOR
ANGIE FOX

MORE BOOKS FROM ANGIE FOX

The Accidental Demon Slayer series
The Accidental Demon Slayer
The Dangerous Book for Demon Slayers
A Tale of Two Demon Slayers
The Last of the Demon Slayers
My Big, Fat Demon Slayer Wedding

The Monster MASH trilogy
Immortally Yours
Immortally Embraced
Immortally Ever After

Short Stories
Gentlemen Prefer Voodoo
(from the My Zombie Valentine anthology)
Murder on Mysteria Lane
(from The Real Werewives of Vampire County
anthology)
What Slays in Vegas
(from the So I Married a Demon Slayer anthology)

To learn more about upcoming releases, sign up for
Angie's quarterly newsletter at www.angiefox.com

CHAPTER ONE

Here's some advice: when a gang of geriatric biker witches tells you they've cleared out all of the spells they left at Big Nose Kate's Biker Bar in 1977—don't believe them.

I was on edge that cold-as-death March afternoon, and it wasn't just the biker witches and their Jack Daniels brand of magic. Something in the air didn't feel right.

Like smoke on the horizon.

I killed the engine on my Harley and planted the toes of my black leather boots on the cracked blacktop. The early spring breeze melted through my riding jacket, sending goosebumps skittering up my arms.

We were on the hunt for a new headquarters for the Red Skull witches. And while I'd suggested a cute bungalow on the shore or perhaps a progressive retirement community, Grandma and the gang had their hearts set on this boarded-up wreck of a place near the New Jersey turnpike.

Dimitri pulled up on my right, handsome as sin in a black leather jacket and shades. "Trouble?" he asked, studying me.

"How'd you know?"

The side of his mouth cocked into a grin. "I know

you."

Did he ever. Heat pooled low in my belly at the thought of exactly how well this man knew me.

The witches hooted and hollered as they dismounted behind us.

"I don't know where it's coming from," I told Dimitri.

I reached out with my demon slayer powers, trying to get a grip on the energies that threatened us.

The low-slung brick building sagged with age. Old beer signs and jumbled blinds crowded the windows. A hand-painted sign read: *Big Nose Kate's—The more you drink, the better he looks.*

It was the last holdout at the end of a long-abandoned road. Woods surrounded the bar on three sides, like an impenetrable barrier. A light fog swirled, making the whole place seem even more isolated and empty.

I held still, on high alert. "I think it's everywhere."

He eased off his bike. "Okay. I'll fly around the perimeter. You check out the bar."

I tried to hide my surprise. "You trust me?" Dimitri was forever trying to protect me.

"I do," he grinned. He knew. "You can handle it."

Dimitri could handle himself too. "Be careful."

His eyes met mine. "Always."

He strolled toward the woods, motioning to Flappy, an adolescent dragon we'd adopted a few months back.

I tugged off my helmet and hung it from the right handlebar of my bike, fully aware of the churning in my gut.

Whatever was wrong here, I'd find it.

Grandma lumbered toward me, gravel crunching under her Drill Sergeant-style motorcycle boots.

"Told you it was a beaut." Her long gray hair tangled over her shoulders. She squinted against the setting sun, making her wind-burned cheeks bunch and look even rosier. Grandma wore suede chaps, an American flag bandana and a black leather jacket with *Kiss My Asphalt* written across the back in rhinestone studs.

"Something's up," I said. The air held a sizzle of anticipation.

"I don't feel anything," Grandma said.

I watched a winged griffin soar from the trees and toward the setting sun. A gangly dragon tottered behind.

"Why don't you all stay outside for a minute?" I asked, expecting an argument.

Instead I got a wink from a tattooed witch named Bettina. "You heard the demon slayer." She let out a whoop and dashed toward a broken-down Ping-Pong table in the parking lot. A dozen others followed.

Grandma peeled off her black fingerless riding gloves. "What is it, Lizzie?" she asked, her voice gravelly as if she'd spent the last century breathing semi-truck exhaust. She adjusted her chunky silver rings. "Because I tell you, Big Nose Kate's is warded like Fort Knox."

I had faith in Grandma and her magic. But I had to trust my instincts too.

The biker witches shouted to one another as they scavenged along the tree line.

"It's hard to say what's wrong yet," I said, "other than the fact that Creely is about to chop down some pool cues."

I nodded toward the giddy engineering witch as she headed for a spindly evergreen, toolbox in hand.

Grandma trundled off to investigate while I swiped the key to Big Nose Kate's from her chrome-studded saddlebag. It was the only way I could do this alone.

I kicked aside chunks of asphalt as I made my way

to the bar.

I didn't like this place. I stiffened as I caught a flicker of movement in the far left window. The haggard blinds began to sway. Maybe it was just a rat, or better yet, a ghost.

Somehow, I doubted I'd be that lucky.

"What are you?" I murmured, the back of my neck prickling as I trailed my fingertips along the barbed wire framing the front door. I felt the familiar hum of my grandmother's wards, left to protect the building against intruders. Yet there was something else as well. It throbbed low and steady underneath.

I braced a hand on the old wood door and listened for subtle changes in the magic. I coaxed it out until I could almost see it.

"Gotcha," I said, running both hands along the door, up to the edge of the barbed wire. This was the same touch of energy I'd felt when we first pulled up to the place. I could almost taste a smoky, burning presence. It was stronger here at the door. "Who made you?"

The barbed wire began to curl toward my fingers and I jerked them back. Just because Grandma's wards recognized me didn't mean I wanted them to get too friendly. Like most of her spells, they were a bit too prickly for my taste.

I took a deep breath and inserted Grandma's key into the lock. The iron bolt opened with a creak and a poof of smoke and sparks.

Big Nose Kate's was cold and dark. I wrinkled my nose at the smell of old bricks and a healthy dose of mildew. But there was something else in the bar.

It smelled like death.

Judging from the laughter and boot clomps echoing up the walk I had about two seconds to figure this out by myself.

I eased past an overturned barstool and shrieked as I

walked right into a spider web.

"Hells bells!" I scrambled to snatch the sticky mess off my face. Yes, I'd gone eyeball-to-eyeball with a demon, a possessed werewolf and a virtual army of imps, but it didn't mean I enjoyed getting bugs up my nose.

"Why, Lizzie Brown," Grandma chuckled from the front door, "you're hopping like a cricket in a frying pan."

"Don't be ridiculous," I said, forcing myself to stand perfectly still. I had a reputation to uphold, however shaky it might be.

I yanked at a piece of web tickling my nose. It ended up being the spider—a big, fat, bubbly-butted spider. This time, there was no mistaking the shriek as I launched it halfway across the bar.

Grandma bellowed in delight as I rubbed at my cheeks, my chin, my hair until I was sure the bug didn't have any friends, and in the process, transferred the sticky mess of a web from my face to the leg of my brand new black leather pants.

Yuck.

Meanwhile Grandma was doubled over, tears in her eyes.

"Cut it." We had real problems here.

"Sorry," she said, trying to catch her breath. "Here you are this bad-ass demon slayer…"

It would take more than a spider to change that.

"Stay behind me," I said as the hairs on the back of my neck began to tingle. I'd been feeling a disturbance for the past fifty miles.

"Look," she said, straightening and wiping her eyes, "we stayed outside while you John Wayne'd your way in here. But take a gander. Our wards held."

True. Still, "something's wrong."

"Tell me about it." Creely planted a hand on the

door jamb behind us. "I don't know how we're going to get the Ping-Pong table through the door."

It was strange none of the witches could sense it. Grandma's coven had spent thirty years on the run from a fifth-level demon. Any one of them could spot a hex from a half-county away.

An icy breeze whipped through the door behind us and I shivered. "I don't like this place."

"Are you kidding? It's perfect!" Grandma said, tossing a Light 'em Up spell. Bulbs flickered to life across the bar, even the ones that had broken in their sockets or fallen to the floor. Nice trick.

I scanned the window where I'd seen movement earlier. There was nothing but mangled blinds and a smudge in the dust.

And then I focused on the rest of the tavern...

A wreck of a Harley lay crushed on top of a wooden pool table in a snarl of green felt and shattered timber. Whiskey bottles covered in three decades of grime hunkered together behind a long oak bar. Pickled egg jars held up a handwritten sign advertising $1.00 drafts.

I wrinkled my nose. "You left it this way?"

"It was easier than cleaning," Grandma said. She slapped me on the back. "Lighten up, Lizzie. The wards in this joint helped us hide from a fifth-level demon for almost a year. We're safe. And we're about to have a very good time."

I surveyed the well-used barstools and the peanut shells still strewn across the floor. "You say this place is soaked in protective magic."

That meant whatever I was feeling had to be coming from outside. I hoped Dimitri was all right.

"Something's been chewing on the Steel Trap wards, but we can fix that tomorrow. Meanwhile, we've got defensive spells above," Grandma said, jamming a thumb toward the ceiling.

I followed her gaze. "Looks like graffiti to me." Black marker scrawls streaked across the orange tiles.

Hell's half acre.

Lusty Lucinda rides like a girl.

Midnight bugs taste best.

"It's not always what you can see," Grandma remarked.

Good point.

"Okay. Fine. Let's stay the night." I was about to let out the breath I'd been holding when a streak of red shot out from under the dusty jukebox and darted straight for my head.

"Incoming!" I ducked and heard it splat into Grandma's leather jacket.

Ant Eater, Grandma's second in command, guffawed behind her. "Hot Foot Spell!"

Grandma cursed, hopping on one foot. "You gonna help me get rid of it?"

"No. I'm going to enjoy it," Ant Eater said.

I stared at Grandma. "You left live spells in here?" I couldn't believe it. Then again, this was the Red Skulls we were talking about.

Grandma ground her steel-toed boot into the floor while she dug the sticky glob of a spell out of her jacket and flung it at Ant Eater.

I was about to tell her it served her right when a wet spell slapped me upside the head. "Ow!"

Ant Eater's eyes widened. "Oh hell."

"What?" I demanded. My forehead stung where it hit. I touched it and felt a hard knot.

She turned to the mess of witches behind her. "We have a situation!"

My scalp started to tingle. "What is it?" Some of these spells could be really dangerous. I couldn't *believe* Grandma just let them fly around loose.

Anybody could have walked in here over the years.
What if the wards had weakened and some kids had
wandered by? What if a homeless person had needed a
warm place to stay? Heck, even a burglar deserved
better than to be hit by random magical incantations.

"Hey!" I protested as Ant Eater mashed her
fingernails against my forehead and pulled away a
quarter-sized piece of flat rubbery goo.

"Ohhh…" A witch with a blond bouffant pushed
her way through a growing number of gray-haired,
leather-clad oglers. She planted a manicured hand on
each of my cheeks and studied the point of impact.
"Tar and feathers, Lizzie," she exhaled, sending out a
waft of cigarette and bubble gum breath. "I don't know
how we're going to fix this."

My stomach churned. "As long as it's not deadly
I'm fine," I said.

"It won't kill you. But it might just make you cry a
little bit." Chomping her gum, she dug through her
white purse until the fringe at the bottom shook. "It's
more of a beauty-product emergency."

She had to be kidding. "Beauty product?" These
witches did mud masks the old fashioned way—by
riding through puddles. Well, all except for Frieda.

"Here ya go," she said, handing me a rhinestone-
studded compact.

I took it and gasped. My hair was gray. Steel gray.
Which would have been fine except it had been black
about a minute ago.

"What did you do?" I demanded.

I'd had three gray hairs in my entire life. Three.
And I plucked them as soon as I saw them. So this?
Well, this was unacceptable.

"It looks nice," Grandma said, not really paying
attention to me as she ran her boot along the bottom
rung of a bar stool.

"It doesn't look nice," I said, panic rising. "That's what people say when they don't know how to fix things." I turned to Frieda. "But you can reverse this because you are a Red Skull biker witch and you know your magic."

"Well..." Frieda chomped at her gum, buying time. "It's less magic and more...hair enhancer. It used to be platinum blonde. I guess it got old." She tested a lock of my hair between her fingers. "Problem is, it's the permanent kind. We brewed it so you don't ever have to worry about dyeing your hair again. No other color will take."

Oh no. Wrong answer. "Well then you'd better figure out how to fix it. Now." I had a big date tonight. Finally. Dimitri and I had been trying to get something going for quite some time now and no biker witch spell was going to blow it for me.

"Okay, okay," she winced, "don't get all Red Skull on me." Frieda brightened. "Hey, you're acting like one of us and now you look like one of us—"

"Frieda!" We didn't have time.

She sighed, as if I was the difficult one. "Okay, darling, here's the poop: you're going to be gray from here on out unless we can get your head under the sink and brew up a counter spell in the next two minutes. Does the water run in this place?"

Soon after, I had my head under a rusty faucet in the ladies room while Frieda rubbed oily gunk into my hair. I'd stripped off my coat and stood freezing in a purple leather bustier, which was my demon slayer trademark of sorts. Although right now I doubted I'd impress too many bad guys with my shivers.

"There's something glowing in the corner," I said, straining to see.

"Head straight," Frieda said, adjusting my neck. "It's only a Lose Your Keys spell and we're already staying put." Her fingers dug into my scalp as she rubbed. "You just be glad your dog was able to get us some dragon feathers, or you'd be a silver-haired beauty for the next seventy years."

"I didn't even know dragons had feathers," I mumbled to the rusted sink.

"That's 'cause you never petted one behind the ears!" I nearly jumped sideways when my dog ran a cold nose under my pant leg and above my sock. "I have a whole collection. Gray ones and blue ones and white ones...I even have a pink one, but it's kind of smushed."

"Pirate!" My Jack Russell Terrier had started talking to me the day I came into my demon slayer powers. Real words. Call it a side effect. Pirate liked to say he'd always talked and it was me who never listened.

He gave a wet doggie snort against my shin. "Why are you getting a bath in the sink? Did you roll in something good? Was it stinky? 'Cause I found a dead chipmunk outside and I don't mind sharing."

"Go get a hair net," Frieda told my dog. "And ask Bob to pour a shot of Jack."

E-yak. The black muck and dragon feathers were bad enough. "You're going to pour whiskey on my head?"

"Nah. I'm just thirsty."

Ten minutes later, I stood with what looked to be motor oil glooped through my hair, with half my split ends stuffed through a two-sizes-too-small hair net. Then Frieda handed me a cowbell.

Oh yes, I was hot date material. I glanced at the door. He should be back soon.

"Is the bell really necessary?" I sighed at the parade of biker witches clomping past me. Most of them were holing up at the bar—Frieda included. The others were gathering the last of the renegade spells and other flying surprises, a little too late in my opinion.

Frieda tossed back a swig of beer and grinned. "That may look like an ordinary old cowbell. But I enchanted it like a genuine egg timer. The dragon feather cocktail must stay on your head for exactly thirteen minutes thirty-seven seconds or I'm not responsible for what happens next."

She paused expectantly. "Okay. You got me, Lizzie. Want to know what happens next?"

"Not exactly."

Besides, I'd already set my Swiss wrist watch. It had been a gift from my anal, adoptive parents to my equally anal self. It was silver, tinted pink, which is how I used to like things. My watch told precise time, was waterproof up to 12,800 feet and I didn't go anywhere without it.

"At 5:20 or thereabouts," Frieda began.

"5:20 and twelve seconds," I corrected.

She waved me off. "You will dunk your head in the sink and I will douse it with water. Capiche?"

At least she couldn't drink much more in the next thirteen minutes.

"Okay. Well try not to get it on the leather." I looked down to my mussed black leather pants. I had some clean ones in my saddlebag, but I'd rather save them for tomorrow. Besides, I'd be changing soon into this slinky red sweater dress I'd found at the Ann Taylor Loft Outlet while the biker witches rode the SeaStreak Ferry, looking for mermaid scales. Evidently, we'd arrived during molting season. Lucky us.

Some days, I couldn't believe the things I had to put up with. But then there were the times that made everything worth it. Take tonight, for instance.

Any moment now, my sexy-as-sin boyfriend would

be walking in the door. Dimitri and I had been to hell and back—twice—but we'd never been on a real date. Tonight would be the first time.

If we made it that far.

Last time we thought we could relax, we were attacked by an army of imps. Then we spent four months in Greece. You'd think we could have squeezed in a date somewhere. But we spent most of our time re-building Dimitri's estate. Then every time we tried to leave, one of the biker witches blew something up. Or my dog got loose with his dragon. Or Zebediah Rachmort, my mentor, decided he needed me *right then* because conditions were perfect for me to levitate or slow down time or visualize.

That last one really got me. It didn't make any sense to sit around and ponder my abilities. And before you say anything, pondering is different than planning. When I outline a strategy, I have a clear goal in mind. I'm not just sitting around wondering about things.

Now that Rachmort had gone back to Boca Raton and we'd landed here, I could move from visualizing my hot-as-sin griffin without his jeans—or anything else—and start realizing it.

In fact, Dimitri and I promised ourselves once we got back to the States, we would ditch the witches and the dog for at least one night a week. We'd talk, we'd cuddle—we'd date.

Although frankly, right now I'd be relieved to see Dimitri whole and unharmed.

He had a habit of picking dangerous assignments and then trying to do them by himself. Yes, he was a big, bad griffin and did just fine on his own. Still, I didn't want to think of him getting into trouble out there.

I rubbed at the tension in my shoulders, my wrist brushing the cold sludge in my hair. *Focus on what you can control.* I simply needed to wait for the bell to jingle, rinse out the spell and get back to normal.

If only things were that easy.

Three loud knocks sounded at the door.

It wasn't Dimitri. He wouldn't have knocked for one thing. And I'd have sensed him for another.

I looked to the witches at the bar. They hadn't noticed, which was strange. I focused my demon-slayer powers and detected the unmistakable scent of death on the other side of the door, like rotten cherries and burned hair.

My throat went dry.

Relax. I was the Exalted Demon Slayer of Dalea. I could deal with this. Even if I'd only inherited the job less than a year ago.

I flung open the door and was hit in the face by the same smoky, burning sensation from before, only this time it was a hundred times stronger. A black crow stood on the porch. The thing was massive—the size of a house cat with a shiny black body. It spread its wings wide and screeched.

"Holy Hades," I gasped, my fingers dropping to the razor-sharp switch star I always kept on my utility belt. That's when I realized the bird was dead. Its eyes were milky and vacant rather than black and beady. As it turned from the porch, I saw it had been run over. The back of its skull caved in and its spine twisted at an impossible angle.

My heart sped up.

"A zombie crow," I whispered, unable to take my eyes off the thing.

It turned back to me. "Reeeaaawrk!"

The dead bird's cry sent new shivers up my spine. "What do you want?"

It uttered another unearthly shriek.

Before I could decide what that meant, a tower of

flames shot up from the woods beyond the bar. "What the—?" It blasted us with a wave of hot wind and flecks of dirt. The crow stumbled against my leg, and I took a quick step back. I rubbed the grit from my mouth and eyes as the fire crackled orange against the bare trees of the forest.

Caw! Caw! The bird beat its wings and urged me to follow.

Sure. A zombie bird wanted me to ditch Big Nosed Kate's Biker Bar and head out into the woods toward a tower of flame, which—I was starting to realize—did not seem to be burning any of the trees.

The door remained closed behind me. It seemed no one in the bar had noticed the knocking or the zombie crow.

Okay, well, I had five minutes.

CHAPTER TWO

I set my watch alarm to give me a two-minute warning and strode off across the parking lot after the zombie bird.

This wasn't a high point in the history of 'great moves.' For one thing, I'd left my coat slung over Ant Eater's barstool. There'd been no way to get it without drawing attention. For another, my hair was sopping wet and slathered in a now-icy spell around my head. I usually—no, strike that—I *always* planned better than this.

At least I was armed.

I had five switch stars and a demon slayer utility belt made by my Great Great Great Aunt Evie. The leather had cracked in places and I'd had to repair some of the side pockets and flaps. But this belt fit as if it were made for me. I liked having something passed down from a great slayer. Besides, who was I kidding? The last time I'd made anything from leather was when I made a wallet at Girl Scout Camp. We won't even talk about how that turned out.

I'd loaded the side pockets with crystals my mentor had given me—most of them designed to help me sit and ponder. Then I'd added a vial of mace and a cell phone with a GPS system.

Too bad I'd left off a flashlight holder.

My emerald necklace warmed against my skin. It was loaded with defensive magic from Dimitri and tended to morph into an interesting shield right before the bad guys flung something at my head.

For now, though, the teardrop emerald merely slapped against my chest as I jogged to the edge of the parking lot. It was as if it had no defense for what was out here.

Lovely.

At least I had my demon slayer instinct for running straight toward danger. Most people avoided large bears, poisonous snakes and angry trolls. I was drawn to trouble like a preacher to Sunday supper. I'd learned to control it in the last few months. I no longer made a beeline toward pushy mall salespeople. Instead, I headed straight for supernatural fire storms.

Dead leaves and sticks snagged at my boots as I made my way through the woods. Every few feet or so, I had to duck around spindly branches and brush. The crow fluttered from one skeletal tree to the next, stopping once in a while to caw at me as if I were cramping its style.

I shot it a dirty look as I stumbled over a root in true horror-movie style. I was going as fast as I could with only the light cast by the wall of flame ahead. Heaven knew I had no reason to take it slow. It's not like I had much time. I glanced at my watch. Four more minutes. I'd make it out in three.

The glop on my head began to itch. I was never late for anything. And truly, if I was going to be on time for doggie day camp and my manicurist, not to mention my last root canal, I was sure going to be there for Frieda to finish her fix-it spell on my hair. I checked my watch. Three minutes.

As we approached a break in the trees, the bird dropped to the ground. It landed in a ruffle of feathers before tottering the last several yards into a small clearing. I stayed a safe distance behind.

A wall of orange fire fanned out from a bluish-purple center. It towered high into the night, snapping and spitting. I raised my hand in front of my face, expecting more heat, but the air around me remained cool. A tingle ran up my palm and my throat burned from smoke, even though I couldn't see any. I squinted into the blaze of the fire, amazed that the flames didn't touch the trees or even char the ground.

The zombie crow shrieked as it broke the barrier of the flames and lumbered toward its master. It nuzzled up against the leg of a dark-haired man at the center of the inferno. He wore jeans and a white button down shirt. And although his strong features put him at about fifty years old, you wouldn't know it by the way he held himself. He opened his hands to me, demonstrating that he was unarmed. Like that was going to make me trust him.

I stopped at the edge of the clearing next to a fallen log and resisted the urge to wrap my arms around my chest for warmth. I needed to be able to unhitch a switch star. Fast.

"Who are you?" I demanded. Faint traces of sulfur hung in the air. If he wasn't demonic, he was close to it.

"My name is Xavier," he said, as if I should recognize him.

"Xavier the demon lord?" I usually killed the spawn of Satan before I learned their names.

"What?" he asked, genuinely puzzled. "No." He straightened. "I'm not a demon."

Yeah, well he didn't look too far off. "Fine. Whatever. 'Shady character of the underworld.' Either way..." I didn't have the time to argue vague semantics.

I sighed. Since time was ticking and I didn't really have enough of a reason to kill him, I began backing up, feeling my way through the woods. I could very well trip and end up on my rear, but I was not about to turn my back on this guy.

His eyes widened. "Wait!"

"No."

"You have to understand, Lizzie," he said as if he were my teacher or something, "I can't hold this portal open much longer."

He knew my name. Peachy.

"Too bad," I said, continuing my backward walk. "Normally I'd love to stand outside on a cold night and chit-chat with a guy inside a fire wall who may or may not have semi-demonic tendencies," My watch alarm beeped. "But I'm busy right now."

If he wasn't going to kill me, then he could move to the back of the line.

At the moment, all I wanted was a normal head of hair, followed by a night on the town without biker witches, zombie crows or entities who got their kicks standing around in towers of flame, gobbling up my time.

He grinned. "You are absolutely gorgeous."

That stopped me. "Are you hitting on me?" That was new. I reached for a switch star. Maybe I'd give him a warning shot.

He laughed. "It's…" He swallowed hard, grinning. "I know I'm screwing this up, but it's such a shock to actually see you. Lizzie, I'm your father."

That stopped me cold.

"Xavier," he said, as if that explained anything. "Your mom never told you about me?"

"No," I drew the word out, shocked to the core. To be fair, my birth mom and I hadn't been able to discuss much.

"Nothing?"

Like where he'd been for the last thirty years?

He stood looking at me as if he couldn't quite believe it.

"No." The one time I'd met mom, she tried to kidnap me. There hadn't been much of a discussion.

He ran a hand through his hair, almost giddy. "I knew she was going to have you. But I just found out about this," he said, indicating my switch stars.

At least one of us found this amusing. I planted my hands on my hips. "It was a surprise for me too." I hadn't known anything about demon slayers until I became one this past summer. Chalk that up to another discussion I needed to have with my mom. She'd shoved her powers off on me and split.

"I thought you were living a normal, happy life," he said, almost to himself. "Phoenix never said..." The words seemed to be coming faster than he could manage. "You have to understand. Your mother is...different."

No kidding.

Hope flared in his eyes. "But you're not."

I didn't know what to say to that. If he didn't consider a demon slaying preschool teacher to be different, I wasn't about to argue.

He swallowed, his Adam's apple bobbing up and down. "I saw your mom this morning. For the first time since we broke up. And she told me what she did to you."

"Okay."

He was saying these things as if it was all so wonderful, but my brain felt like cotton. I tried to wrap my head around it. My parents had kept track of each other. They still talked, at least they had this morning. My dad was magical.

But I could still smell the sulfur.

What did he want?

My wrist watch dinged. I touched a button on the side. 5:20. "Time's up."

My dad didn't notice. "Your mother and I were never meant to be. But you? I would have given anything to have you in my life."

The tingling on my head eased into a slow burn.

It was too much.

"How do I even know this is true?" I asked. I had to get out of here. "How do I know you aren't some demon in disguise, telling me what I want to hear?"

He dipped his head. "Your mom said to tell you it's okay about the portal. Although she misses her white heels."

Shock zinged through me. Mom had been wearing white heels the day she'd tried to drag me through a portal and away from my destiny.

He was telling the truth. He was my dad. My body felt like lead. "Where were you?"

"I was," he searched for a word, "busy."

Oh help me, Rhonda.

"She thought she was hiding you. For your own good," he added. "But she was wrong. I know you need a dad."

I couldn't say anything around the lump in my throat.

My dad wanted me.

He found me.

His eyes were glossy with unshed tears. "And now, I need a slayer."

Hold up.

"I went to your mother. She was supposed to be the Demon Slayer of Dalea. Then she told me she'd passed it on to you."

Very convenient. "How did you find me?" Was the disturbance I felt from him? Or from something else entirely?

"Lizzie, I got mixed up in something bad."

"Demonic?"

He cringed. "In a manner of speaking." The zombie bird circled his legs like a cat. "But it's not what you think. No deals with the devil or anything like that," he said sheepishly.

"Just come out with it."

He barked out a laugh. "Over an insecure transmission?" He saw my face and lost the attitude. "I need you to come see me in Pasadena. Will you help me? We can fight this thing together."

Heavens to Betsy. "We just got here." And I barely knew him and I had no reason to help him.

His expression was earnest. "I'm sorry I wasn't there for you. But that's in the past now. Lizzie, I need you. I want to get to know you." He gave a sad smile. "We've lost too much time as it is."

I wanted to say yes. I really wanted to.

"I don't know." It was too much too fast. I needed to think.

His gaze touched my switch stars and a corner of his mouth turned up. "You're the last of the demon slayers."

He would have to say that.

My mentor had already told me I was the last of my line.

If my dad truly needed a slayer, I was it.

"Please." He lifted his shirt sleeves away from his wrists.

Holy cow. Someone had burned a mark of the demon into the tender skin above the bend of each wrist. I'd had to get rid of a similar curse. The charred skin formed three swirls, in almost a floral pattern. Squat sides together, lines reaching out to form 6-6-6.

I let out a slow breath. "Jesus, Mary, Joseph and the

mule."

He pulled a thin silver lariat from the back pocket of his jeans. With practiced movements, he tied it into the shape of a hangman's noose. "Take this," he said, hand shaking as he held it out to me. "It will lead you to me."

Tempting.

He certainly knew my weakness—I loved to know exactly what was going on. Then I could plan, which I enjoyed way too much.

I wanted to take my father's silver lariat. Badly. Which probably meant it would either strangle me or poison me, if it didn't fling me straight to hell.

After all, I didn't trust my mother. Why should I trust my father?

He was surrounded by evil.

But was it his fault?

I couldn't be sure.

When I didn't move, the crow took the silver rope and broke the barrier with a screech. It scurried up to me, my dad's present in its beak.

"Drop it," I said.

The bird's milky eyes lolled back in its head as it deposited the rope at my feet. It dipped its mashed head sideways before trotting back to the fire wall.

Slow and steady, I retrieved my father's gift with the tip of a switch star, watching the rope bend and swirl with a life of its own.

My father's image began to fade. "I won't be strong enough to reach you again," he said quietly.

I held his gift out in front of me and watched it try to curl itself around my switch star.

Fabulous. I was a grey haired biker with what appeared to be yet another magical creature clinging to me.

"Then I'll see you in Pasadena," I said, wondering

if my life could get any stranger and knowing this was just the beginning.

Chapter Three

One step at a time. I made my way back to Big Nose Kate's, holding the lariat out in front of me like a poisonous snake. It kept trying to weave itself around my switch star, taking one shock after another as my weapon repelled it. Whatever my father had given me, it wasn't exactly friendly—or smart.

The gloom of the night settled around me.

I had a potentially evil pet, a semi-demonic dad and gray hair.

I tried to look at it objectively.

Maybe I could handle my father. I refused to touch the rope. Which left my hair. I'd never been vain, but still—my hair?

What would Dimitri say?

Just when I was starting to feel attractive and confident. Now I was going to have to wear a hat for the rest of my life. Or one of those turbans you see on old movie stars. Somehow, I doubted they made them to go with cute red sweater dresses from the Ann Taylor Outlet.

My only hope was Frieda got it wrong and we had more time.

I clung to the thought until halfway across the parking lot when the spell on my head sizzled one last time and gave a large poof.

It was pretty much the theme of my life as a demon slayer—forward motion and then—poof.

Maybe I could keep my muddy, smelly outfit on and wind my new red dress into a turban around my head.

Rather than think about my future as a silver-haired beauty, I banged open the door of the bar and headed straight for my grandma. She was running down a checklist of to-do's with Ant Eater and a few other witches. Perhaps I was related to this woman after all.

Her eyes widened and she almost dropped her clipboard as I held up my prize.

"What the hell is that?"

"You tell me." Seeing her, showing her, made it all too real. "It's a gift," I said sarcastically, "from Daddy."

Grandma whooshed out a breath. "Xavier is out there?" She banged her hand on the bar. "Hey, Bob, I need a Critter Trap!"

A ponytailed biker in running pants and a *Ride to Survive* T-shirt dug around in a cabinet below the liquor bottles. He reached up from his wheelchair and sent an empty jelly jar sliding down the bar, Old West style.

"Is Dimitri back yet?" I asked.

"No," Grandma said, worried.

He'll be okay. Please let him be okay.

Grandma held the lid open and I dropped the rope inside.

I watched the whole thing with a sort of numb fascination. "What do you know about him?"

"What I told you," she said, as if I'd whacked my head on a tree.

That she'd barely known him. My mom had never talked about him. I'd spent years craving any scrap of knowledge, any kind of connection. Did I have the same hair as him? Yes. The same eyes? Hard to tell. Would he be as organized as me? I had to have gotten it from somewhere.

Why had he left me?

I didn't know any of the important things and I might not find out even if I did help him.

The lariat bucked and hissed as Grandma popped the lid on top.

I watched her. "If it makes any difference, I asked him for a pony."

Grandma held up the jar and watched the rope attack the glass. "What's he like?"

"I don't know," I answered truthfully. "He seemed to care about me."

She patted me on the shoulder. "Buck up. We'll figure this out."

That's what I was afraid of.

Hells bells. It was bad enough my mother abandoned me when I was just a baby. Now my father, who couldn't even stick around for my birth, just zapped into my life asking for salvation.

"Convocation time, people!" Grandma shouted over my shoulder.

Chairs creaked as the witches clambered off their barstools.

"Wait," I said, planting a hand on her shoulder as Grandma started to take off.

There was one more thing she needed to know.

"He wants me to go see him," I said.

She gave a sour look. "I'll just bet he does." She shook the jar. "We're going to find out what that man really wants."

"You can trace him?"

"Hell, yes." She grinned.

"He made some kind of bad deal. He didn't tell me what." He probably didn't want to scare me off.

"Dang it, Lizzie," she said, flat out frustrated. "You ever think of bringing me out there with you?"

"You weren't invited," I said. She hadn't sensed the presence of my father. She wouldn't have even known he was there if I hadn't just told her.

Two witches leaned past us as Sidecar Bob started handing over candles from underneath the bar. Out of the corner of my eye, I watched Frieda stalk up to me, hands on her hips.

Her blue-shadowed eyes narrowed. "Where in hell's knob did you go?"

"It's a long story."

"Don't worry, Lizzie." Grandma clapped me on the shoulder. "We're going to find out exactly what's going on."

I hoped.

Frieda wrinkled her nose. "Well my spell is fried." She took me by the arm. "Come on."

Grandma walked past me. "Convocation in five minutes," she said over her shoulder.

"Where?" I asked. "In the bar?"

"Nah, we got a better place." Ant Eater showed Grandma a jar full of brackish liquid and the two walked off together.

"Bathroom first," Frieda said, leading me by the neck to the sink in the ladies room.

"It won't do any good. I missed the deadline."

"Don't be such a baby," Frieda coaxed, angling my head over the ancient industrial sink.

I'd blown the cure. "I felt it poof." Frankly, I didn't want to know what was under the black goop on my head.

Frieda snapped her gum and thought about it. "Let's just see what that poof meant." She turned on the faucet and sprayed my head and neck with cold water. "I don't like to make my spells too precise or you lose the element of surprise."

I gritted my teeth against the rivulets of water trickling around my neck and down the front of my kick butt demon slayer bodice. "Did I ever tell you I don't appreciate surprises?" I shouted from inside the sink.

"My stars, where's the fun in that?"

I watched the black water run down into the sink. The biker witches didn't take things seriously enough. Yes, they'd saved my butt more than once. Sure, they could be a kick to hang with. But I just wished they could be a little more focused.

As if answering my unspoken request, Ant Eater banged into the girl's room. "C'mon. Everybody's in the Bathtub Club waiting for you."

I lifted my sopping head. "You've got two dozen witches stuffed in a bathroom?" I wouldn't put it past them.

"No, Einstein. It's the name of Creely's momma's speakeasy. This used to be her bar. When Prohibition hit, they had to improvise." She planted her hands on her silver studded belt. "Grandmamma Creely was a witch too. We're good at winging it."

No kidding.

Frieda shoved my head into the sink. "They brewed gin in the bathtub upstairs, hence the name."

I tilted my head enough to see out. "Don't tell me you've got booze going." They'd barely cleared the Harley off the pool table.

"Nah," Ant Eater waved me off, "we just use it for spells. It's the only badass secret place here, which is what you need for what we're about to do." She grinned, her gold tooth glinting. "Now get. Demons don't worry about hairdos before they attack."

Ant Eater turned to go.

"My dad's not fully demonic," I called after her,

knowing how bad it sounded, "and he's not going to attack."

"If you say so," she said over her shoulder.

I stopped, water running down my back. "Do you know anything?" I asked Frieda.

She shrugged. "I know he showed up when he needed you."

"True. But he didn't realize that I wasn't living a great life with my mom." It sounded lame even to me.

Frieda tossed a towel over my head and I rubbed myself dry. "How does it look?" I pulled the towel back and nearly fell over.

The blonde biker witch cringed.

"Purple?" I bleated. "You were supposed to make my hair black and you made it purple?"

I touched my hair gingerly and fought the urge to cry on the spot. It was lavender, like the flower. Only this was not beautiful and it smelled like motor oil. I ran my fingers through my roots. Every stinking hair on my head was the color of an Easter egg.

Enough. I turned away from the mirror to once again face my hairdresser. Frieda's overdyed blond bouffant suddenly seemed the height of normal.

"I didn't do anything," she protested. "You left it on too long." She leveled a pink-tipped fingernail at me. "I told you to rinse it on time."

"What about non-precise spells?" I demanded.

"I gave you a cowbell."

I was not about to go tromping out in the woods with a cowbell. "And now my hair matches my bustier."

"Hey yeah," Frieda said, impressed. "You might start yourself a new fashion trend."

"Lizzie!" Ant Eater yelled from out in the bar.

"Oh, I'm coming," I stomped out of the bathroom.

Ant Eater stood inside an old wooden phone booth

near the back. A year ago, I would have thought that was strange. Now I was just glad there were no creatures or roadkill souvenirs in there.

"Inside," she said, shoving me past her. She dialed a combination on the rust-flecked rotary phone and a wooden door on the wall slid open.

What was this? Maxwell Smart?

A spiral staircase led straight down. "Welcome to the Bathtub Club," she said as she led me inside. Her leather pants and jacket whooshed loudly in the enclosed space. "It's not as classy as the Cotton Club, but the gin tastes the same."

The old iron staircase shuddered and the air temperature dropped at least ten degrees as we wound our way down. I touched the damp brick wall and it was freezing cold. "Did people use this place?"

"Are you kidding?" Ant Eater gave a sandpapery laugh. "It was the hangout for Monmouth and at least three more counties. I hear the women were loose. Don't tell Creely."

She kicked open an unmarked wooden door and we found ourselves in a 1920s supper club.

The ceiling hung low and I felt the tang of paraffin in the back of my throat. A gorgeous carved bar stood in one corner, a raised bandstand in the other, both of them layered with candles and lounging biker witches. Betty Two Sticks raised her glass to me and winked.

Brass and crystal chandeliers hung with an array of candles. The motley shapes and colors of the tapers clashed terribly with high rent fixtures. Soft light from the flames danced across their faces as their whoops and hollers echoed off the damp brick walls.

"You made it." Ant Eater thwacked me on the arm, her skull and crossbones do-rag hanging crookedly over her forehead. "Finally. Now let's get a move on."

Sure. Why not?

In another life, I would have loved to get a better look at this place. Maybe I'd take Dimitri down here after our date tonight. My insides warmed just thinking about it.

We gathered in a semicircle around a discarded wooden barrel Grandma had commandeered. She'd placed my father's gift on top—still inside the protective jar. It bucked and hissed against its magical cage.

"Nice hairdo." Creely the engineering witch sidled up to me.

I didn't know whether she was serious or not, seeing as Creely had green streaks running through her hair.

It was always the quiet ones.

Frieda took the place next to me.

"Pipe down, people." Grandma eyed the open back door. "Bob, seal 'er up."

I hadn't even heard him come down behind us.

"Just a sec!" He hollered. "I got a wheel stuck in the dumbwaiter."

A rattle sounded, then a series of dull thuds.

Bob's weathered face popped up on the other side of the door. "Easy peasey." He gave Grandma a thumbs-up before the unmarked wooden door hissed closed like an airlock.

The candles burned brighter in the darkness surrounding us.

"Join hands," Grandma murmured.

I took Creely's warm hand and Freida's chilly one. The crowd of two dozen witches drew closer. They closed their eyes and concentrated. The temperature in the room began to rise.

Swallowing hard, I tried to do some thinking of my own. As much as I had every right to grouse over the events of the night—and believe me, I liked to brood—

I needed to let it go for the moment. I closed my eyes and tried to be one with this coven, this place.

For the first time that night, I felt warm.

A grinding noise shook me out of my thoughts. Two of the Red Skulls, along with Bettina the library witch, huffed and struggled as they dragged a battered footlocker to the center of the group.

Bettina wasn't even a hundred pounds soaking wet. She drew her silver hair out of her eyes and kicked the box twice with a steel-toed biker boot. The box groaned and opened with a creak.

She shot us an apologetic glance, still catching her breath. "I haven't had a chance to feed my ingredients tonight. They get testy when they haven't had their supper."

"Are there live animals in there?" I whispered to Frieda, horrified.

"No, honey," she said, her breath tickling my neck. "Live spells. They eat just about anything. Cracker crumbs, leftover lasagna, motor oil. They like to graze. Only Bettina keeps 'em locked up. For obvious reasons."

My head began to itch, but I knew better than to break the circle.

Grandma lit three red candles around the jar of rope. She blew out her match and deposited it on the table. Eyes on the jar, she held out her hand. "Okay, give me the enchanted eyeballs."

My stomach squinched. "From what?" I whispered.

I could feel Creely's impatience. "From your dinner last night. Or did you forget how you went to town on that poached salmon?"

Okay. Never mind.

The biker witches never let anything go to waste. Bettina had soaked the eyeballs in something clear and I suddenly felt bad for ever liking croquettes with lemon glaze.

The flames burned brighter as the silver rope began to growl and hiss. It threw itself against the glass like a wild beast. Boy was I glad I hadn't tried to touch it. And for about the tenth time, I wondered just how desperate my dad had to be to give me such a gift.

Maybe I should be glad he was never around at Christmastime.

The other ingredients clacked together as Bettina unscrewed the lid. With two bony fingers, she plucked a single eye out of the mixture and examined it. "Oh yes," she crooned at it like a pet. "Nice and fat. You'll do a good job for us, won't you?"

"Now?" Grandma asked.

Bettina nodded as Grandma pulled out an old Swiss army knife. It was as long as her palm, with an unending number of gadgets. She drew out the corkscrew and, as the rope reared and attacked, she drilled a tiny eyeball-sized hole in the top of the jar. "Ready everybody?"

The witches drew together, and I felt the magic build. For a moment, the room was completely quiet except for the hissing of the rope. The air grew heavy as candles leapt and danced.

Grandma bowed her head and the witches followed suit. "We, the witches of the Red Skull bind together now. We call on the magic that has sustained our line for more than twelve hundred years. In it, we find warmth, light and eternal goodness. Without it, we perish. This night, divine the true nature of this gift before us. Let us seek the greater good for our sister Lizzie and for the magic that empowers us."

I sucked in a breath. For all my abilities, it always amazed me just what these witches could do.

Grandma drew her hands around the jar once, twice, three times before she dropped the eyeball inside. We watched with rapt anticipation as the eyeball latched on to the enchanted rope and burrowed until we could no longer see it.

The rope thrashed like a stuck pig. It slammed against the side of the jar, squealing before it shuddered and fell limp. Grandma held her hands over the concoction, her eyes closed tight.

"Ostendo," she uttered, as if forcing the words from somewhere deep inside. *"Ostendo!"* She repeated, louder this time.

I stared at the jar in front of her, then back to her face. Her skin had gone pale. Red color rose to her cheeks. *"Ostendo!"*

Her face contorted. "The man you saw *is* your father, Lizzie. He came to you because he needs your help."

I'd already known. I'd felt that connection.

The rope began to smoke and hiss in the jar. Grandma struggled to maintain her hold on her vision.

"What your mother didn't know. Wait. She knew! What your mother didn't tell me is your father saw... No. Knew... No –" Her eyes flew open. "Holy crap, your dad is a fallen angel."

"What?" I blurted.

Frieda clutched my hand harder and yanked.

"Ow!" A fallen angel? I'd detected death and sulfur. I'd never met an angel before, but I doubted they smelled like demonic minions. And another thing—if he was an angel, that meant I was half angel and that was too impossible to contemplate.

It had taken almost a year to get used to the fact that I was a demon slayer. I was still learning to control those powers and now I might be something completely different.

Being a demon slayer meant I could levitate, slow time and fry bad guys on occasion. But it still meant I was fully human.

And now?

If I was part angel, I wasn't all human.

I wanted to leave. I had to get out of there and think about this. I had to tell Dimitri. He'd know what to do. We could turn our date into a therapy session.

Heaven above.

I looked around the room, to the circle of witches. They watched Grandma.

"Hold it together, Gertie," Ant Eater warned her.

Grandma shook her head, focusing hard. "Damn it, Phoenix. Why didn't you tell me?"

Because Phoenix, otherwise known as my mom, was a royal jerk. Not only did she shove off her demon slaying powers on me, it seemed she neglected to tell anyone she'd been running around with a fallen angel.

Grandma swallowed, collecting herself. "Sorry."

Considering the circumstances, she was doing better than I was. My mind could barely hold a thought. I forced myself to slow down.

Relax.

Focus.

I'd always prided myself on my control, and if there was ever a time to shut up and take it in, it was now.

The rope grew still and began to smoke as Grandma redoubled her efforts. "Why, Xavier? Why did you come back now?" She struggled, her mouth hanging open, her eyes fixed on something none of the rest of us could see.

"Grandma?"

Her eyes bugged out. "Your dad's been fiddling with the wrong side, Lizzie. He made some bad friends." Sweat beaded on her forehead. "He might not have known what he was doing. Hell, he'd better *not* have known what his jackass friends were pulling. Either way, he got demoted."

"Before or after he had me?" It was a selfish thing to ask, but darn it, I needed to know.

She just shook her head, concentrating. "He tried to work his way back, but now he's really struggling. Dang it. I can see why he needs you. Hell and damnation!"

"What?" I demanded.

She struggled to pull out the last bit of information as the enchanted lariat caught fire. Grandma fought as it burned to ashes.

When it was gone, she lifted her head and stared right at me.

"What?" I repeated, leaning as far as I could without breaking the circle. "So I'm a half angel." Or half fallen-angel. "He's a fallen angel." I was good. "He has to have some good, right?"

Grandma trembled slightly. "He does." She glanced at the charred remains of my dad's gift. "Even after this booby prize. I think it was hexed to compel you straight for Pasadena."

"Like a magical lasso?"

Grandma frowned. "Or a noose."

"Did he know I'd find all this out?" I asked.

"Nope. Most people don't see us coming."

Frieda grinned, but Grandma wasn't in the mood. "I don't want you going. I don't want us to go," she said to the group. "It's foolhardy, and it's dangerous. Xavier's soul is not our problem."

Okay, so I could tell Grandma had never been too keen on Xavier, but since when did she give a fig about foolhardy and dangerous?

I could tell there was something else. "What is it you're not telling me?"

She eyed me. "If you don't go, your father is going to fall farther," she said, automatically. "He can't help it. Forces are in motion against him."

I didn't understand. "But how can he fall more? He was an angel and now he's not."

Frieda squeezed my hand. Grandma planted her hands on her hips, searching for words. Ant Eater took the blunt approach. "He's going to go demonic."

"What?" I stopped for a moment, shocked.

Oh geez. Who was I kidding? Hadn't I detected some demonic tendencies? Didn't I smell the sulfur on him? He'd allied himself with death.

Grandma sighed. "I'm sorry, Lizzie."

"Yes, well so am I." This was my father we were talking about. Yes, he was creepy and I didn't care for the way he'd tried to compel me or how he'd tried to trick me. But I wasn't going to damn him to hell for it. "You say he's going to go demonic unless we do something about it."

"We?" Grandma balked.

"Fine. Me." I was the demon slayer.

"Lizzie, you don't owe that man anything."

"Only my life," I said. Technically, it was true. Even if I didn't know him, I couldn't help but feel for him. I owed it to him to at least see if I could help. If I didn't try, I'd never forgive myself.

Grandma watched me, unhappy.

Dimitri would understand. Why couldn't Grandma?

She could frown until her face froze that way. There was no way to ignore the final, awful truth. "You realize if he does fall all the way and becomes a demon, I am a demon slayer."

"I know what you are," she snapped.

I'd have to kill my own father.

I opened my mouth to say it and realized I couldn't. She knew.

It was too much. My head hurt. I rubbed at my temples, knowing it wouldn't make a lick of difference. "Do you want to be on the run again?" I asked. "What if he comes after me because I didn't help him?"

What if he came after me and I couldn't destroy him?

I'd rather not have to find out. I really didn't want to know that yes, I could kill my father. To save my friends and my new family, I would. It would be gut wrenching and horrible and I knew I'd never be the same person again if I did it.

"Face it, Grandma," I said to her and the rest of the Red Skulls. "Saving him is a lot easier than the alternative."

Besides, it was the right thing to do.

Grandma stared at me long and hard.

"We just got here." A witch in the back protested.

"I know." It was a lot to give up. These witches hadn't had a home in more than thirty years. "We can come back," I said.

"When?" Another witch grumbled.

I didn't have an answer to that. I was asking them to sacrifice for a person they didn't know. Heck, I had barely met him. They'd worked my entire lifetime to get back to the place where we now stood and I was asking them to give it up.

"Can it wait?" Frieda asked. "I haven't even finished cleaning the cobwebs out of the shower curtains."

That, I could ignore.

"This isn't our battle," Grandma said to the group, her eyes still on me, "but I haven't known any of you to walk away from a fight that needs to be won."

She dug her hands into her pockets. "I'd like to settle down too, but I don't think I could relax knowing we could save a man from eternal damnation. Lizzie hasn't always asked for our help, and sometimes we've wanted to skin her for it. Now she's asking. I'm not going to say no."

The witches began murmuring among themselves. Grandma spoke louder. "Anybody who wants to stay here, that's fine. You've earned the right. We won't say a word about it." She drew a deep breath and let it out. "Anybody who sees fit to join us, we're leaving tomorrow morning at dawn." She paused, her eyes fixed on the floor, finding the words.

"I always used to think we were running and fighting because we had a demon on our tail. And that's a damned good reason."

The biker witches chuckled.

Grandma shook her head. "It was more than that. Somewhere along the line, we stopped fighting for just us. I don't want to eek out a living hidden behind wards and our spells. I want to look the devil in the eye and kick him in the teeth. I want to say to these creatures, 'No. You will not win. You will not corrupt us or enslave us. You will not own us.'"

She climbed up on the keg. It rattled with her weight, but Grandma was beyond caring. She stood, her black Harley flame boots planted firmly on either side. "We are in charge of what happens in this world. Not them. *Never* them."

"Never!" Several witches bellowed from the back.

"We owe it to everything good to stand up and fight," she bellowed. "So I will go to Pasadena. I will take that man back from the demons. And I will tell them to *go to hell*."

The walls echoed and chandeliers swayed with the stomps and cheers of the biker witches.

Creely slapped me on the back. "I'm there."

"Me too, honey." Frieda hugged me from the side. "We'll get your daddy back."

The flood gates opened as the witches shouted out their support. The circle broke, gin glasses clinked and

I stood there like a fool with a smile plastered across my face. I had a whole coven of bikers behind me.

"We're in this," Frieda brushed a lock of lavender hair from my shoulder, "whether you want us or not."

I did. The decision was made. Dang it all. We were going to Pasadena.

Heaven help us when we got there.

Chapter Four

I stepped out of the phone booth and let it slide closed behind me. Most of the biker witches were still celebrating downstairs, and probably would be for a while. Me? I had some things to figure out.

So far in my time as a slayer, I'd killed the baddies instead of trying to rescue them. I wasn't sure how rehabilitation worked. Even if we could track down my dad, what would we do next? What would we be facing?

I took stock of what remained of my dad's gift, still in the jar. Judging from what he'd given me, I wondered how badly Dad wanted to be saved.

The ashes had settled into a circular groove along the base. I shook it out so they spread across the entire bottom. Within seconds, the particles had flickered back to the edges.

Maybe it was just gravity.

Yeah, right.

Grandma said my dad's creature couldn't harm me now. She told me it was as dead as the zombie crow. I wasn't so sure.

Before I became a slayer, a pile of ashes was a pile of ashes. Now a jar was a magical trap, a spell meant a new hairdo and I still wasn't sure how the biker witches were playing "Freebird" on the jukebox when we technically had no power.

My Jack Russell Terrier bounded up to me amid tables crowded with Burger King takeout bags. Sidecar Bob was in charge of catering. My dog followed him everywhere.

"It's a feast!" Pirate said, skidding right into my leg, his tail thwacking my shin at a hundred and eighty beats a minute. "We have French fries and cheeseburgers and double cheeseburgers and double bacon cheeseburgers…"

"Chow time!" Bob yelled down to the speakeasy. Boots thundered on the metal stairs.

"Bob, have you seen Dimitri?" I asked. He should have been back by now.

Bob tossed Pirate a French fry and shook his head 'no.' "Don't worry," he said, as the first of the biker witches clambered out.

Easy for Bob to say. I scooped Pirate up and buried my nose in the wiry hair of his neck. The heavenly aroma of flame grilled burgers and piping hot fries made my stomach rumble.

Pirate licked my fingers, my arm, my shoulder, pretty much anything he could reach. "You smell fantastic. Smells like you've been roasting meat. Of course you burnt that one," he said, sniffing my jar, "but that's okay. I'll eat it."

That wasn't saying much. Pirate would eat anything. In this case, he couldn't have my dad's crispy minion.

The front door banged open. Everyone in the bar jumped, including me. Dimitri Kallinikos, my long-awaited griffin boyfriend stood in the doorway with a massive white dragon behind him.

"Oh thank God," I said. He was here. He was safe and he was mine.

Dimitri was well over six feet, with the broad

shoulders and sculpted body of an ancient Greek statue. He had a square jaw, olive skin and striking green eyes. Dimitri was out of place in this dingy biker bar, even though he wore jeans and a dark black T-shirt stretched over his broad shoulders.

He had the ability to hold perfectly still, which is lost on most people these days. Even now, his movements were precise as he peeled one of Grandma's thorny wards away from his leather jacket.

I let the tension leave me as I started for him, amazed he still managed to look polished after flying for two hours. Maybe it was the way he carried himself, back straight and always alert. Or maybe it was simply the fact that he really was from another world.

"Flappy!" Pirate scrambled out of my arms and broke into a run the second his paws touched the concrete floor. My dog dashed straight for Dimitri and through his legs as he greeted the dragon.

Flappy's happy squawk ended in an adolescent croak. As usual, Pirate blew the curve when it came to happy reunions.

Still, I wasn't too shabby myself.

"Hey there," I said to Dimitri, feeling my mouth quirk into a grin. Heaven knew I'd missed this man. I didn't like him going out in search of trouble, and not just because it could be dangerous. I just wanted him with me.

"Lizzie," he said with a slight Greek accent that made my name sound almost lyrical. He looked me up and down. "Nice hair," he said without a trace of irony.

Heat crept up my cheeks. Yes, it was ridiculous. I was embarrassed enough. The last thing I needed was for him to remind me.

"I don't want to talk about it." I'd just found out I was part angel. That trumped the hair thing. Besides, it was good having him back. I'd been more worried than I wanted to admit.

"What happened out there?" I asked as he touched his forehead to mine and closed his eyes.

He'd been fighting. The emerald in his eyes betrayed him.

"I'll tell you in a minute," he said. "Not here." We savored a quiet moment and when he opened his eyes again, they'd gone back to a rich chocolate brown.

I reached for him and noticed his ebony hair curled with moisture at the ends. I ran the damp strands between my fingers.

He replied with a melting brush of his lips on mine.

"Why do you always assume we have trouble?" he said against my mouth.

"Other than the fact that we usually do?"

He rumbled out a laugh and pulled me into his arms. "You're just worried about our date." He smelled like warm leather and campfires. I snuggled against him as a toasty feeling wound through me.

Yes, well I had every reason to worry. Ours hadn't been what you'd call a typical relationship.

We'd met when he pulled me out of a hole. I'd wrecked my Harley in an encounter with seven imps and a particularly nasty water nymph. We'd ended our first fight with a trip to hell. Personally, I would have preferred make-up sex. And now we were in another mess. The more things changed, the more they stayed the same.

Call me an old-fashioned girl, but it would be nice to be officially courted.

And then his mouth was on mine, hot and possessive.

Okay, so maybe I wasn't complaining too much.

I curled toward him as he slid hands up the exposed skin of my arms, up my shoulders to cradle my chin. It was a rash, claiming kind of kiss and I loved every second of it.

As if he knew what I was thinking, Dimitri drew me closer until I was flush against him. One of us groaned—I think it was me—as he nipped my neck.

This man was sin wrapped in leather. There's no telling what I would have done if I didn't sense half the bar gaping at us.

I eased back, as the cool air seeped between our bodies. *No need to make a spectacle*, even as my mind conjured up images of us heated and naked and sliding against each other. Sweet heaven.

"Thanks," I said, a little unsteady, "I needed that." I needed him.

His breath came quickly. His eyes were closed and when he opened them, the warmth in them nearly melted me into a puddle on the floor. "My pleasure," he said, making it clear there would be more to come.

My inner vixen did a little happy dance.

"First I have something I need to tell you." He wound his hand in mine.

Pirate jumped up against our legs. "Is it about Flappy?" he asked. "I told him to stay away from your boot laces. I've been training him, see?" Pirate thumped his butt on to the floor. "Flappy's not good at 'sit' and he doesn't know how to 'fetch.' I thought I had him at 'play dead,' till I realized he was sleeping. But I know for a fact I told him to stay away from your boot laces."

To his credit, Dimitri barely cringed. "The way that dragon can spot an ambush, the shoelaces are on the house."

I knew it. "What happened?"

Dimitri bent and rubbed Pirate between the ears. "Look over there," he said, as if letting my dog in on a big secret, "Sidecar Bob ordered extra bacon on his burger, just for you. I'll bet he can find something for Flappy too."

Pirate dashed away, toenails clacking and tail wagging. Dang griffin knew my dog. Seemed everyone did. Pirate was a lot thicker around the middle than he'd been when we started our adventures. Perhaps a doggie diet was in order.

"We found something you need to see," Dimitri said against my ear.

He led me through the maze of witches crowded around tables to the back door of the bar. It was flanked by two rusty lanterns with green floss wound between. One of Grandma's protective spells, I'd be willing to bet. I wondered why she felt the need to re-enforce the back wards rather than the front.

An unearthly howl erupted from the other side of the door. It was a female voice, like a caged animal, only worse.

I rubbed at my arms, and at the goose bumps prickling my skin.

Noticing my discomfort, Dimitri slipped off his coat. "Take this," he said, sliding it over my shoulders.

It felt warm and comforting. Better still, it smelled like him.

"Before we go out there, let me tell you that given the choice, I wouldn't show you this."

"Have some faith," I said, in part to stomp out the dread swelling inside me. "I've scorched imps, fried curses, beheaded a werewolf. I ripped out the blackened heart of a fifth-level demon, for Pete's sake." And I'd potty trained a bus load of three-year-olds. I was actually more proud of that than anything else. "Or wait. Did Grandma tell you about the spider?"

I wouldn't put it past her.

There was no shame in it. I liked things clean,

which meant I hated spiders and their webs.

Dimitri ran a hand through his hair, his shoulders stiff. "This isn't about bugs. This is about our agreement that I tell you everything. Always."

Good. Dimitri had tried to protect me for far too long. It was in his nature as a griffin—fierce, vigilant and loyal to a fault. Still, I had a right to know what was going on, even if the things I'd seen so far in the magical world hadn't been what you'd call pleasant.

Dimitri opened the door to a green-skinned, blue-haired creature chained to the concrete patio. Its gangly fingers and limbs curled as it reared back. A second later, it leaped straight for me.

I whipped out a switch star as chains caught it in midair, holding the monster taut as it hissed and swiped at me, an arm's length from my neck.

Sweet heavens. I clutched my switch star in one hand and braced against Dimitri's wide forearm with the other. "What is that thing?"

It had an almost human appearance, save for an overlong face with sunken eye sockets and razor cut teeth.

"She's an Icelandic banshee," Dimitri said, his voice tight. "They're native to the mountains and glaciers of the high land. When the ice cliffs began thinning out a few years ago, they started migrating south."

The creature shook with predatory menace, her entire body straining against the chain around her neck.

The emerald at my throat began to hum, its bronze chain warming against my skin. Its energy flowed through me like a soft touch.

My stomach twinged. I stood motionless as the bronze metal slid over my skin, snaking down my chest, my hips, my legs and reforming into a pair of soccer-style shin guards.

Against a banshee. I shuddered.

The protective necklace had never been wrong before.

I glanced back into the bar, at the biker witches feasting on Burger King, at Frieda with a cigarette dangling from her lip as she told a story, Pirate eating French fries from Sidecar Bob's unfolded Whopper wrapper. I closed the door, feeling the wards sizzle into place. It would be a disaster if this thing got loose in the bar.

"How strong is the chain?" I asked, watching the rusted metal plates rattle where they attached to the porch.

"It'll hold her," Dimitri said, not sounding as confident as I would have liked.

He couldn't have had much experience with these things. I know I'd never seen one.

"Flappy killed two. I got three. And then we captured this beauty."

"That's a dangerous souvenir."

"I'm hoping your Grandma can take a look at it, tell us who sent it."

The banshee spit. I jumped back, but not before a hissing glob of black tar landed on my shin, right on the bronze guard. It sizzled like a fried egg.

"Don't move." Dimitri had one eye on the creature as he made it to my side.

I let the banshee slobber burn itself out on my armor-plated shin as my attacker stalked me with hungry purple eyes.

My breathing quickened. "This thing is seriously messed up."

"I couldn't agree more," Dimitri said, favoring his side. I hadn't noticed before.

"What happened? Are you hurt?" He let me push his shirt away to reveal a fist-shaped gash in his lower abdomen.

"Banshee bite," he said.

"It looks awful." It was red and raw, his skin seared around the edges from the banshee's saliva.

"Thanks," Dimitri groaned. "The cold air makes it sting even worse."

That wasn't a sting. That was real pain. The creature had sunk its teeth into Dimitri. It was like nothing I'd ever seen before. "It tried to *eat* you."

He cringed against another wave of pain. "They're feral creatures, Lizzie. Eating things is what they do—animals, pets, people."

The banshee struggled against the chain, stretching it tight. It watched me. It wanted me. I could see it in its eyes. I cringed as the rusted metal plate ground eerily on its hinges. "Tell me why we're keeping this one?"

I had a split second of *oh no* as the chain snapped.

It leapt straight for me.

Lizzie!" Dimitri threw himself between me and the creature.

It attacked in a blaze of fury, lunging for Dimitri's throat as I fired a switch star.

Dimitri reared back just as the churning blades of my weapon caught the creature between the eyes. The switch star sliced a clean hole through its head. Wet brain matter splattered onto the patio as the banshee fell on top of Dimitri. The creature's jaws slackened and released him.

"Nice aim," he grunted, throwing the corpse off. Black saliva ate at the threads of his torn T-shirt.

"Are you all right?" I rushed to him, with half an eye on the banshee.

Dead wasn't always dead.

Dimitri eased his shirt off smeared the toxic spittle off his shoulder and arm, his skin firm and strong.

"The saliva doesn't affect you?"

"Just the bites," he grunted, inspecting the one on his stomach. It could have been a whole lot worse. "That's why I wear leather."

The jacket that he'd given to me. I ran my fingers down the coat and found gouged leather and bite marks. "You have to stop saving me."

He laughed at that, which didn't make sense at all.

The banshee would have been on me in a heartbeat and if I'd been without my switch stars, a fraction of a second slower, distracted in any way, Dimitri might be dead.

The creature bled mucus onto the ground as I tried to catch my breath. "I hate killing things."

Before I'd come into my powers as a slayer, the worst thing I'd done was stomp a cockroach. Now I killed things all the time. In my defense, they were creatures who wanted to eat me or possess me. Still, it didn't make it easy. The dead banshee reminded me a little of a smashed insect, leaking out its grape jelly insides.

What would happen if I had to kill my own father?

"I don't think the six we killed tonight are the only ones," he said, with a touch of resignation. "Someone knew we were coming and brought a small army here to take us out. Best I can figure, the original drop point was on the driveway out front, less than an hour before we pulled up."

"You don't think they just happened to migrate here?"

He scowled at the creature, broken and bloody on the pavement. "One, maybe. But six? No way. They tend to be loners."

"And if you're going to release six…"

"You'll release a lot more," Dimitri said, finishing my thought.

I sucked in a breath. I didn't want to be running into any more of these things.

Dimitri rose to his feet. He stood shirtless in the glow of the porch light. His chest, well muscled but not overdone, gave him an air of understated sexiness.

He walked toward the beast and squatted over it. "Whoever did it isn't used to working with banshees," he said. "They didn't realize how fast the creatures scatter."

"And we have no idea who set these things loose?"

He shook his head. "That's what I was hoping to learn by bringing this one to your Grandma."

We stared down at the dead banshee.

"Wait." I had to wonder. "Are they after the group, or are they after me?" The banshee had attacked me first, before Dimitri had gotten in the way. It had watched me, as if it were tracking me. And it had gone for the kill. If someone or some*thing* wanted the witches and their magic, it would need them alive.

Dimitri shook his head. "Either way, I don't think we should wander far tonight."

"Which means," I said, my heart sinking to my toes, "we're not going out."

"I don't think it would be smart," he said, looking as sorry as I felt, "at least not tonight."

"I know."

We stood there a moment next to the dead banshee with nothing else to say.

I touched his chest. "We have to bandage that bite," I said, his skin warm against my fingers. A swirl of black hair traced its way down his lower stomach toward a place I knew well.

"Come on." He ran a hand along my back. "Let's get back inside. We'll let your grandma know what's up. After that, you can play Nurse Fix-it and we'll get something to eat."

"Okay." I slipped my hand into his. "But this is not a date."

CHAPTER FIVE

While grandma and the witches buried the banshee, Dimitri and I sat across from each other in a booth at the back of the bar. My crown-shaped chicken tenders didn't taste as good with banshee spit on my shoes and creature dust in the jar on the table in front of me.

But seeing as either one of us could have gotten killed tonight, I supposed we were holding our own.

Dimitri had been pure business as I'd bandaged him up, which had been bad enough. Worse, he'd found a new black shirt.

Rather than think about the attack or our failed first date, I reverted to the most basic of womanly complaints. "I wanted to look good for you tonight and now all of this," I waved a hand at my hair, my ruined pants, heck I probably had a booger in my nose too. It was that kind of night.

If Dimitri was fazed, he didn't show it. "Bob told me what happened."

"It's awful, isn't it?"

He shook his head slowly. "It's more like biker chick sexy."

Right.

Dimitri grinned. "You're a wild woman, Lizzie."

More like wildly embarrassed.

What really killed me was that I wasn't the type to

worry about how I looked. I used to wear basic, sensible clothes. I went for tidy and presentable. Dependable. I didn't waste time on this season's "in" hairstyles or worry about the latest lipstick colors. Long ago, I decided the entire fashion industry was designed to make women feel insecure.

Yes, I admit it—it had felt good to slip into my first pair of leather pants. I felt powerful, sexy. But in the end, it was only a pair of pants. It didn't change who I was.

So why did I care so much about this?

"I just wish I could do something," I groaned.

I needed control.

And it would help if Dimitri stopped staring at my rock star hair. If I didn't know better, I'd think he was turned on.

I found a rubber band in my pants pocket and used it to pull my hair back into a ponytail.

As much as I wanted things to be normal, we had bigger things to consider, like the dead banshee out back and exactly what kind of trouble my father had gotten himself into. Dear old dad showing up and the creature attacks had to be connected somehow.

Before tonight, we'd gone months without being ambushed. Of course we'd been hanging out at Dimitri's villa in Greece. I tried to remember exactly why we'd insisted on coming back to the States. Oh yes, because I needed more than an idyllic life on the islands—sleeping in, sunbathing, watching the witches build small castles—literally—out of the black sand. The Red Skulls never could do anything halfway. Of course it had been hard to explain to the beach patrol.

Even that seemed like fun compared to this.

"Can we go back to Santorini?" I asked, stuffing the remains of my dinner into a Burger King bag.

Dimitri looked thoughtful. "Do you want to return?"

"No," I answered on a sigh.

It was his destiny, not mine. I wasn't quite sure where I belonged.

As much as I loved Dimitri, I couldn't just take up the life of a griffin housewife. Not that we'd ever talked marriage. That was the problem with him—with us. Our past was fiery. Our present was toe-curling, but our future was anything but certain.

I couldn't live in a griffin clan on Santorini. I'd tried. And I didn't think he wanted to spend the rest of his life tearing around on the back of a Harley, hunting demons.

Who would?

Creely slapped both hands onto our table, rattling everything on it. "You got any beer cans?" She reached for my Diet Coke, and shook it. "Good enough."

"Hey," I protested, "I still have a little more in there."

"I can fix that," Creely said, drinking it in a swig.

"Gee, thanks."

But she was already jogging back to Bob, Pirate and a group of witches who were building a beer can tower by the bar.

"You see what I put up with?" I was about to get up and get another soda when the ashes of the rope twitched in Grandma's jar.

Holy Hades. "Look at that."

The particles in the jar rolled over each other as if blown by an invisible wind. They twisted faster and faster until they shaped themselves into a paler version of the silver rope. One end poked against the glass, reminding me of a blind snake, arching and finding its way. It stretched up into thin air, as if looking for something, and then wound back around itself, forming a noose.

"Unreal," I murmured. Of course so was a zombie crow.

We stared at it, waiting for it to do something else, like_I don't know—make rope animals. I was up for anything at that point.

I wished Rachmort were here to see this. He not only had generations of experience mentoring slayers, he was also a necromancer who specialized in lost souls and spiritual apparitions.

Maybe there was a way to contact him. I'd have to talk to Grandma once she finished building the Budweiser tower of Babel.

Dimitri didn't say a word about the reconstituted rope, which was telling. In our half year together, I'd learned he didn't like to state the obvious. We both knew it was evil.

We watched the jar to see what it would do next. Yet once the rope made itself whole again, it seemed content to wind itself around the bottom.

Across the bar, the biker witches let out a collective hoot as Ant Eater launched a dart at the wobbling tower of beer cans.

"So listen to this," I said, in a futile attempt to ignore them. I told Dimitri about my dad, the zombie crow and everything else he'd missed while he was out on patrol.

He placed his hand over mine. "I wish I could have been there."

I nodded, swiping at a few tears.

"We'll fix this," he said.

The kicker was, he meant every word. Leave it to Dimitri to save the world.

I could do it on my own, but thanks to this man, I'd abandoned the notion that I should.

Single kick butt demon slayers who were mad at the world and did everything on their own were fine in the movies, or in books. But in real life, I needed a partner. I wanted Dimitri by my side. Not because I had trouble handling things on my own, but because I wanted someone to share this life with.

I ducked as a dart hit the wall between Dimitri and me.

"The beer can tower is that way," Dimitri said, yanking the dart out of the wall and taking aim himself. His shot went wide. The Red Skulls cheered anyway.

The witches were getting rowdy, which meant it was time for Dimitri and I to turn in. It was either that or try to control them.

Ha.

We stood. "Thanks for killing banshees for me," I said.

Dimitri brushed a kiss along my shoulder and let me step in front of him. "You do a pretty good job yourself."

We waved at the witches, who toasted us and started giving us bedroom tips as we headed for the second floor.

Dimitri placed a protective hand on my back as we navigated the narrow stairs, lit by broken light bulbs. "I don't want to judge my girlfriend's family before I meet them, but let's just say I have a few questions for your dad."

Join the club.

I waited until we reached the top of the stairs before I leaned close. "You'll never believe what Grandma discovered. Turns out I'm half angel."

"Angel?" He nearly sputtered.

"Now why is that so hard to believe?" I asked, enjoying the sight of my mighty griffin nearly speechless.

He leaned back against the brown paneled landing,

"I'm…"

"What? Shocked? Amazed? Freaked out? Take your pick. I'm still trying to decide."

He took my hand and drew me close. "I always knew you were special," he said, caressing the soft spot at the base of my palms. "But angelic?"

"Bona fide," I said, running a finger down his arm. Maybe that's why I'd always been so keen on following the rules.

We began walking down the hall toward our room. We had the third on the left, according to Grandma.

"Now tell me," I said, "What do you know about angels?"

He seemed to search for the right thing to say. "I've never met one."

"Until now," I teased.

He tried to appreciate the joke, but was still too shocked. "Most view angels as agents of the divine, representatives of everything good."

I snorted. "Instead of the things we usually run into."

His mouth twisted into a smile. "You could say that."

"Grandma says dad is a fallen angel," I added.

"A being who has willfully turned away from the light."

He came up with that a bit quickly. "Wait 'till you meet him." And until I was through with him.

We stopped in front of our room.

"It's extremely convenient that your dad didn't tell you what he's done," Dimitri said.

"He said he'd tell me in person. He didn't want any supernatural eavesdroppers."

"We'll see."

"Dimitri, he's my father. I have to help him."

And if I couldn't, if I failed, would I have the

courage to slay him?

"Your father tried to compel you to go see him," Dimitri said.

I really didn't want to talk about this. "What a power," I said, trying to lighten things up. "It's every parent's dream come true."

Dimitri didn't take the bait. "You understand what's at stake here, Lizzie. He wants you badly. He's holding the threat of his damnation over your head." He paused, as if he didn't want to say the rest. "He didn't search you out until he needed you."

"I know." It hurt to admit it even to myself: if my dad truly wanted me, he would have found a way to see me during the last thirty years. "But maybe this is a fresh start, a way to re-connect."

Dimitri frowned. "I hope so. I want that for you, Lizzie. But just remember, he may be your dad, but that doesn't mean you're similar souls."

"It doesn't mean we're not," I reminded him.

For as long as I could remember I'd wondered what my real dad was like. I'd given up on the idea of perfection a long time ago. I wasn't a child.

I'd also learned in my time as a slayer that things weren't always as they appeared. Sure my dad hadn't been there for me in the past, but he needed me now and I owed it to him and to myself to at least give him a chance.

Dimitri's expression remained dark. He'd gone into full protection mode. Heaven help us. "It also says something about him that he'd rob you of your free choice," he said.

"Kind of like the time you chained me to a tree?"

He looked unimpressed. "That was for your own good."

It sure didn't feel like it at the time.

I flicked the light switch in our room and was

disappointed when the room remained dark. Grandma must have forgotten to hex our place. Or maybe the light-em-up spell didn't have an off switch.

"Lizzie." He brushed a lock of hair from my forehead, "I'm always behind you. No matter what."

He truly was my rock, my other half.

"But I wonder if it is a good idea to get involved with your father."

He was the bane of my existence.

I leaned against the door jamb and looked up at him. "You did it for your family."

Dimitri went to hell and back to end the curse on his sisters. Then he fought a rival family's army in order to keep them safe. He'd sacrificed years off his life to train me as a demon slayer, even when he barely knew me, so I could help the people he loved. He wasn't in any position to tell me what I could or could not do for my estranged father.

A muscle in his jaw twitched. He realized it too, even if he refused to admit it. "I want more for you," he said, towering above me in the narrow doorway.

"Believe me." I ran a hand down his chest, stopping above the place where the creature had bitten. "I have everything I need." Despite the mess with my father and the banshee, I was happier than I'd ever been in my life. For the first time, I knew what I wanted—this life, him.

Did he even know what having him meant to me?

His eyes narrowed down to tiny slits as he weighed the options. "If we do this, I want to protect you."

"You already do."

"It's not enough," he said, moving closer.

Yum.

"I'm always willing to accept more emerald necklaces," I teased.

"That's not what I meant," he said, gruffly.

"Leather jackets?" I asked as he nipped at my neck.

He brought his body flush against mine. Double yum. Heat pooled in my belly. "Well if this is some kind of one-on-one body guarding, then I'm all for it."

He touched the emerald at my throat. "Will you accept more of my protection?"

"I can't."

Dimitri's powers were different from mine. While I could levitate, he could shift and fly. When I slowed down time, he could speed it up. It made us formidable. But it also made us weak. When I'd fallen, he'd gone down with me.

It gnawed at me that I could expose him and get him killed.

"We need to each maintain our own strength," I told him.

"Don't risk, don't get too close," he said, completing my thought with a scowl.

I flattened my back against the hard wooden door jamb. "It's not like that." I could see he was hurt, and I hated it.

It wasn't fun, but it was the responsible thing to do.

And there was also a deep, dirty secret I didn't even like to admit to myself: when our relationship ended— and I knew it would—I didn't know what I'd do without Dimitri. I didn't need to make it any worse by entwining my powers with his.

"You think I'm going back," he said, accusing, but not denying he was needed elsewhere, away from me.

"Your destiny is in Greece with your sisters." No head of a griffin clan had ever left their homeland for long. Griffins were conquerors. They craved land and security, and Dimitri had left his holdings wide open. Even being here could leave his sisters open for attack. I cared about him, and them, too much to ignore it.

He ran his hands through my lavender hair. "Why

don't you let me decide what's best for me?"

Stubborn man. "You always do."

Then he leaned in and kissed me and for a second I wanted to pull back and have our conversation. I wanted to tell him I did know what's best and I could handle myself and I didn't really need him but instead I yanked him closer and ground my body against him and never wanted to stop.

His arms wound around me with a resolute, almost bruising strength. He slanted his mouth over mine, deepening the kiss, pulling me against him until suddenly I was on top of him and we were inside the door and on the bed.

"Are you okay?" I tried to move away from his injured side.

"Hush."

He lay over me, heavy and strong and I kissed him wildly. He had way too many clothes on. I nipped his lower lip and he groaned. Yes, yes. He was mine.

I slithered away from him long enough to help ease his shirt off and toss it over his shoulder. Then I went to work on his belt buckle, a little too eager for my own good, but who cared? My body was on fire. Everything in me screamed for this man. For the second time tonight, I knew exactly what I wanted.

And I'd have it as soon as I could master the buckle. "Is this thing welded on?"

Meanwhile Dimitri was at work on my neck, layering hot kisses until I feared I'd melt from it all. "You'd think you'd have enough practice by now."

I gave up and ran my hand along the hard ridge below his buckle. He groaned into my ear.

"And you'd think you'd have an incentive to help."

"I was busy," he gasped, solving my problem with two tugs and a tumble out of bed.

He landed with a thud.

"Are you okay?" I sat up to see my powerful griffin on the floor.

"You'd better be naked by the time I get back up there."

I happily obliged.

He rewarded me with a wet mouth on one breast and then the other, his tongue tugging at my nipples, hot, hungry and oh so skilled. I didn't care if he dragged me down with the dust bunnies as long as he didn't stop.

His cock strained hard against my thigh and I shifted and curled, bringing it into contact with my sex.

"Patience," Dimitri groaned against my breast. He kissed up my chest. "Or I'm not responsible for what happens next."

Silly man.

I kissed him long and deep.

It had been a rough night. I needed him. Now.

"Come here," I said, easing the tip of him into me.

"By the gods." He strained his entire body away from me, but couldn't quite bear to move himself from between my legs.

"Got you now," I whispered, nipping his neck.

He swore in Greek.

I had him. I knew it from the way he moved over me, hungry and wild. "Give it up, griffin."

"Yes," he said, thrusting home.

He dug into me hard and I savored every second of it, urging him on. Whispering his name in short, frantic breaths. He was so whole and so good and so *alive* it made me want to scream.

My heels dug into his back, his fingers clutched my butt, holding me, positioning me just so. It was rough and hard and exactly what I needed.

I jolted into a spine-bending orgasm. He shuddered hard groaning as he spent himself inside me.

Afterward, he lay on top of me, holding just enough of his weight away on his elbows. I felt possessed, protected and wonderfully tingly as he planted a precise line of tiny kisses along my collarbone.

"You must accept more," he murmured.

I ran my hands through his thick black hair. Perhaps. But not yet. Right now, I just wanted to savor the moment.

This man made me feel safe. And needed. And loved.

At present, that was more than enough. As for tomorrow, well, we'd see what happened beyond the old brick walls of Big Nose Kate's.

CHAPTER SIX

The next morning, I headed downstairs with renewed confidence. Dimitri had helped me forget my troubles two more times, with spine-tingling results. My, I loved dating an overachiever.

He'd brushed my lavender hair and he'd even helped me rig up a flashlight holder on my demon slayer utility belt. The Maglite hung heavy on my waist.

Downstairs was deserted, save for a grumpy fairy bent over a ginormous fold-out map.

Sid could have been Danny DeVito's brother. He was shorter than most and balding. What was left of his hair circled his head like a wiry black halo. He'd tried to cover his natural bubblegum scent with Brut for Men. Trust me, it wasn't a good combination.

"What?" he demanded without looking up from his map.

He'd flung the enormous thing over two bar tables. It still lopped over the edges. The Martha Stewart in me didn't know how he was going to fold it all up again.

We'd picked up Sid in Las Vegas a few months back. Actually, Ant Eater had swept Sid off of his little sparkly feet. They were like Ozzie and Harriet on a Harley.

"What's going on?" I asked the fairy.

Dimitri had headed out back to double check our bikes. I could hear the witches in the back store room, loading up everything they'd unpacked yesterday afternoon.

"Do you mind?" Sid scowled at me as if I'd eaten the last Oreo. "I'm getting us out of here."

"Good." I scooted in to get a better look.

Highways and smaller connected roads zigzagged across Sid's map. They ran between major cities and smaller towns and seemed perfectly normal—until you added a network of winding green fairy trails, with names like Hobblers Knob and Limey Crook's Shaft.

Maybe I hadn't gotten enough sleep last night. "Nether Wallup Way? You've got to be kidding." I pointed at a particularly nonsensical route that wound in corkscrews between Trenton and Philadelphia.

"Cut it, Lady Gaga."

He didn't have to bring my hair into it.

Sid glared at me. "Nether Wallup Way happens to be the fastest path out of here."

"Path," I repeated, taking a second look at the map while at the same time resisting the urge to touch my head. "Oh no. We're not taking any paths. We need the interstate." I had to get to my dad as quickly as possible.

His bushy brows shot up, deepening the cascade of wrinkles etched into his forehead. "Last I heard you weren't in charge of trip planning, demon slayer."

I snorted. "I am if you're going to lead us down Willy Wallup Way."

"Nether Wallup Way," he said through clenched teeth.

"Whatever." It was ridiculous no matter how you said it.

Ant Eater cracked an egg into a glass of tomato

juice and handed it to Sid.

"Your boyfriend is trying to lead us down the primrose path," I protested. "And what's with the eggs?"

"Protein," she answered. "And what's the deal? You think Sid doesn't know his stuff?"

The short, stocky fairy gulped at his power drink and slapped Ant Eater on the rear. She tittered and wiggled her hips at him, which I really didn't need to see.

I ran a finger down the corkscrews and roundabouts that made up the fairy path in question. "What I'm saying," I said, assuming my teacher voice, "is Nether Wallup Way would mosey us about two hundred miles south instead of west," and mostly in circles.

If we were going to get to Pasadena any time soon, we needed to take the most direct route, which meant interstate highways. "Look," I said, bending over the map, "we take I-80 all the way to Sacramento. Hang a left at either 99 or 5, preferably 5…"

Sid shook his head, sprinkling silver glitter onto the map like a bad case of dandruff. "That's all fine and dandy, but the fairy paths run through Philly and then down south." He pointed to a series of winding trails through Virginia and Kentucky. "We'll take a short detour down Filligan's Rut into Nashville, and then head west from there," he said, as if it were obvious to anyone with a touch of otherworldly intelligence.

Not happening.

"The interstate works just fine." I was all for magical hoo-ha. It had saved my rear plenty of times, but, "we have banshees on our tail and time issues to consider." Magic for the sake of magic was just plain foolish.

He looked at me as if I had a screw loose. "About

those banshees, I had to clean up the mess you left outside. Poison skin, poison fangs, poison spit. I'll bet those suckers even have poison poop and you just want to rocket down the highway and see if they can catch up to us. Not me. I'm going with fairy magic. If you want to be stupid about it, then you can go by yourself."

"Oh sure, let's break up the group," I said, realizing just how serious he was. What was with this guy? We needed speed as well as safety in numbers. "We're in a race to save my dad's soul. We don't have time to fool around."

"Lizzie –" Grandma clapped a hand on my shoulder.

But I was on a roll. "Give me a fast Harley and a belt full of switch stars."

"Now you sound like a biker witch," Grandma said, her gravelly voice ringing with pride. "I hate to tell you that in this case, Sid is right."

Oh please. "Did you hit your head on something pointy?"

"We're talking about ancient protection here." She shrugged. "Fairies have been running these routes since George Washington was in diapers."

"Try Ramses," Sid smirked.

Grandma ignored him. "Every fairy that travels a route deepens the magic. We're talking generations and generations of strength and protection."

Okay, well, Sid hadn't bothered to explain that part. "Have you done this before?" I asked.

"Hell, no," Grandma said. "We never knew where they were. Now we do."

Frieda handed us both a glass of tomato juice. "Drink up."

I took a sniff. It held the bitter tang of something besides tomatoes. Of course knowing the biker witches, it could mean they'd added anything from vodka to vitamins.

Nothing could be simple. "Will fairy magic protect us against banshees?" I asked.

And anything else that might be hunting us?

Grandma took a long drink, considering the question. "It'll muddy up the waters, make it harder for them to track us. And hopefully we'll run into lots of other magical folks who can tell us what's ahead."

When she put it that way, it wasn't such a bad idea. I could use some extra knowledge about what we were facing, especially after the attack outside, and what my dad had tried to pull.

Sid threw his stubby hands out in front of him. "Do you trust me, or not? Because I don't have all day to sit around and decide who's going to lead this parade."

"Okay, fine," I said, depositing my tomato juice surprise on the bar.

If Grandma trusted him, so did I. We were heading out into the open, and if the fairy magic could act as a shield, we'd be crazy not to take advantage.

Besides, I had a feeling Ant Eater would use my head as a bongo drum if I harassed her main squeeze.

"Let's leave in ten," I said, pulling my gloves out of my back pocket. If all else failed, we could always head back to the main highways.

"No problem." Sid shook a bit of dust from his sleeve. The map shivered and began folding itself.

Nice trick.

†††

We assembled the witches in less than five minutes, which never failed to amaze me. I strapped Pirate to my chest in true biker dog style and adjusted his Doggles riding glasses.

"You'd better lay off the puppy treats," I said, knowing the problem was probably donuts. I scratched

Pirate between the ears. He'd eaten two this morning and we were on our last notch on the black leather baby-style carrier.

He ran a cold nose along the inside of my wrist. "Are you kidding? I can't pass up a donut. You know anybody that can say no to a chocolate long john?"

Not my dog.

"Besides, I'm using them to train Flappy and he hasn't been getting many of his tricks right. So I have to eat the donuts. Well I do give him *some* donuts, whether he sits or not, because well, I can't just eat donuts in front of him." Pirate's tail thumped against my leg. "Sometimes Flappy even sits down when he eats them so that sort of counts."

Flappy. I craned my neck back at the dirty white dragon licking water out of a battered gutter of Big Nose Kate's. Good thing only magical people could see Flappy. He wasn't exactly subtle.

His snaggletooth dredged entire shingles off the roof.

According to Dimitri, the dragon's wings should have been the size of a man and sparkle like glass. Flappy's were less than half that size and they only sparkled the one time Pirate decided to play dragon makeover and sprinkle them with glitter. Flappy didn't care either way, but Pirate had been a glittery mess and I was still finding sparkly bits in my bedroll.

In short, it was pretty safe to assume Flappy had been the runt of the litter, abandoned by a sleeker, sparkly clan. We had no clue which because as far as anyone knew, there were no white dragons.

I'd rescued Flappy from the side of a cliff while he was still in the egg. At the time, I hadn't planned on adopting a dragon. Of course plans change. I should know that by now.

The dragon let out a juvenile *skreeek* as the Red

Skulls began cranking up their bikes.

"Oh yeah," Pirate hollered, "you like to ride, now don't you Flappy?"

Teeth-rattling engines roared on all sides as I made sure Pirate was strapped in safe and made a final check on my helmet.

My bike wobbled slightly as we revved out of the battered driveway and toward a series of side roads that would take us to Nether Wallup Way.

Sid and Ant Eater led the group, followed by Dimitri, Pirate and me. Grandma took up the rear position, with Flappy above her. I snuck a glance past the line of bikers behind us to the hulking mess of Big Nose Kate's.

It still didn't look like much from the outside. The witches warded it extra tight this time, careful not to leave any live spells behind. As the morning mists rose off the woods, I could feel the comforting whispers of the magic we'd left in our wake.

Every single witch had chosen to come with us. It was a humbling show of support— one that I would never take for granted. I just hoped that sooner rather than later, the Red Skulls could return. They deserved a place to call home.

Right now, it was probably better we were leaving. I doubted they wanted their home overrun by banshees. Just the thought of tangling with them again made my stomach clench. The fairy paths would protect us only for so long.

We cruised up Service Road D until Sid called us to a halt on a dirt shoulder littered with rusty soda cans and holes. A wooden fence twined with barbed wire ran the length of the road, separating us from an empty farm field. The shorn stalks of last year's crop huddled close to the ground as far as the eye could see.

My front tire caught on an extra deep rut and I

started skidding sideways. I caught myself—barely.

Meanwhile Frieda had run her sidecar into a prickly bush. "Sorry, Bob!" She winced at her passenger.

Bob put a leather clad shoulder to the worst of the brambles. "What's the idea, Sid?"

"A thousand apologies, mister prickly pants." Sid lumbered off his bike. "Next time, I'll make sure the fairies in these parts landscape the highway entrances. What else do they have to do? Maybe they'll plant some petunias or lay out pillows for you guys." He rolled his eyes and muttered something under his breath.

Sid planted both hands on a section of the fence. He spread his fingers, making sure he had a solid grip.

"Nether Wallup Way," he said, laying on the Jersey twang, "land of fairies. Path of fae." He scowled with his entire round body, daring me to so much as crack a smile. "Release the latch upon this door. That we may wend forth evermore."

The fence cracked open to form a door. Green grass spilled out, inching out over barren rocks and dirt.

"What?" Sid waved his arm. "Are you just going to stand there?"

Ant Eater and I slid off our bikes and helped him pull the heavy gate back. Sunshine flooded out, warming my hands and face.

Where there had been dead grass, a rich black road wound its way through a canopy of trees. Tiny purple flowers cropped up in the grass on either side of the path and around the low stone wall mounded on either side. The flat rocks—stacked as if laid by hand— formed intricate patterns. Ivy climbed the trunks and moss dripped from immense green conifers.

The air smelled sweet, although not in a nature-type way but in a bakery way.

Amazing.

I'd had a fairy godfather once. When I first met him, I imagined him showing me hidden fairy places like this. He'd died before I could even get to know him. As strange as it sounded, I felt Uncle Phil here. Seeing this trail, this fairy magic, made me feel closer to him somehow.

Too bad opening the path hadn't affected Sid in the least. "Lookie here," he said, "a demon slayer with nothing to talk about. You'd better get a move on. I can't keep this thing open all day."

The witches grinned at each other as they revved their bikes and took off down the fairy trail. I cranked my motorcycle and joined them. As soon as my bike hit Nether Wallup Way, it picked up speed. Trees whizzed by. The road was so smooth it felt like glass under my tires.

"Yyy-yes!" Pirate whooped.

My dog had a need for speed.

I tried to slow down, but it was no use. We zoomed straight for a slate stone fairy bridge. I detected a slight sizzle of energy as we passed up and over a deep, narrow creek.

Riding a Harley is the nearest most of us get to flying, but in this case, I could feel my tires lift from the ground.

My stomach dipped and I held on tighter.

We made it through Tennessee and into Arkansas and Oklahoma. Now and again, we'd pass a minivan load of fairies, or fairies on ten-speed bikes. They flew past in a blur of color, light, and *I brake for squirrels* bumper stickers.

You'd think someone could have mentioned fairy paths were faster than regular roads. Sometimes, I think they just liked to see me squirm.

We passed a pair of fairies on rollerblades, headed the other way. No one blinked an eye at Flappy. And we didn't even have to stop for gas.

I couldn't help but think of what fairy paths could do for the energy crisis. If only the fairies would be willing to come out of the closet.

Maybe I'd have a talk with Sid when this was over.

As evening neared, we stopped in Colfax, New Mexico, which blew my mind because we'd basically covered half of the United States in a day. One day. My route would have taken at least three times that long.

Sid had us pull over in an abandoned heap of a town just north of Cimarron. It sat on a grassy plain with a spectacular view of red mountains in the distance. The sun was beginning to set, which meant the Red Skull's magic would be the strongest if they wanted to set up wards around here.

Then again, maybe they shouldn't because, er, this place was a dump.

Sid eased his bike to a stop outside the Colfax Hotel, a two-story wood structure with a second-floor balcony overhanging a wide porch.

A plaque on the side of The Colfax said it had been built in 1872. I didn't doubt that for a second. From the look of the place, it was being held up by fairy magic and good intentions.

Half the white paint had chipped off and where it was missing, rotted gray wood lay exposed to the elements. The front bay window sported several broken panes of glass and the dented front door knob held on by a single rusty screw. A wooden half-circle sign on the roof read *Hotel* in faded block letters.

Grandma and Dimitri eased their bikes onto the dirt patch that passed for a parking lot and we shut off our engines.

"So this is it?" Grandma scowled, not taking off her helmet. The dust of the town swirled around us.

"I've seen worse," Dimitri said, easing one long leg over the seat of his bike.

Of course, we'd all seen worse. We'd been to hell.

Then again, this place probably had cockroaches the size of demons.

"I told you to trust me," Sid said, with no small amount of pride. "You wanted to make good time and we did. You want a place guaranteed to be free of people in case we get the banshees, here you go."

"Ohhh…" Pirate trembled in his harness, his tail thumping against my chest. "It looks like a ghost town!"

"That's because it is a ghost town," Sid said. "Well, a fairy town. Intra Magical Matters Charter number Five-o-Three says we can take over if nobody else is using the place."

"I wonder if they have an ice cream parlor!" Pirate said, struggling against his carrier and making it quite clear he was a bit hazy on the details of a ghost town.

Sid led us up the crumbling brick steps of the Colfax Hotel. He paused in front of the rough wood door, hunting in his pocket until he pulled out a handful of what looked like dirt.

"Do you mind?" He glared at us.

We stepped back and Sid stuffed a pinch of dirt into the rusty lock and muttered a low chant.

"Cow's beestheens, nettles, tweenies and twine, ye be to open and be mine." The door clicked open.

"Let me down," Pirate said, scrambling against his doggie carrier.

"We could have just busted it," Grandma said, first in the door.

"Just a sec," I said, reaching for the flashlight on my demon slayer utility belt.

But there was no need. Gas lamps shed warm light over a turn-of-the-century lobby. Rich floral wallpaper in pinks and greens gave way to high plaster ceilings. Padded benches and intimate seating areas were clustered throughout the cozy room. A boxy piano in the back began to play Down By The Old Mill Stream.

"Welcome home, girls," Sid said, with no small amount of glee.

"They could have better taste in music," Grandma said, hands on her hips as she eyed the place, "but I'll take this over Motel 6."

"It's the nicest place I've ever stayed," Ant Eater said, pinching Sid on the bottom.

I didn't doubt it.

"So this is normal," I said to no one in particular.

Twenty-four hours ago, I was content to open up an old biker bar. Now I'd carted my half-angel self to fairy town. I shuddered to think what tomorrow would bring.

"I've heard of fairy hideaways," Dimitri said, unclipping a grateful Pirate and tucking my dog under his arm. "I never thought I'd see one."

"This doesn't feel like a hollow," I said, running a boot over the polished wood floor.

"That's just a term." Dimitri inspected the room, rubbing Pirate's back as we took it in. "It's more of a window to the past. Fairies can call up wooden structures if there is enough left."

"How much?"

"Depends on the fairy."

I knew this place didn't really exist, but darned if it didn't look comfortable. And safe.

My protective necklace hung warm and steady against my neck.

Grandma had found a crystal bowl of peppermints and held it out to me.

"No thanks," I said.

Who knew how old those were?

She popped one in her mouth. "I think we put some miles between us and those banshees."

Grandma was right. I could feel the weight of the threat easing. Still, we were stopping and I didn't think the ancient minions of evil would be kicking back for the evening.

"Maybe we should keep going," I said to Dimitri as we made our way past the lobby to a hallway in the back.

"It's not safe," he said. "We can't drive for two days straight, even on fairy paths. We need to be alert if something decides to jump us." He glanced back at the witches rearranging the lobby. "Besides, the Red Skulls aren't as young as they look."

Good point.

He slipped his hand over mine and gave a tug. "Come on, angel."

I couldn't help grinning at his comment and at the sight of his butt in blue jeans as we went to explore the back hallway. That man was temptation in the flesh.

We counted a dozen rooms in the back, which should be enough if we doubled up. That way everyone was on the ground floor, bikes at the ready in case we needed to make a quick escape.

There was no dining room, so we ate our MRE's out on the front porch I didn't bother heating my beef ravioli. Pirate talked his way into my toaster pastry. I never understood why they put Pop-Tarts in with Italian food anyway. Pirate, the charmer, also managed to snag Dimitri's peanut butter crackers and Sidecar Bob's maple muffin top.

"I'll take first shift," Dimitri said as we wound down for the night.

"I have second." I volunteered fast, before Grandma or Frieda tried to stay up. It's not that I didn't want them to help, but I'd feel better tonight if they left it up to me and Dimitri.

Heaven knew we'd both slept soundly enough after our encounter the night before. I wanted to fan myself just thinking about what that man could do with his hands, among other things.

As if he knew what I was thinking, Dimitri kissed me lightly on the nose. "Scram. I have work to do."

"Yes, sir, your manliness."

I left him to scout out a perimeter location while I walked back inside with the witches. He wouldn't want me to hover.

"Well, then I'm sleeping with Bob again," Pirate announced, accepting yet another peanut butter cracker.

I would have felt sorry for my dog if both of us didn't have it so good.

My cell phone rang as I watched Pirate retreat. "Electric Avenue" pulsed through the Wild West hotel. The biker witches groaned at my ring tone as I dug in the back of my utility belt.

Hillary Brown. My mom.

Well, the mom who had wanted me.

My thumb clicked it over to voicemail.

I wanted to answer her. I did.

I hadn't called Hillary since Greece, when I'd had to make up a story about traveling to find myself. I couldn't tell her I was dating a griffin or hanging out with biker witches. I didn't want to explain that yes, I was back in the States, but I had more important things to do than return to my old life in Atlanta.

Still, she called every other Sunday.

I watered your plants.

I planted your bulbs.

I took a look at that statement from your bill paying service, although I don't know why you pay for cable when you never watch it.

She was waiting for me to come back to a life that didn't exist anymore and I really didn't know how to tell her that while standing in a fairy hollow.

I stuffed the phone back into my utility belt and eased down into a wing-backed chair close to the bay window. I could see Dimitri's shadow as he inspected the remains of a building across the street. It was just the foundation, really. He looked fine and I didn't sense any evil in this place.

Yet something didn't feel right.

Let it go.

We set up the guard so that we'd each take a four-hour shift. I checked my watch. It was not even ten. Dimitri would be on until 2:00 a.m. I'd take over until dawn.

I was probably just being jumpy. Maybe it was fairy magic messing with my demon-slayer sense, but it felt as if I was waiting for something to go wrong.

It began as a tingling in my stomach and spread until my whole body practically vibrated with it.

I walked out to the porch and listened to the night. Cars zipped by in the distance, but other than that, silence.

Dimitri stood with one foot on the ruined foundation across the way.

"You okay?" I called to him, just to be sure.

"Go to bed," he chided.

I braced a hand on the door frame. He probably assumed I was having a hard time going to sleep without him.

He was right.

Maybe I was suffering from a case of nerves. I walked back through the comfortable lobby of the hotel, looking both ways before I eased into the back hallway.

It paid to be careful. I unhitched a switch star as I

turned the key to room 113.

"Scree!" Frigid air blasted out of the dark. Claws seized my shoulders.

"Holy Hades!" I thrust my switch star up into leathery skin.

Claws scrambled before the thing hit the floor with a dull thud.

Heart racing, I pounded on the lights. A shadow of a creature curled on the floor. It resembled a snake with legs, only as seconds passed it seemed to be made of black smoke more than anything else.

It had been solid. I'd felt it.

It wound its neck back and smirked at me with glowing red eyes. "That wasn't smart, Lizzie," it cackled as it dissolved into thin air.

I hit it with a switch star to the chest.

"Too late," it crooned as my switch star buried itself into the floor, "too late."

I stood, shocked and sweating and shivering.

It knew my name.

And it was gone. I dug my switch star out of the floor, the pink blades still churning.

It looked like some new kind of an imp. I'd never seen one that could speak before. At least, none had chosen to talk to me. The way it leered at me left me feeling very uncomfortable. It wanted to call me out, threaten me. With its dying breath, it wanted me to be very afraid.

It had worked.

A door opened down the hall to the right. "You okay?" Grandma called.

"Yes," I said, straightening. Holding my switch star against my left leg.

Grandma narrowed her eyes at me.

I shivered despite myself. "It was just a bug," I assured her.

"You and your bugs." She shook her head, her gray hair tangling around her shoulders as she closed the door behind her.

I turned back to the charred spot on the floor.

Grandma might have been able to tell me more about this imp, but I doubted it. I was getting pretty good at spotting evil. She and the others needed their sleep. The last thing I wanted was a biker witch meeting about a creature I'd already eliminated.

Besides, it hadn't been after them. It had called me by name. This thing had waited for me alone. I just needed to find out why.

Chapter Seven

I tried to get a few hours sleep before it was my turn to stand watch, but it was no use. It's hard to close your eyes when the rug smells like burnt minion.

With the sigh of a true martyr, I stuffed a pillow under my lumpy demon-slayer utility belt and studied the outline of the iron chandelier hanging above my bed.

Why was I even trying to take it easy?

I blew out a breath. Because I needed to rest or I wouldn't be good for anyone.

Dimitri was standing guard. He wouldn't let the boogeyman in. I should be able to close my eyes. Every time I did, the smell of bitter ashes grew from acrid to overpowering.

I didn't know much about supernatural soot, but I'd seen it come back to life in a jar. Why not on a carpet?

That was it. Wrestling with the covers, I scrambled out of bed. I turned on the light and stared at the charred Aztec carpet. I was tempted to toss it into the hall, or even out the window. If we'd been staying in a regular hotel, I would have.

Oh, who was I kidding? I would have taken it to the dry cleaners. But that was beside the point.

There was nothing I could do in an enchanted hotel. It was hard to know what gave power to these kinds of places or what would upset it. We had enough trouble.

I needed to get some sleep. If it was going to come back to life, it would have by now.

Right?

I sat with my back to the headboard, a hand on my switch stars, as the snake-like creature tap-tap-tapped its stubby end against the top of the jar.

The glass jar rattled on top of the dresser.

"I'm not letting you out, you know."

He responded with a tap-tap-a-tap.

"You're like a woodpecker."

Maybe I should call him Woody.

No. I would *not* name it.

I wouldn't even think about it—or my dad, or what it meant to be a half-angel or what could happen if we didn't make it to California in time.

And so I waited.

I supposed it was a positive sign that I couldn't just ignore my zombie friend, or skewer a smoky imp and then go right to sleep with potentially enchanted ashes on the rug. If I wasn't on edge, I wouldn't be good at my job. I just wished demon slaying powers came with a little peace—or at least a vacation. Maybe even a date.

It wasn't happening tonight.

Relief swamped me when my watch alarm beeped at 1:30 a.m. By that time, I was groggy and stiff. I sat up and planted my feet on the floor. What little rest I'd gotten was more of a tease than a refresher.

Sometimes it's better not to sleep at all. I'd just have to let my fear of the unknown keep me alert.

After what had happened in the last forty-eight hours, it wouldn't be hard.

"What do you think?" I asked my undead buddy, wincing as I turned on the light. "You want to go on guard duty?"

I wasn't leaving it alone.

Letting my eyes adjust, I ran my toes along the floor, searching for my boots. They'd been the only thing I felt comfortable removing.

I pulled them on, checked my switch stars and one yawn later, was ready to go.

"Come on," I said, stuffing the jar into a holder on the side of my utility belt. I was going to clank like a biker witch. And I really shouldn't be talking to a piece of zombie rope. Call it a habit. I missed my dog.

Pirate was still there for me, of course. He always would be. Yet over the last year, he'd also become a part of the Red Skulls. He was the coven's dog too. It made me grateful and a touch sad.

At least he hadn't been with me when I arrived at my room tonight. I paused over the charred remains of the Aztec rug. Pirate was always the first one in the door. Even if he had to wait for me to turn the lock, he'd squeeze past as soon as it cracked an inch.

He would have run straight into my attacker.

I shuddered, locking my room behind me. I should have listened to my instincts tonight. I'd known something was wrong. That churning in my stomach, that heaviness in the air, it told me I was in deep trouble.

I'd felt it before we'd walked out to see the banshee too.

Hold on a minute.

My mentor told me I needed to get out of my own way and let my abilities surface. I had more power than I could imagine, confined only by what my mind could see. I'd spent my life knowing my limits, making sure not to cross the line.

What if I had the ability to sense attacks before they happened?

My heart swelled. Finally, something that could

help keep the people I loved safe.

I strode through the darkened lobby with a new purpose. Maybe I really could change things. I at least had to try.

The heavy front door squeaked as I opened it. Dimitri stood where I'd left him on the ruins of the building across the street. The bright moon outlined his form—and that of another.

I stiffened. He was arguing with a man. Both were obviously agitated and equally large. The stranger gestured wildly, making some kind of a threat.

My feet hardly touched the stairs. "Dimitri!"

Both of them turned.

"Lizzie," he said, not at all welcoming as he stepped away from the stranger.

I hurried across the dirt road.

The man watched me with glowing yellow eyes. He wasn't human.

Then again, I'd stopped expecting it.

"What's going on here? You have a problem?" I asked, ready to draw weapons. Dimitri's adversary faced me. Oh my word. He was stark naked. He didn't even seem to care. A long collar of red jewels set in gold hung low on his muscled chest.

He turned back to Dimitri. "Think about the stakes," he said, with a heavy Greek accent that punched every word.

My griffin glared at him and I realized that I wasn't helping. I was interrupting.

The other man practically snarled, his bare shoulders quivering with tension. A tattoo of a gold sword wrapped in fire wound up his neck and disappeared underneath his shaggy black hair. "My terms are non-negotiable," he said, low and menacing. "You know it is the only way."

He turned his back on both of us, bent his head and

shifted.

Feathers cascaded down his back, catching in the moonlight, shining eerie shades of gold and red. Claws erupted out of his hands and feet, and thick lion's fur raced up his arms. Bones snapped and reformed as his body expanded. An immense set of wings unfolded from his back.

I'd seen griffins shift before—from men and women into creatures with the bodies of lions and the heads and wings of eagles. It was a powerful, awesome sight to watch these beasts emerge.

The stranger took off on a massive set of wings. He flew east, toward the coast, calling out like a giant predator.

"Damned fire griffins," Dimitri muttered.

"Who was he? What did he want?" I asked, realizing I'd been holding my breath.

"He's a pain in my ass." Dimitri clenched his jaw as he watched the griffin fade into the night. "You're early."

Ha. "You're surprised?"

He checked his watch. "I shouldn't be."

It was a half hour before I was set to relieve him, which was early even by my standards. I usually arrived only twenty minutes before schedule.

"Look, you don't have to give me details if you don't want, but I really would like to know who just flew away."

It was important to know who was venturing in and out of camp, even if I didn't want to be reminded of Dimitri's obligations to the griffins.

I touched his arm. Warm muscle flexed under my fingers. "I know you've had to make compromises."

"Rest assured," he said, tucking a lock of hair behind my ear, "it's not a sacrifice."

I didn't believe that for a second.

Of course I liked to think I was worth a few risks. What Dimitri and I had was amazing—and rare. But I wasn't naïve enough to think love conquered all.

It didn't change the fact that Dimitri was needed in Greece. He'd spend most of his life trying to ensure his family's health and stability. He'd saved his clan, but he'd barely reached out to the griffin community before Grandma and the Red Skulls had grown restless. We'd stayed on Santorini a scant four months before we'd returned to the States.

He'd have to return home eventually.

Dimitri had work to do. He loved his home and his sisters. One of these days, I was going to be brave enough to let him leave and fulfill his own destiny.

We stood side-by-side, watching the moon. "Any sign of banshees?" I asked, moving on to a more pleasant topic, or at least one that was not so explosive.

We at least had clear answers on evil creatures. You saw them. You killed them. End of story.

"Nothing yet," he said, wrapping an arm around my shoulder and drawing me closer.

I reached up and kissed him, for comfort really. I loved the feel of his chest and the rub of his leather coat on my skin. I eased into the jacket, careful for his injured side, and savored his warmth.

I'd take this man for as long as I could have him.

He deepened the kiss. Hallelujah. Heat shot straight to my toes—and other parts—before I was able to gather my wits and pull away. The stubble on his chin scratched my cheek.

I caught myself before I leaned in for more. "I'll meet you after guard duty," I whispered.

"I'm not going to be able to sleep now." His voice sounded rough.

He cleared his throat. "I did some investigating while I was out here. We're standing over the ruins of a church. There isn't much left, but I'm assuming it's blessed ground. It should be easier to defend if anything comes calling."

My opinion of Sid clicked up a few notches.

"The hotel backs up to a cliff, plus your Grandma had enough leftover ingredients to ward it pretty well. Flappy is trying to contribute, or maybe he just likes the smell of turtle knees and swamp mud. Either way, he's perched out there on the edge of the canyon. I've been basing myself here, and then doing a full lap every few minutes."

"Okay," I said, scanning the area. The plains surrounding our location would help me spot anything before it arrived. Unless it came out of thin air—or a wall of flame—but I had to think I'd feel it first. I'd pay special attention to my instincts tonight.

"One more thing," Dimitri said.

"Yes?" I tried to ignore the thump of the glass jar against my leg. The zombie rope was getting restless.

"I love you."

Did my boyfriend know how to give a briefing or what?

He gave me a lingering kiss before heading back inside. Mmm…that would keep me warm.

The night was chilly and clear. After watching Dimitri walk back to the hotel—What can I say? The man could certainly fill out a pair of blue jeans.—I gave my dad's gift a place of honor on a broken out window ledge.

I had to give Sid credit. He'd not only gotten a coven of biker witches more than halfway across the country in a day, he'd also found a relatively secure place to spend the night. I'd make sure it stayed that way.

My belly quivered. It wasn't quite into threat mode. In fact, my stomach reminded me quite heartily that I probably should not have given my Pop-Tarts to Pirate. Yet I could tell something in the night air had shifted since I came outside.

Unhitching a switch star, I decided to circle the hotel and investigate.

Halfway around, just as Dimitri had predicted, I found an immense dragon. Flappy sat watch over the canyon like a great sphinx. His mottled white scales looked gray in the moonlight.

He whipped his massive head and his black button eyes lit up when he saw me. "Rrr-yow!" He hutted out a billow of smoke.

"Hiya, Flap."

Rocks crunched under his scales as he rolled onto his back and arched his tummy.

"This isn't a social visit," I said, reaching up to scratch him across the leathery plates of his stomach. "You see anything strange out here?"

He lolled his head back and began kicking his left rear leg. "Urfle."

"Yeah. You like that."

"Grrr..." Smoke trailed from one nostril.

"You gonna eat some banshees if they come calling?"

"Grrr..."

"I'll take that as a 'yes,'" instead of 'please keep petting me and I'll agree to anything you say.'"

Flappy was shameless when it came to tummy rubs, same as another four-legged creature I knew.

I just hoped the dragon could take care of himself. "Keep an eye out." The air had grown heavier in the few minutes I'd stood with Flappy. I could sense the storm moving in.

"You see something, you come get me." I strolled up to his head and gave him a scratch behind the ears, just to see. Wouldn't you know it? Tiny feathers prickled against my fingers. "Don't be a hero."

I'd already been attacked once this evening. And my enemies tended to be persistent.

The dragon sat up and shook the dirt out of his wings as he watched me walk away.

I was glad he didn't try to follow. I needed an extra set of eyes at the back.

A smoky, burning presence weaved its way around the front of the hotel. Blackness shrouded the road and the desert beyond. My insides tightened.

"Dad?" I stepped into the darkness. It smelled of rot and death. "Dad, are you out there?"

I didn't dare move farther forward or go back. I paced at the edge of the sinister cloud, listening to the wind swirling over dried grass, the occasional call of coyotes.

My boots crunched against the sandy soil as wisps of black, darker than night, curled around my ankles. Something was out there.

Whatever it was, I knew without a doubt it wanted me.

The ground was rougher than it looked. Crab grass sprouted in tufts. Every few feet, a hidden dip threatened to trip me. Stiff grass and nettles brushed my ankles.

The black silence crawled up my spine and settled behind my shoulders.

"Show yourself," I called out into the night.

Let's do this.

A wave of banshees screeched straight for my head. "Flappy!" I screamed as I hit one with a switch star. It flew backward as another banshee knocked me to the ground. Breath whooshed out of me as I hit hard sand and dirt. Razor sharp jaws thrashed, acidic spittle rained down as I took out the one on top of me, my switch star propelling it back into at least two more.

I scrambled to my feet and saw that Flappy had one in his jaws like a chew toy. The creature shrieked as the dragon bit it in half. I knocked out the last two with switch stars to the head while they tried to scramble away from Flappy, who'd chomped another one.

He tossed the creature out into the night. "Rrr-yee!" Flappy called, triumphant.

Biker witches poured out of the hotel, Grandma in the lead. I could tell it was her by her lavender housecoat, flapping behind her as she ran.

"Now they come," I said, out of breath, turning a circle to make sure we didn't miss any bad ass creatures of the night.

One of my pant legs sizzled with toxic banshee spit. Just when I was about to try and find a rock to scrape it with, Flappy licked it off.

"Thanks," I said slowly, waiting to see if I had to take care of a sick dragon.

Flappy panted, his breath hot and wet against my shoulder as he watched me.

"Dimitri was right. You are a fighter." I reached up to pet the dragon behind an ear, flicking my wrist to avoid a glowing red moth that wanted to land there.

Fairy moth?

"Shoo," I brushed it off my shoulder and cringed as it landed on my neck.

It chomped down. Hard. "Ow!"

I grabbed it. That's when, to my horror, I saw it was missing half a wing. Its entire body was rumpled, as if it had been smashed and its eyes were milky white.

It was a zombie bug.

Sweet Mary.

It zipped away as I went for a switch star. Jagged teeth sprang from a bulbous, larvae-like body. It reached for me with countless scarlet tentacles.

I tried to dodge sideways, but it crashed down on

my leg. Before I could say demon-insect-from-hell, it bit a hole in my pants and sunk its teeth into my thigh.

"Ow!" I recoiled as it dug its fangs into my flesh. Pain seized me as it burrowed its head into my skin.

In a panic, I pulled at the creature's fat body as it sank, fraction by fraction into my flesh. I could feel it biting, wriggling inside of me.

My mind went foggy and I had an insane desire to stand up and run—to where, I had no idea.

I screamed like a banshee, or so I was told.

The biker witches propped me up. My mind was numb, shocked as I tried to pull the creature away from me, watching it move under my skin.

"Kill it!" Grandma hollered.

Flashlights blinded me.

"No," Dimitri ordered. "Put it to sleep."

Glass broke over my leg and a cold spell oozed down my pants. My entire leg went dead.

"I've got you, Lizzie," Dimitri said, his words clipped and crisp. I closed my eyes and focused on his voice. "Slowly. We want to get it all."

I squeezed my eyes tighter. My head pounded. I was burning from the inside out.

Bit by bit, Dimitri pulled the hot agony out of my body through the hole in my leg. It felt like he was taking part of me with it. Sweating, I ventured a look. My thigh was laid open and bloody as Dimitri worked the fat pulp of the creature out by the neck.

I leaned my head back against Grandma. "Oh, ick."

Dimitri grunted and plunked something into a jar. "Come on. Let's get you inside."

A few minutes later, I hunkered in one of the wing-backed chairs by the window with my leg propped up on the opposite chair. My brain was starting to clear, the muddiness replaced by a throbbing ache at the base of my skull.

I looked around to Grandma, Dimitri and about a dozen or so biker witches.

"How's your leg?" Dimitri asked, inspecting the bandage.

"The feeling is starting to come back," I said, the greatest understatement of the year. My entire leg burned from the knee up. It was like coming off a giant dose of Novocain.

The insect snarled inside a jar on the side table. The zombie rope had disintegrated to ash along the bottom, no doubt trying to hide. "Any theories on what this is?" I asked.

"It's a pressure bug," Grandma said. "I'd never seen one, but I've read about them. They try to get under your skin. Literally. Then they hijack your free will."

No kidding.

"What is Dad caught up in? This was worse than the banshees." And here I thought a mini-horde of acid spitting creatures was my problem.

Ant Eater held up the jar, watching the bug slam against the glass. "No angel, fallen or otherwise would have access to something like this." She gave me a stern look. "It has demon written all over it."

"So what do we do with it?" I asked.

"Test it," Dimitri said to Grandma.

She blanched. "I can't touch something that evil."

"Then what do we do?" Ant Eater asked.

I watched the creature attack the lid of the jar. "I don't know."

CHAPTER EIGHT

"Lizzie!" Pirate dashed through the crowd of witches and jumped right onto my leg, nailing me with a prickling pain.

"Baby dog." I let him nuzzle under my arm and sniff Grandma's jar on the table next to me.

"That's it? That's the bug? Shoot. I've eaten bigger bugs than this for dessert. You want me to chomp it?"

"Thanks for the offer," I said, "but not this time."

I'd spare my attacker from death-by-dog. I wanted to observe it, learn more about it. Besides, Pirate didn't need to be eating enchanted creatures.

It was bad enough he'd adopted a dragon.

"He looks crunchy. I like crunchy bugs," Pirate said. "You change your mind, you tell me. 'Cause you know I'll eat anything."

Did I ever.

"Ho-boy." Pirate scrabbled against me. His whole body quivered as he attempted to slather every inch of the jar in dog nose. "You didn't tell me it was magic!"

"What are you talking about? It's not—" Jesus, Mary, Joseph and the mule. "Grandma. Take a look at this."

My attacker was no longer a red insect. It twisted upon itself, chest heaving, wings collapsing. It bent and flattened until it morphed into a fleshy, plasticky lump. It reminded me of the silly putty I used to play with as a kid. But this thing was hard. It shimmied against the glass, sounding like a wobbling penny.

Frieda, Sid and a half dozen other biker witches scooted back. Grandma, Dimitri and I moved closer.

She whistled under her breath. "Pressure bugs can't do that."

Dimitri watched it as if he'd cornered a viper. "That was never a pressure bug."

A bad feeling crept over me. For the love of Pete. "I can't believe it's worse than a demonic bug."

The rope cowered as the bug-turned-blob gained momentum and began slamming against the side of the jar.

I stood to get closer, trying not to wince as pain shot through my thigh. As long as the leg didn't buckle, I'd be okay. If I was going to be a big, bad demon slayer, it would look better if I didn't wipe out on the floor.

Grandma pulled out a pair of reading glasses with rhinestones clustered in the corners and went nose-to-nose with the jar. "I hate it when Dimitri's right."

"Then what is it?" I asked, wanting—no, needing—answers.

Grandma lowered her glasses. "Dunno. I've never seen anything like it."

Wonderful. We were now testing the limits of biker witch knowledge.

Grandma spoke slowly. "We spent thirty years dealing with everything Vald had to throw at us from the fifth level of hell. I thought I'd seen everything."

"What? Could this be from a deeper level?" I asked, sharing a glance with Dimitri.

He didn't like it. I didn't either.

"If it is," Dimitri said, "we need to know what level it's from so we know what we're dealing with."

Ant Eater looked as shaken as I'd ever seen her. "If

we're up against anything over five, we need to go into bunker mode."

"Or if we're facing a two, we need to keep on to Pasadena," I reminded her. We had no reason to jump to conclusions. "How far is Las Vegas?"

"What does that have to do with the price of tea in China?" Ant Eater demanded.

"Max is in Vegas," I answered.

"What?" Dimitri thundered.

"Now?" Grandma balked.

"Oh please." I thought we'd called a truce.

I watched the middle of the creature pulse into a flat disk.

This thing was evil and Max knew evil.

Max Devereux was the only person I knew who made it his life's work to navigate the murky waters between heaven and hell. "He's been killing demons longer than I've been alive."

"That's not hard," Grandma muttered.

"Sid," I said, locating the fairy over by the window, "you have any fairy paths that can take us through Las Vegas?"

Sid looked at me like I'd asked him to tap dance across broken glass. "We can take Gooey Gumdrop Lane."

Grandma tapped a silver ringed finger against the jars at her belt. "Lizzie, you have to admit Max is a long shot. And the guy's not completely right in the head."

This coming from a biker witch.

Grandma, Dimitri, and the rest of them had never liked the hunter, and for good reason. Max was half-demon. He wasn't what you'd call trustworthy. And he was on the edge of giving into the dark side himself—if he hadn't turned already.

He was a cambion, a half demon, half human I'd

met during a succubi invasion in Las Vegas. Max was on our side, mostly. I never knew what he was going to do, but he did get a kick out of killing demons, so we had that going for us.

Okay, so Max wasn't Dudley Do-Right. "You didn't even have to watch him eat a demon." I'd never forget it. "Still, he's a hunter, which is as close as we're going to get to another slayer. He's survived for a century on his own and if anyone can tell us where this thing came from, it's Max."

Nobody looked happy.

Dimitri looked fit to be tied. He knew I was right and it was killing him. "Let's go," he ground out. "I hate the bastard, but I'll go."

"Thank you." I knew he'd stand by me. Dimitri always did. Now we just had to convince the rest of the group.

Or go it alone.

"What if you hole up and it gets you anyway?" I asked. "We don't know what level of hell this is from or what it's capable of doing. This is life or death, people."

Sure Max was dark, dangerous and sexy as hell (not that I'd admit that last part to Dimitri). Max was also the one person who could help us.

I needed to be a leader here. I finally knew what I was doing and nobody wanted to listen. My preschoolers used to listen to me. Mostly. Pirate listened. Sometimes.

Why couldn't I just make them understand that this is the way it had to be?

"Our answer is in Las Vegas," I said, as sure as I'd been of anything in my life. "We need to go. Now."

No one moved.

Dimitri turned his back on me and walked away, through the crowd of witches. The front door creaked as he held it open. His dark eyes caught mine and held them. "Come on, ladies. Sid. Let's hit the road."

† † †

As soon as the last biker had left the hotel, it reverted back to a crumbling wreck. Flappy sniffed at the rotted-out porch as we climbed onto our bikes.

Even though I'd gotten my way, I couldn't help but fume over how it went down. They followed Dimitri out the door. Not me. He wasn't even part of the Red Skulls.

I knew what it was. I'd come into this group with no knowledge of my abilities and no experience in the magical world. We'd fixed that. I'd grown into my powers. Sure I still had some things to learn but I knew what I was doing—especially when it came to Max. Still, it seemed like I'd always be seen as the newbie.

Maybe that would change after they saw what was waiting for us in Vegas. And maybe Ant Eater would braid my hair and tell me a bedtime story.

We took Nether Wallup Way to Greeny Bits Drive up to Gooey Gumdrop Lane. I found myself in awe each time Sid swung open a new fairy gate.

The paths were similar in that they let us travel at ungodly speeds. Most of the time, my bike tires didn't even touch the ground. Yet each of the trails had a personality of its own. Nether Wallup Way felt like old Ireland. We sped over a cobblestone road, past soaring cliffs and fields of emerald green. We turned left at a low stone wall—heaven knew how Sid could distinguish it from any other.

There Sid eased away a section of stone to reveal Sunny Dale Drive. Just like that, we were speeding over sand and seashells. Palm trees swayed, colorful macaws sang and I could taste the ocean on the breeze.

It was to the point where I almost expected a candy store when Sid opened the gate to Gooey Gumdrop

Lane.

Instead, large pink and yellow mushrooms sprouted as far as I could see. They even covered the road. Sid broke off a chunk of the nearest one and stuffed it into his pocket.

"And that is?" I asked.

"None of your beeswax," he shot back.

We fired up our engines and took off down the lane.

As night fell, Sid pushed open the bamboo gate that opened onto Las Vegas Boulevard. A few tourists paused outside, expecting a show as we roared our bikes out of a row of palm trees and past the Treasure Island Casino pirate ship.

If they only knew.

It wasn't the first time I was glad non-magical humans couldn't see large scaly dragons.

Sid closed the gate with a grunt as Dimitri pulled up next to me.

"Look," I pointed to a billboard, "Dale Fiehler is building a new mega casino." He was the Donald Trump of Las Vegas, only with better hair. The twenty-foot-tall Fiehler smiled down on us, not knowing just how close we'd come to having no Vegas at all.

Dimitri revved his bike. "Let's keep moving."

I knew Dimitri wasn't happy about being back in Las Vegas with Max. Worse, the last time he'd been here, he'd nearly been consumed by she-demons. Succubi look at griffins the same way Pirate sees pork chops—the ideal snack. I'd exterminated them, but it didn't make for happy vacation memories.

We eased into the traffic on The Strip. Cars streamed up and down, honking over the sound of tourists calling out to each other. Bright lights from dozens of casinos and restaurants flashed up and down the street.

I wouldn't have dragged us here if I'd had a choice, but we needed to know what level of demonic creature I was carrying around. The jar on my belt rattled as the plasticky creature threw itself at the glass. Vicious little beast.

"Max could be anywhere," Dimitri said.

"I know where to find him," I said.

"You do?" He didn't sound happy.

"I know where he lives." He'd be there, unless he was out hunting. If that was the case, we'd just have to wait. "Follow me."

Dimitri and I took the lead. Grandma and Flappy moved to the rear of the line. My bike shook and rumbled. Asphalt under my tires felt strange and slow after the speed and exhilaration of the fairy paths. Sid was going to spoil us.

I glanced back at the line of biker witches behind me, and to the dragon chasing the swooping spotlight on Paris Hotel's Eiffel Tower.

We snaked down Las Vegas Boulevard in bumper-to-bumper traffic. Flappy dove low over New York, New York, clipping the top of a skyscraper with his big toe. "Rrr-eek!"

Oh geez. I winced as bits of plaster rained down.

Flappy didn't notice. He'd perched at top of the Empire State Building to inspect his stubbed toe.

He was like a snaggle-toothed, naked King Kong. Without the girl. Which was good. I didn't need to find any more dragon eggs.

"Hey," Pirate called from Sidecar Bob's lap, "maybe I should ride with Flappy."

I took one last look at the dragon, whose face lit up as soon as he noticed me watching. "Not on your life."

We turned onto Highway 70 out of Vegas and followed it until the neon and strip malls ceased and we were instead surrounded by desert scrub and emptiness.

The headlights of the other drivers became scarcer and disappeared completely when we turned off onto a lonely side road. We cut through the dry, cool desert night until we came to an abandoned prison thirty miles outside of Harrison.

I'd known exactly where it was. I could feel the demons.

Gray metal guard towers loomed above rusted fences. Barbed wire twisted along the tops, its loops capturing Styrofoam cups and fast food wrappers. Weeds littered the ground and sprouted between the concrete basketball courts in the yard. A dented sign read *South East Nevada State Women's Minimal Security Correctional Center*.

I'd never forget my first and only other trip here, mainly because I'd hoped it would be my last.

We parked our bikes along the side and I fought not to choke as the pungent stench of sulfur burned the back of my throat.

"This place is wrong," Grandma muttered, tugging off her riding gloves.

"It only gets worse," I said, dread seeping through me.

Dimitri held open a cut in the fence and we slipped inside.

"Set up a guard around the perimeter," Grandma said behind me. "Ant Eater, Frieda, you guys take point. Pirate, see what the dragon can sniff out."

"Aye, aye, captain!" My dog exclaimed with enough get-up-and-go for an entire platoon.

I couldn't believe she was giving him a job. Then again, he always wanted to be a guard dog. And it would keep him out of the way. The real trouble lay inside those walls.

The biker witches scattered. Soon everything was

silent.

I stopped for a moment, taking it in. No crickets chirped, no night animals called. It was as if anything that could walk, crawl or slither away had long abandoned this place.

I didn't blame them. The deadness here made me want to sprint back to Vegas. The prison crouched like a half-eaten husk, an unnatural blight on the endless desert beyond.

A chill sent goose bumps skittering up my skin as my memory traced back to the last time the silence of a place had swallowed me whole.

Dimitri and I had been dumped head first into the wastelands of hell.

He glanced back, as if he were thinking the same thing. Over his shoulder, I saw a flutter of red light behind a darkened window. They were watching us.

We sounded like an invading army as our boots crunched over the crumbling parking lot. Ragged weeds pushed out of craters in the cement. Signs reserving spots for VIPs and visitors lay crumpled and rusting on the ground.

I focused on the building in front of us and reached out with my mind, honing in on the stickiest spots, or basically, anything that might be crouching and ready to pounce. Grandma's jar clanked against my leg. While I wasn't crazy about faceless, featureless, Silly Putty minions attacking out of the blue, it was better than skulking around, waiting for them to come to us.

The true horror rested low in the building. I counted at least three demons, twisting and angry, down in the caverns under the prison. No sign of Max—unless he was one of them.

Don't even think it.

We hurried behind a row of dead bushes at the edge of the parking lot and past an old prison cemetery on the side of the building. I stiffened as a cold presence slid down my back. It was just a ghost—I hoped.

We'd come to Max for answers. I didn't need any new battles to fight.

Sid tested the padlock on the iron industrial door with a window of chain-linked safety glass. "Houston, we have a problem."

Grandma groaned. "I'll go back for the lock eaters."

"Hold up," I said, feeling the cold steel under my hand. "Max," I called. He had to know we were here. "Max," I repeated.

"He must be out hunting," Dimitri said.

"Or he's compromised."

There was only one way to find out.

Sparks flew as I incinerated the padlock with a switch star. Max always said to act first and apologize later. Let's see if he'd be glad I took his advice.

We found ourselves at the entrance to a large industrial kitchen. Stale air mixed with the last of the fresh as we eased our way inside. Dimitri swung the door shut and darkness enveloped us.

Grandma stiffened next to me as the scarlet light of an orb hovered near a row of metal soup spoons. It moved between them, causing them to sway as if touched.

"Ignore it," Dimitri said.

He was right. We didn't need to waste our energy, unless it attacked. I pulled the Maglite out of my utility belt and shone it down, away from the windows.

The beam cut through the night and illuminated a pool of dried blood on the floor.

I caught my breath and followed the blood to a spatter on the rounded leg of a stainless steel counter, and up toward the ladles, serving spoons and tongs hanging over the metal counters on each side of us.

Please don't let it be Max.

The orb hovered, watching us, as I traced the blood back to a body slung over the kitchen tool rack.

The black claws of an imp shone under my light. The beam of my Maglite trailed up a gnarled hand, along a spindly arm up to a cutting board, where a knife protruded from the creature's leathery neck. Its weasel-like face snarled, even in death. Its thick, dark hair matted with blood and gore.

"Something is very wrong here," I said around the lump in my throat.

Grandma whistled under her breath. "You just figured that out?"

I took a step back. "Max would clean this up."

Unless he couldn't.

A glance at Dimitri showed he shared my concern.

Number one: imps answered to demons, so if there was one here, we could be walking into a trap. Number two: if Max hadn't cleaned up the body, he wasn't just out for the night. He was compromised.

"Come on," Dimitri said, stepping over the blood. "Let's see what we find."

"It can't be worse than a banshee horde," I said, knowing that wasn't true at all.

Focus. I worked to keep my breathing even as we took a left down a deserted hallway. I was responsible for this and for the safety of my friends. They were here because of me, because I needed answers. I'd proven myself as a demon slayer enough to be a target. Now I just had to learn to trust myself, and hope that a little knowledge wasn't worse than none at all.

"*Look to the Outside,*" I said to myself, trying to find comfort in the Three Truths of the Demon Slayer. "*Accept the Universe.*" Okay, we could skip the last one—*Sacrifice Yourself.*

We hurried down a narrow service corridor, our lights casting strange shadows on the cement block walls. The orb followed, just over my left shoulder. Anger radiated off it in waves. It hovered at the edge of my vision, a constant threat. But frankly, I had bigger worries.

I was alert almost to the point of being strung out as I led the way into the unknown. With every click of my heels against the linoleum of the forgotten passage, I felt like a rabbit lured into a trap. I could sense the demons below us, waiting until we had no chance of escape before they unleashed their fury.

Of course that's when the hallway dead ended into a gaping stairwell. The black maw led straight for the mass of evil.

I stopped at the top, the toes of my boots peering over the edge. Sulfur scoured my nose, along with mildew and decay. "I hate this part."

Dimitri stood at my back. "Want me to go first?"

"No."

I didn't want to go at all. Therefore, I rumbled straight down before I had a chance to dwell on it. It was like diving into cold water.

Our lights dimmed against the overwhelming darkness as I led us down the first stairway, the second, the third.

The orb burned brighter.

"You done this before?" Grandma asked, as if we were playing trivia.

She could pretend all she wanted. I didn't miss the breathless undertone in her voice.

"Yes," I said, chest tight as we reached the concrete floor of the prison basement.

"Your job sucks."

Oh yeah, now she tells me.

I flipped on the lights with a sudden, blinding brightness.

When my eyes adjusted, I saw more blood against

the stained concrete walls. Just what were we walking into?

"Get behind me, Lizzie," Dimitri said.

Nice thought, but, "you don't know the way," I reminded him.

These walls had been aqua once and still were in some places. In others, large chunks of paint peeled away like dead skin onto the floor. A massive network of pipes loomed overhead.

"This way," I said, following the splotches of shiny dark blood, leading us through what had been the prison laundry. The walls held ghostly outlines of machines ripped from their stations, leaving bare concrete and rusted pipes jutting from the walls.

My heart fluttered when I realized where the trail of gore was leading.

"Max houses his demons in the old steel cells. He picked this place because the cells have an unusually high iron content." It certainly wasn't for the décor.

Would the steel cells still hold the demons if Max ceased to be?

And what would I do if I found Max had finally turned into the enemy?

I forced myself to breathe steadily, in and out, as we crept down the last hallway, to the prison hole, put out of commission long before modern renovations. The overhead pipes didn't even reach this far into the underbelly.

Door upon door, at least twenty, led to a dead end. Each was a perfect steel box.

"Welcome to hell on earth," I said, stopping in front of the first set of massive steel doors. The wards in this place were amazing. I couldn't even sense them until I touched the door in front of me. It stung like dry ice.

On the other side, a demon shrieked and pounded against the metal, screaming when it came into contact with iron.

The second door held the same.

I lifted my hand against the third and was greeted with silence. I drew a switch star as I pulled it open. "We've found him."

A figure lay huddled in the corner of the cell. His honey blond hair hung in tatters over his face. Blood caked his temple and ran in dry rivers down his neck.

I drew a switch star. "Max?"

He raised his head, his angular features even sharper in the harsh shadows cast by my light, his eyes devoid of emotion.

Max dipped his chin by way of greeting. "Lizzie Brown." The platinum cross, designed to draw succubi, lay sideways over his bare and bloodied chest. "You look worse than I do."

Chapter Nine

I ducked under one of Max's arms. Dimitri took the other side as we pulled him to his feet. "What happened to you?" The man was a dead weight.

He groaned, dirty blond hair tumbling over his eyes. "Ate something that didn't agree with me."

"What? Like a demon?" I stumbled and Dimitri pulled more of Max's weight his way.

Max angled his head toward me. His lips curved in a slow, sensuous grin.

Oh for Pete's sake.

Max wasn't a demon slayer. He was a hunter. That meant he couldn't kill demons. He had to consume them. I watched him draw the life force out of a succubus once and it was the most erotic and disturbing thing I'd ever seen.

Of course, given a choice, he captured and imprisoned them down here in his holding cells.

Every evil being Max took into himself corrupted him. No one knew what his breaking point would be. Eventually, the wickedness he consumed would overpower what good he had left in him and Max would turn as evil as the things he killed.

I didn't want to be around when it happened.

Dimitri and I dragged Max out of the demon holding area, with Grandma guarding our rear.

"Whose idea was it to come visit?" Max asked, as if we'd stopped by to have a glass of lemonade on the porch.

"Mine," I told him.

That's all it took for the hunter to be way too satisfied with himself. "You see? She needs me."

"Fuck off," Dimitri growled as he pulled Max further away from me.

Well it seemed these two had taken up where they left off.

Dimitri didn't approve of the way Max consumed demons, or the fact that Max's mom had been a succubus. I could understand his point. But seeing that the sex demon had also killed Max's dad, the hunter had a huge chip on his shoulder when it came to evil beings. I liked that.

I kept my face neutral as Dimitri and I shuffled Max down a narrow cinderblock hallway to an old guard's station turned bedroom.

Yes, he lived with these things.

"In here," I said, kicking open a flimsy metal door. Next to it stood a stack of Campbell's chicken noodle soup cans.

Grandma gave the room a quick once-over. "You do what you have to do," she said. "I'll stand guard."

I hesitated. "Just you?"

She patted her brown hide bag. "I brought some friends."

I loved my grandma.

Max's bachelor pad hadn't changed since I'd seen it last. A narrow military-issue camping cot hugged the far wall. Underneath, shoved to the back, was a steel lockbox. Other than that, it was clear that nothing else in the fading office belonged to Max.

We deposited the hunter onto his cot. It crackled under his weight as he eased his way down. He was near collapse, but he still managed to radiate power. I'd never seen Max lose control. He carried himself like a Navy Seal. Even now, he refused to lie down in front of us. He remained upright with great effort, his back ramrod straight against the wall.

"Come for some demon target practice?" he asked, out of breath. "I got two in the back."

I'd sensed three. And the fact that he was lying sent a chill through me. Either he was hiding one, which I doubted, or Max didn't have much time.

"We came to ask you to look at something. But first," I said, bracing myself, "what did you mean back there when you said I was worse than you?"

"Lizzie, Lizzie." He pulled himself off the wall, wide shoulders shaking from the effort. "Come here."

I took a step forward, then two. A minute ago, I trusted this man. Now, I wasn't so sure.

His eyes were still amber. The small bend on the bridge of his nose tilted harder, as if he'd broken it again. Demons didn't heal crooked. The ones I'd seen had coal black eyes as well. He was still part human. For now.

Still, something about him wasn't entirely right.

He took my hand, running his thumbs along the soft spot under my wrists. "You've been touched. You don't feel it?"

"No."

Max's fingers radiated warmth. I resisted the urge to pull away as they lingered on my wrist.

His jaw set hard as he studied me. "I can tell it was inside you."

God bless America.

"How?" Dimitri demanded.

Max released my hand. "She's tarnished." He fixed on me. "What did you do?"

I had no idea. "Take a look," I said. My fingers

shook as I untied Grandma's jar from my demon slayer utility belt. The rubbery disk shot straight up toward the lid and bounced off with a sizzle. The rope cowered.

Max held the jar with both hands, like a rare piece of art. "Where did you get this?"

"It attacked me after I took out a horde of banshees. The disk can morph. It was a pressure bug when I found it. It changed when it hit the neutralizing magic in the jar."

Max's eyes narrowed. "Fascinating." He turned the jar over and over in his hands, sending the former bug into fits and the zombie rope into a dead faint.

He held the jar at eye level. "Your witches should show me this neutralizing magic."

Somehow I doubted that would go over well.

Dimitri wasn't amused in the slightest. "Lizzie's father is mixed up in something evil. We need to know how evil so we can be ready. Are you going to help us or not?"

Max didn't bother to hide his satisfaction.

"How bad is it?" I asked. "And why did it need to hide behind a half dozen banshees?"

The former insect slammed into the jar at every point Max's fingers touched. It was as if it wanted him more than anything.

The hunter didn't seem alarmed—or surprised.

"This, my dear Lizzie, is called a dreg." He tapped at the glass as the creature slammed into the other side. "I'm willing to bet it hid so it could get a good shot at you. Apparently to mark you."

"Mark me?" I hadn't seen any marks. But Max had.

Max glanced up. "So a demon can find you," he said, as if it were the most obvious thing in the world.

I had to think about that. "What? Like "X" marks the demon slayer?"

"In a manner of speaking." He tipped the jar over so the creature conked its head on the lid. Max seemed to enjoy riling it.

"A dreg is," he searched for the words, "a vestige of a demon meant to compel."

"Wait." I needed this in English. "You mean this is a piece of a demon?" I didn't even know they could break apart. This presented a whole new set of problems.

"No," Max said. "Think of it as a demon's personal assistant. In miniature form. It does what the unholy one wishes and holds much of its power."

Dimitri moved closer. "As in the ability to morph."

"Exactly," Max said, quite satisfied with himself. "Now here's the bad news —"

Oh mercy. "Because what you just told us was so fun."

He ignored my attempt at distance, drawing me closer, as intense as I'd ever seen him. "Dregs mean you should run, love. Run far, run fast. Because—" His breath touched my cheek as he moved to whisper in my ear. "—you don't want to know what's after you."

I couldn't move. "I'm not your love," I said low and angry, in case he was getting any ideas.

Naturally, Max didn't listen. He leaned back, giving me space. "It takes immense power or immense conflict to create a dreg. I haven't seen one since the Great War of '66."

"1966?" I asked.

Max shot me a look. "1866."

That's it. I was going to corner him for a demon slayer history lesson. Later.

Right now, I had my answer. "If it takes some sort of fantastical power to create a dreg, that means my dad couldn't have sent it." He hadn't slipped into demon status yet. I hoped. The idea of losing my dad before I even found him was too awful to imagine.

Of course, that meant we had a badass demon after us. I took a slow, shuddering breath, then another. I'd suspected as much after the creature had attacked me in my hotel room. It was another thing to have it confirmed.

Max still hadn't answered our most important question. "What level of demon are we talking about?"

Max tipped the jar, sending the dreg into another frenzy. "That's the million dollar question, isn't it?"

"Stop playing, Max."

He looked at me with mock innocence. "You said it changed into a pressure bug. That's not a very serious creature. They barely skim the first layer of hell." He returned his attention to the jar. "We'd have to watch it change again to see if it was toying with us, or if it can turn into something more fierce."

"What do you want to do?" Dimitri grumbled. "Ask it to change?"

Max gave a small smile. "I think it would like to attack me very much."

"Who wouldn't?" Dimitri wondered aloud.

"We'll take it to one of my holding cells," Max said, "and let it loose."

He had to be kidding. "We barely captured it the first time." It might be too powerful to be contained again. "We could have gotten lucky."

Max glanced up at me, the guile gone from his expression. "It's the only way we can observe it. You want answers, don't you?"

Yes, I wanted to know how bad this was, and if it could teach us more about who was after my dad. But let it out? We didn't know what level of hell we were dealing with.

I'd barely killed the fifth-level demon that had gone after Grandma. And I'd only eliminated the Las Vegas succubi after a struggle that I wasn't sure I could go through again. I couldn't imagine how powerful this new demon could be or what it wanted.

"My holding cells are secure," Max said, groaning as he planted both feet on the floor.

"Dimitri?" I asked.

"I don't know, Lizzie," he said, "it's a calculated risk. We need to keep moving forward on this."

It wasn't what I wanted to hear.

"Okay. Let's do it." Dimitri and I hoisted Max off the cot. With one of us on either side of him, we led him down the dark hallway and into the demon holding area where we'd found him.

"Wait. Where are we going?" Grandma asked, trailing behind us.

"Max wants to show me something," I said, not about to explain. If I had to lay out the details, I might change my mind and we couldn't afford that.

"There," he instructed, "last cell on the left."

"Any particular reason?" I asked, eyeing the lone bulb casting dark shadows on the wall.

"It's my lucky cell," he managed.

I didn't want to know why.

We eased Max down onto the floor. He still gripped the jar. "This will be an intimate exercise. It's best if it's just me," he gave me a penetrating look, "and Lizzie."

"No," Dimitri and I said at the same time.

Dimitri closed an arm around my shoulders.

"You don't know how to have any fun, Lizzie." Max cringed against a wave of pain.

"Max. Answer me straight. Do you have enough power to deal with this?"

If he were a beast he would have snarled. "I wouldn't be here if I didn't."

I glanced at Dimitri. "Grandma's outside," I said.

"If things go south in here, we have backup."

Dimitri swore under his breath.

I knew what he was thinking: my seventy-eight-year-old granny as backup. It didn't matter anyway if we had one witch out there or fifty. It was time to act. We needed to get a leg up on this new threat—and whoever sent it.

"You know I'm right," I said. We needed to do this.

He shook his head. "Damn you and your need to know everything."

"It's part of my charm," I said, realizing I'd won.

He trailed his fingers up my spine. "It's going to be the death of me."

"Probably not today."

"Is that a promise?" He leaned in close enough to kiss.

I couldn't help but smile. "No."

Max cleared his throat. "When you two are done having verbal intercourse, I'd like to get back to the dreg."

Dimitri closed his eyes. "Tell me again why you wanted to find this guy."

"Brace yourselves." Max began to twist the lid of the jar.

"It's not going to open for you," I said. He didn't have biker witch magic. "Only with me."

"Have it your way." Max shrugged, planting his elbows on his knees. "Again."

I reached for the jar. Dimitri let me go. Still, he eyed me nervously "Be careful. Remember what happened the last time that bug got loose." He'd had to dig it out of me.

I found myself wishing I could hold a switch star and open the jar at the same time. I'd just have to be fast.

It rattled in my hands as the dreg lunged for me.

The demon hunter dragged himself to his feet.

I didn't know what was going to come flying out when I opened the jar. The dreg might become a pressure bug again and fly straight for my face or neck this time. Or it might change into something worse.

My palms slickened with sweat.

Opening this jar, freeing these creatures, went against every instinct I had.

What would I do if I didn't have enchanted glass between me and the monster?

"Second thoughts?" Dimitri asked.

"And third and fourth," I said, twisting the lid.

"Lizzie?" Grandma banged on the door.

"We're fine," I called, right before all hell broke loose.

The disk shot out of the jar like it was on fire.

I drew a switch star as it dove straight for us. But my shot went wide. It was too small, I saw, horrified as the dreg slammed into the floor, shattering concrete. I leapt backward. Dimitri surged forward as it reared for another attack.

He was going to get himself killed.

My fingers closed around a second switch star. *Focus. Take it out.* I didn't think I'd get another chance.

I fired as it shot straight up.

Hells bells. Another miss!

My first switch star zoomed back to me and I caught it as Max plucked the dreg out of the air with inhuman speed.

Before it could bite him or burn him or burrow into his living skin, Max stuffed the dreg into his mouth and swallowed it whole.

"You –" I said, out of breath and staring as the lump of the dreg trailed down his throat.

He swallowed hard. "Not my fault," Max managed,

trying to work the dreg all the way down. "I assumed it would go for me first."

"What made you think you could eat it?" Dimitri demanded.

Max gripped this throat, still struggling to force the dreg all the way down. "It's what I do. I'm a hunter. I eat bad things for breakfast." He choked, pointing at his throat. "This one's from purgatory."

Dimitri seemed surprised. "How can you tell?"

Max made a strangled sound. "Tastes like chicken."

I stared at him for a long moment. "This is why you're going demonic."

Max shrugged, panting as the last of it went down. "So what? It's gone. Every one of them needs to be wiped off the face of the Earth."

"Well that's just super." I threw out my hands like an Italian grandmother, not caring a bit.

On paper, I understood Max's obsession with eliminating evil. But come on. I slammed the lid on the jar before the zombie rope could escape too.

"And you," I said, turning toward the immense griffin, "Stop being brave." Demons eat griffins like candy. I recognized Dimitri's insane desire to protect me. But if he jumped at another demonic creature, I was going to skewer him myself. Neither one of these lug heads wanted to look at the big picture—at the cost.

"Lizzie," Dimitri dashed past me to catch Max. He grasped the demon hunter by the shoulders and helped him slide down the wall.

Max gasped for breath. He rocked backward clutching his stomach, his eyes rolling back into his head.

"What's going on?" I asked, drawing a switch star.

Max's eyes bulged. "It's still alive," he gasped, fighting for breath.

"Impossible." Max ate things. Max destroyed evil.

"Remember how it burrowed into you, Lizzie?" Dimitri asked, checking Max's eyes. "He introduced it straight into his system."

Holy Hades.

"How do you feel, Max?" I asked, taking three steps backward. If the dreg had turned him, I needed a clean shot.

Max doubled over and screamed. He clutched his stomach, the corded muscles of his arms bulging with the effort.

My fingers tightened around the holes of the switch star.

"Stop it Lizzie," Dimitri checked his pulse. "It's the dreg."

"Are you sure?"

"Yes." I could tell from Dimitri's expression that he'd watched this before—when the dreg had taken hold of me.

Max writhed on the floor, his muscles twisted, his head slamming back against the concrete. His eyes fixed on a faraway place and blood mixed with spittle trickled from the corner of his mouth.

Fear welled in my throat. This is what would have happened to me if Dimitri hadn't dug the abomination out of my leg. I remembered the burning pain, the sheer terror. Max was suffering a nightmare meant for me.

"How long does it last?" I asked, worried, guilty and more than a little scared.

"I don't know."

I wanted to take some of the pain away, or to at least comfort him. Max didn't have anyone. I did the one thing that felt right given the circumstances. I reached out and took the hunter's hand.

He clutched it hard as another wave of pain poured

through him.

Dimitri's expression hardened. "I didn't say he wasn't going to turn."

"I have my switch stars right here."

"He doesn't need your help."

That was the thing—he did. Dimitri might be the one I loved, the man who gave until it hurt, but right now Max was the one who needed me.

I stayed with him until the worst of the pain passed. He shuddered one last time and cleared his throat as he lay still.

"You don't need to get up right away," I said.

Sweat beaded his forehead. "Yes, I do."

Max opened his eyes. They were still amber, thank the lord.

He forced himself to sit, his arms shaking. "I need to go that way," he said, pointing at the steel wall of the vault.

I swallowed, my mouth dry. "It's compelling him." Max had said it earlier. The dreg made you go places.

"Stick with us," I said, "we'll help you."

This thing was supposed to be in me, making me go.

Max winced. "I'm not sure I trust myself to travel."

"You don't have a choice," Dimitri said.

He was right. Max gave that up when he swallowed the dreg.

We knew it was from purgatory now, which meant we could go on to California.

Maybe Max could lead us to the one who sent the banshees, the one who'd hurt my dad. Besides, I reminded him, "you can't do your job if you're battling a demonic compulsion." I didn't want to leave him here alone. And I sure didn't want him letting any of those demons out.

"We'll help you destroy it," I promised. I hoped.

And if he turned, I was the only one who could keep him from going rogue. I'd step up and put Max out of his misery.

Max groaned and threw his head back as a fresh wave of pain hit him.

This could have been me.

Dimitri seemed to be thinking the same thing. He cringed as he watched the hunter fight through it.

I squeezed Max's arm. "We owe you that much."

He'd helped us defeat the demons in Las Vegas, he'd let us know what we were dealing with tonight. And he was suffering.

"We don't have much of a choice," Dimitri said, resigned. He came from a warrior's philosophy—you're either on our side or you're not. Dimitri didn't have much time for creatures like Max, or the complications they could trigger.

"Dimitri," I repeated.

A muscle in his jaw twitched. He had to see the truth that I didn't want to say out loud: the torture could make Max turn.

"All right, hunter." Dimitri bent down and eased an arm around Max, pulling him to his feet. "You're with us now."

Chapter Ten

Now all I had to do was convince the fairy to let Max tag along.

Grandma and I kept alert as we ducked out of the darkened prison and hurried across the broken down parking lot. Dimitri and Max stayed behind to dispose of the dead imp and mop up the blood.

We'd left just as Max had begun giving my griffin instructions. That was bound to go over well.

"I don't like it," Grandma said.

Truth be told, I didn't either.

"We don't have a choice. We have to bring Max with us," I said, glancing over my shoulder.

A glowing red orb had followed us as far as the kitchen. We certainly didn't need any supernatural troublemakers on the road. A clumsy dragon, a talking dog and a zombie rope were plenty, thank you very much.

The night had grown colder. I rubbed my arms for warmth as we hurried toward the bikes. I couldn't wait to get beyond the fence line—and as soon as Dimitri and Max joined us—away from this place all together.

"I can't believe you let him eat your bug," Grandma huffed.

'Let' wasn't the right word in my opinion.

"There's nothing we can do about it now," I said,

allowing her to slip through the hole in the fence ahead of me. "We need to focus on getting to California."

She nodded, taking note of the lights from the patrols. "I'll convince the witches. You take Sid."

An entire coven versus Sid? Somehow, I think Grandma got the better end of the deal.

When she saw my expression, Grandma just laughed and slapped me on the back.

She knew what was coming. So did I.

A minute later, Sid and I stood by the bikes. He crossed his meaty arms over his chest and scowled. He'd gone from smelling like bubblegum to reeking of burned cheese. And I was pretty sure he was about two seconds from siccing Ant Eater on me.

"I am not taking that degenerate down a fairy path."

"Heavens to Betsy, Sid. It's one more person."

Sid narrowed his eyes. "He's not a person."

"Just because he's half demon," and slightly possessed, "and he lives in an abandoned women's prison does not mean we can't help him out."

Out of the corner of my eye, I saw Max staggering across the parking lot with a lockbox in one hand and a pack slung over his shoulder. Dimitri followed like an immense, angry shadow.

We didn't have much time before this was going to turn into a very personal discussion.

"Look, Sid." I leaned in close and tried not to choke as I caught a waft of charred brie. "The sooner we fix this with my dad, the sooner you and Ant Eater can get back to New Jersey."

"Newsflash, princess. I can do what I do with my lady in Jersey, Vegas or Timbuktu." He jabbed his thumb behind him, toward the prison. "That guy is our worst nightmare. Fairy paths aren't indestructible. He'll clog up the lines."

"I also have a taste for Mag Mell Mushrooms," Max

said over Sid's shoulder.

The fairy jumped a foot, showering glitter on my shoes.

"Smooth move," I said to the unrepentant hunter. "Wait. You've been on the trails before." How else would he know about the mushrooms?

"I've been around."

The man was frighteningly intense, even when he was about to keel over.

Sid took a step backward, one beefy arm out in front of him. "Well, you're not coming with me."

There was no way around this. Max had to come. Of course Sid didn't have to open the fairy path, but frankly, I was used to gliding on air. Which gave me an idea.

"What if he doesn't touch the trails?"

Sid rolled his eyes. "Aside from that being impossible—"

"I can levitate," I said.

Dimitri's mouth split into the first grin I'd seen on him all night.

He'd told me I didn't use my powers enough. It had been so hard to wrap my head around the idea of being a slayer that I sometimes tended to go with familiar solutions. Not this time.

Maybe I was getting the hang of these powers.

Sid knew it too. Still, he wasn't about to go down without a fight. It was the principal of the thing. "You promise you won't let him touch a path?"

"You got it."

"Not a blade of grass."

"Or a Mag Mell Mushroom," Max added.

I elbowed him in the ribs. "Not helping."

"Fine," Sid muttered. "But he's finding his own way back from California."

"Agreed," Max said.

"Fantastic. It's settled." Frankly, I hoped he'd make it that long.

As we gathered up the coven to leave, Max eased onto the back of my bike. It felt strange to ride with a man who wasn't Dimitri. Max wrapped his arms around me.

"That's a bit tight," I said.

His warm breath brushed my ear. "Any looser and I'd fall off."

From the expression Dimitri wore, I don't think he would have minded Max falling off—and getting run over while he was at it.

We rumbled away from the abandoned prison, kicking up dust as we hit the road. Sid led us farther into the desert, down highway 95 until we came to a sign that advertised The Red Hot Rockettes. I hoped they weren't like the real Rockettes because these girls were lounging on a bear skin rug, posed strategically in nothing but their smiles. They did not look like they should be forming a kick line.

Sid pulled off near the sign and we followed him. My bike bumped over several ruts in the shoulder of the road and Max jostled behind me.

"Is that a cyanide injector in your pocket are you just happy to be riding with me?" I joked.

"Is that demon slayer humor?" he asked, amusement finding its way into his voice.

"I'm trying," I said. "How's the pain?"

"Don't ask."

"Let's focus on the road," Dimitri muttered next to us. "And on your powers. You remember what to do?"

Dimitri had given up his position in the back and was riding a tight shotgun. Any closer and he'd qualify as a sidecar.

"You worry too much," I said, desperate for levity. It was bad enough we had my dad to cure, banshees on our tail and a semi-possessed hunter at my back. Now Dimitri had to question my ability to get this bike airborne.

Truth be told, I was a little concerned myself.

My mentor had taught me how to levitate by making me jump out of a tree. The landings weren't pleasant and that's when I only had myself to worry about. But Max and I weren't leaping off high branches or coasting down a cliff. I just had to get the bike airborne a few inches and hold us there.

Frieda pulled up on the other side of us. "You okay?"

"Of course." The worst thing about wondering, worrying if I was going to pull this off was that everybody seemed to have the same doubts as me.

They needed to have some faith. So did I.

I clutched the handlebars of my bike.

Sid groaned as he dragged open a sliding door straight out of the billboard pole. Inside, a fairy path bloomed.

"Let's do this." I kicked my front tire up and reached deep inside of me.

Accept the Universe. There was no other way to get to Pasadena by morning. This had to happen.

I found the flicker of power I needed and with a wince and a prayer, the front tire of my bike lifted off the ground and onto the moonlit fairy path. I tried to hide my surprise and delight when the back tire did the same.

"Let's move, people," Sid called, jogging to his bike. Max and I whizzed past him, and just like that, we were off.

We rode Bumpy Jump Junction through purple desert canyons and on to Limeny Quick, a trail flush with pink hummingbirds and mounds of wild honeysuckle.

The highway ran greener and wilder as we approached the coast. The trees bloomed with exotic flowers and dripped with red and purple fruit.

Levitating came surprisingly easy after I'd convinced myself I could do it. It was like taking a separate road—a better one. This way, I didn't rumble over the stone fairy bridges. Max and I went up and around them.

The hunter shuddered against my back as we zoomed past a field of rainbows.

"You okay?" The spasms weren't coming as often the nearer we got to Pasadena, but they seemed more violent.

Max didn't answer.

Don't go changing on me. Not on the back of a hog.

The closer we came to the coast, I could also feel my dad. I sensed him in the same burning way I'd felt him that night outside Big Nose Kate's.

I gunned my bike.

When I was a kid, I had fantasies about what my real parents would be like. They wouldn't make me study so hard or stand so straight, or eat Grandma Renquith Noxington IV's paté. My true parents would love me even if my room wasn't clean and I smelled like last night's horse riding lessons.

If only they hadn't given me up.

But they had.

I'd convinced myself for years that it had been for some great cause that I couldn't understand.

Someday, they'd come back for me and they'd see how wonderful I was and they'd want me. They'd regret giving me up. We'd be a family again.

I wasn't that naïve anymore. I didn't believe anyone was perfect, much less the people that left me to be raised by someone else. My adoptive parents had done their best, but it was obvious we didn't have much in common.

Now the only thing I wanted from my birth parents was some sort of validation for who I was. Some reason for what I felt and what I'd become. My mother had set me on the path to becoming a demon slayer. My father had supernatural powers

I'd save him. I'd show him what he'd been missing in the last thirty years.

And maybe, just maybe, if I was really lucky, I wouldn't have to prove anything. He'd see it on his own.

"Hold up. Hey." Sid zoomed up on my side. "Exit to the left."

Sid rumbled his bike ahead of us. He slowed and came to a stop under a willow tree next to a babbling brook.

"Damned side exits," Sid grumbled as he lurched off his bike and began splashing through the creek. He dug his fingers into a brown gate at the edge of a meadow and pulled it open.

We were immediately assaulted with rap music. The thump-thumping beats of "Jump Around" blared into the meadow, accompanied by the smell of gasoline and McDonalds French fries.

Personally, I was a bit disappointed to be exiting from paradise but at least now I could keep my tires on the ground.

"Welcome to San Fernando," Sid said like an overly proud tour guide.

"We wanted to go to Pasadena," I protested.

"This is a fairy trail, not door-to-door delivery." Sid grumbled. "We'll take the 210 south and we'll be there lickety split."

We exited the fairy path and found ourselves in an alley behind a row of fast-food restaurants. It was a world of grease, packed Dumpsters and car horns. The zombie rope leapt inside the jar, thunking it against my leg. Either he was a fan of McDonald's fries or he knew we were close.

Sid led us to the 210 south and we took it into Pasadena.

We rode down a main street, teeming with car dealerships, more fast-food places and a surprising number of dry cleaners. It was newer than the valley, but not too different.

"Let me drive," Max said against my ear.

I nudged him out of my personal space. "Not on your life."

"Then make a left at the Taco Bell."

"Gotcha." I made the turn. Half the witches made it through the light with me. The rest waited in the middle lane with Flappy the dragon. Somebody was going to have an accident. Dimitri circled back to try and get Flappy in the air.

We pulled over to wait in the back parking lot of a Bed Bath & Beyond. "How much farther?" I asked.

Max strained, as if looking for a sign. "How should I know? I didn't swallow a road map along with the dreg."

The zombie rope banged against the lid of the jar like a Mexican jumping bean.

"Why am I following you anyway?" I asked. If the dreg didn't come from my dad, I should be following my own instincts.

The zombie rope banged harder. "See?" I said, pointing at the jar. "Look who agrees with me."

Max balked. "You're going to take the advice of that thing over me?"

I considered it for a moment. "Yes."

Even though we'd made it to Pasadena, I couldn't seem to get a direct lock on my dad. I tried to sense the burning from before, but near the busy street, I was only coming up with car exhaust.

"This way?" I asked the zombie rope, turning left.

The zombie rope banged his head on the top of the jar.

"Over here?" I asked, doing a full 180.

The zombie rope danced.

We might be onto something. "No kidding? He's that way?"

"You can't be serious," Max groaned.

"I've never heard you whine before."

"Keep it up and I'll be forced to do it a lot more."

The rest of the gang made it through the light and I gunned my engine. "This way," I said, heading across the parking lot and down a back alley.

The rope led us through the alley and back up Mesa Avenue. He took us through a maze of crowded streets flanked with strip malls, drive-through banks and at least twelve In 'N Out Burgers. Every time he banged his head against the glass, I knew we'd taken a wrong turn.

Finally we exited onto a narrow, tree-lined street. Pale stucco houses lined up behind immaculately kept lawns. If an angel lived in Pasadena, I could see him living here. The neighborhood was gorgeous.

Of course now I didn't even need the zombie rope to tell me which house belonged to my dad. A lonely brown house cowered at the end of the street. Paint peeled from it in small sheets. It sat on a hill held up in part by a concrete retaining wall. The near side had rotted completely, leaving rusting metal rods. The lawn was brown. The bushes on either side of the front walk had died and it was a wonder no one had called the city and reported the awful stench of burned hair and sulfur.

The only color heck, the only thing that remained whole and untouched—was the blue front door. It stood in stark contrast to the rest of the house.

Even the zombie rope shuddered.

I shut down my bike.

"This isn't where we're supposed to go," Max said behind me.

"This is my stop," I told him, getting off.

I'd never seen anything like it. It was as if death radiated from this place.

"It's not worth it, Lizzie," Grandma muttered, pulling off her riding gloves.

"It is to me."

"Let's get it over with," Dimitri said, heading straight past us.

Zap!

The moment his booted foot crossed onto my dad's front lawn, an unseen charge hurled him back to the street.

"Dimitri!"

He landed flat on his back and barely missed cracking his head on Frieda's bike.

I rushed up to him. "Are you okay?"

He rubbed at his head. I helped him up, giving him a quick kiss on the forehead. He felt hot.

"It's solid," he muttered.

Which meant Max had to try it.

Zap! The unseen wall threw Max flat on his back a few feet away.

H-e-double-hockey-sticks. I half expected my dad to come to the door and see what the commotion was about. But the curtains in the windows didn't even sway.

"Don't I get a kiss?" Max dug his elbows into the dead grass and struggled to sit up.

In his demon-hunter dreams.

"Let me try something." Grandma dug at the chain around her neck. A Ziploc bag dangled on it, held up by a safety pin. Inside, living spells twisted and curled, practically falling over themselves as they vied for her attention.

They were like living pulses of energy, flattening, lengthening, and twirling as the mood saw fit. One lime green spell kept leap-frogging the others, as if it knew she'd pick it.

Grandma eased open the bag and snagged a hot pink spell.

I watched it curl under and try to rub up against her fingers. "What does it do?"

"Oh this is just a simple, 'get your butt to dinner' spell. Good for when Battina wanders off looking for wild lavender." She winked. "It'll also tell us what we've got going here or at least who can get in."

She flung the spell at my dad's house and it zapped up against the invisible barrier. The spell flew back and smacked Pirate in the chest.

"Now what was that all about?" He paused for a moment, stunned. "You know I could go for a burger? Maybe three. With mustard and cheese and more cheese and crispy bits."

"Nothing can get through," Max said.

"I don't buy that." I was called here. I drove three thousand miles of fairy paths to be here and I wasn't about to just walk away.

There had to be an explanation.

Dimitri came jogging around the side of the house. "The entire place is warded."

"Are you sure?"

He glanced back. "Unfortunately."

"Stand back, Lizzie," Pirate said, kicking up brown grass with his back legs. "This is a job for a dog."

"Oh, no you don't," I said. "Stay." Before he could protest, I walked straight into it.

I made it partway through until my switch stars hit

the barrier and a giant electric shock slammed into me and sent me reeling onto my butt. I landed hard on the sidewalk, my teeth rattling.

"Ohh…" Pirate rushed up to lick my face. "Are you okay? I told you I'd go too. Did you know you didn't get zapped back as far as anybody else? I saw that. In fact, I saw you didn't get zapped at all until your belt hit it. And then whammo—goodbye, Lizzie. Lizzie?"

I brushed him aside and stood. "Did anybody else see me go through?"

Dimitri stood with his arms crossed, a thundercloud of mistrust.

"You saw it!" The only thing that snagged me had been my switch stars. I could go through.

If I surrendered my weapons.

On second thought, that might not be the best idea. I chewed at my lip, studying the house. It didn't look as if anyone lived here.

"My dad has to be here," I said.

Dimitri frowned. "Because the zombie rope said so."

The zombie rope and I had come to an understanding of sorts, but I wasn't about to admit that to Dimitri. Not right now anyway.

We didn't travel this far not to check it out. "I know it's crazy to go anywhere unarmed." Some days I didn't even want to shower without my switch stars. But extreme situations called for extreme measures. "You're going to be right out here."

"Where we can't get to you," Dimitri said.

"And you'll have your weapons."

"Which we probably can't fire through your dad's wards," Grandma said, lining up next to Dimitri.

Hells bells.

"He may be hurt in there," I told them.

"Or it could be a trap," Dimitri said.

But they knew I'd already made up my mind.

Grandma dug through her leather bag. "Take this," she said, handing me a jar of brackish yellow sludge. "Throw it."

"What will it do?" I asked.

"Nothing."

"Grandma," I warned.

She shrugged. "It might singe his lawn. Look. The point is to see if you can get a spell through the barrier."

"Fine." I launched the jar, cringing as it sizzled past the barrier and exploded onto my dad's lawn, leaving a Pirate-sized crater. None of the dust or rocks made it past the wards, which was really creepy.

"Good," Grandma said, rummaging through her bag as if we hadn't just launched a small explosive at my dad's house.

"If you're going in there, take this." She handed me a jar of red sludge.

It felt slippery. I held it with two hands. "This is a death spell."

"You walked through a death spell before," she reminded me.

I wasn't worried about myself.

"I can't use this on my dad," I protested. "Haven't you always said I shouldn't carry a weapon if I'm not willing to use it?"

Grandma planted her hands on her hips. "Oh for Pete's sake, Lizzie. What's the difference between this and a switch star?

I wedged the jar under my arm as I unbuckled my utility belt and handed it to Grandma.

Dimitri frowned. "Bring the spell, Lizzie."

"Does this mean I have your blessing to go in there?"

"Does it matter?" he asked.

I didn't know how to answer that. This wasn't a committee. This was me saving my dad, or at least finding out what kind of trouble had him contacting me after thirty years of silence.

"Okay. Let me get organized." I took the jar with the poor cowering zombie rope and shoved it into my right pocket. Then I wedged my flashlight down the front of my pants.

Pirate jumped up on my leg. "You can do it!"

"Thanks, doggie," I said, picking him up for a quick head rub before handing him off to Dimitri. No way I wanted my dog following me in there, even if he could make it through the barrier.

And I wasn't about to put anything past Pirate.

I picked up the death spell. Butterflies danced in my stomach. "Here goes nothing," I said, closing my eyes as I stepped into the ward.

This time, it felt like walking through warm butter.

I looked back to Grandma, Dimitri and the biker witches. They couldn't help me now.

It was me, the red jar and the zombie rope.

I clutched the death spell, praying I didn't have to use it, as the blue door creaked open.

Chapter Eleven

God. Everything was dead. My boots crunched over wilted weeds still reaching out from between the flagstone walk. Abandoned birds' nests hung crookedly from bare trees. I wanted to see a bug, a leaf, anything. But nothing lived in this yard.

We'd see about inside.

I'd never felt the absence of my utility belt as I did right then. It was like going in without a part of me. I missed the familiar weight of it, the unspoken energy.

As the air touched my skin where the belt usually hung, I hoped I'd done the right thing. My dad would never harm me. I hoped.

I clutched Grandma's spell jar.

My mother had been less than trustworthy when I'd met her. But that had been early, when I'd first become a demon slayer. She'd sought me out to warn me and when I didn't take her advice about quitting the job, she'd grown insistent in her own creepy way.

This was different. It had to be. My dad called me. He needed me.

Maybe he even wanted me.

My boots echoed on the concrete porch. This place was eerie in its silence. I knew the biker witches were behind me, watching. Their silence was disturbing to say the least. Since when were the biker witches the quiet types?

"Here goes," I said to myself, just to hear something, anything, as I pushed open the blue door.

"Dad?" I stepped onto the straw welcome mat and felt a movement underneath. "Yak!" I almost fell over backward as the mat skittered away. It moved like it was on legs, but that was impossible because it was a straw welcome mat with strawberries and blueberries and birdies on top and straw mats did not move.

Heart pounding, I surveyed the rest of the small entryway. A brass stand held a sturdy looking black umbrella. My adoptive parents would approve.

Be prepared and you'll never come up short, Cliff used to say.

Boy did he have a thing or two to learn about the supernatural world. As it stood, I just hoped the umbrella wasn't alive. I half expected it to take flight in front of me.

"Dad?" I called, not really wanting to venture any farther. He had to have heard the explosion on the lawn. If he was here.

"What do you think?" I asked the zombie rope. He curled around the bottom edge of the jar. "I see you're not as gung-ho as you were." He didn't say anything, just lifted his frayed end and sniffed the air.

Death and sulfur. It was about the worst combination you could have. I'd also detected it on the night I'd first seen my father, but it was stronger in here.

They say animals know things. While the zombie rope didn't necessarily qualify, I didn't miss the fact that he'd been excited as heck to get here and not so happy once we'd arrived.

Things had gotten worse, I knew it. The question was—what kind of evil were we looking at?

Believe me, there were degrees. I'd witnessed that

myself.

The place had very few windows to begin with. With the curtains drawn, it seemed like twilight. I switched on my flashlight.

My dad still hadn't come out to greet me. Was he even here? Was he alive?

Even worse, had he turned?

"Okay, bub." I patted the jar. "Onward and upward."

Or merely forward, which was going to be hard enough. The rope curled into the back of the jar. I could see his point. I really didn't want to go farther into this house, either.

Still, we'd come this far. I needed to learn more about the man who'd had me, the important things, like how I could save him, and the not-so-important things like how he met my mom, how he spent his time and why he decided to let me go.

On our left, we came to a small living room shrouded in quilts and desperation. Books and journals littered the floor and side tables, their pages spilling open with symbols and colorful diagrams.

Letters scrawled across the walls in dripping dark sludge. I winced. The room held the coppery tang of blood.

Subvenio arranagnato Zatar unum levis letum

I took a deep breath. You didn't need to be a supernatural genius to know the good guys didn't scrawl their prayers in blood.

The word *Zatar* dripped from the side of an oak bookcase, the ceiling above me and—I realized in horror—slashed into the door I'd closed behind me.

Who was this Zatar?

I edged into the room, careful not to touch the books, or step on them or even look too long at any one of them. I could feel the power radiating from them. It sizzled up the walls from the words scrawled with hideous affection.

Gold script scrolled across the pages. Demons danced with the damned in blackened wastelands. They tore at their captives, shredding skin and emptying bowels as they laughed and cavorted. They ate the flesh and drank blood from gold cups.

One demon in particular made me pause. He had the scaled body of a lizard and face of an angel. Handsome and strong, with a crown of golden hair, he must have been magnificent before his fall. The silver and white wings of an angel sprouted from his leathery back and I froze when I realized this was not a drawing. It was a photograph.

Inscribed below it were the words *Zatar, Earl of Hades*.

Goose bumps shot up my arms. Just who was my dad hanging out with? And why was he asking me to save him from hell when he was calling these people into his living room?

I glanced at the book again. I couldn't help myself. *Zatar, commander of sixty-six legions of dark angels.*

Hell.

Here I stood, without my switch stars, holding a death spell that would only work on a mortal—my dad, who had been calling demonic royalty into his living room.

Any help I could hope to find was trapped outside behind the strongest ward Grandma had ever seen and frankly, that was saying a lot.

As much as I wanted to save my biological father, this was too much. The place was too horrible and too wrong, and I wasn't about to walk around a corner and face a demon.

"I'm leaving," I said to anyone who might be listening. "Come on, buddy," I said to the rope, who had curled up into a teeny tiny ashen ball.

I backed out of the room slowly and just as my heel hit the hardwood entryway, a voice threaded from the back of the house. "Wait."

My throat caught. It wasn't Zatar. I'd be able to feel it if a demon entered the house. Still, the voice sounded wrong. It echoed, detached from humanity.

"Who is it?" I asked, taking another step backward.

"It's me, Lizzie," the disembodied voice echoed, "your dad."

My heart caught in my throat. "I was afraid you'd say that."

My hand wandered down to where my switch stars used to be. What I wouldn't give for one now. Even if this wraithlike voice did belong to my long-lost dad, I didn't want to face him without protection—not with the company he'd been seeking.

"Come out here," I said, two feet from the front door. I could run if I had to. I'd never been the fastest kid in school, but minions from hell can do wonders for your speed and agility. Well, that and a few new demon slayer powers.

"I can't. Lizzie, please."

"If you can get out here to write on the walls in blood, you can come out now."

I was answered with silence.

"Dad?"

Nothing.

"I'm out of here," I said, wincing. I hated to leave him, but I wasn't crazy. I couldn't follow him farther and farther into a house with demonic incantations scrawled in blood on the walls. I may read a lot of novels where the heroine does brave and reckless things but in real life, those things are beyond stupid and I refused to be killed or damned because I wasn't bright enough to stay out of an obviously hellish situation.

"Goodbye, Dad." I turned the knob on the door behind me.

"Lizzie." He shuffled around the corner.

Holy heaven.

He hunkered under a dirty bathrobe caked with dried blood. Dark circles ringed his eyes. He'd lost at least twenty pounds and clutched at the wall as if he'd fall over if he let go.

Roaches skittered across the floor. It was everything I could do to lift my eyes away from the advancing insects and to this shell of a man who called himself my father.

"What happened?"

He folded his lips over his teeth like an old man unable to speak.

"Answer me," I said. If these roaches were enchanted I was going to be ticked.

I advanced on the nearest insect, a brown one at least two inches long. I stomped it with my boot before it could scuttle closer. I felt a satisfying, cringe-worthy crunch and lifted my boot away. At least it wasn't magical.

My dad fought for every word. "I'm being punished."

"No kidding," I uttered, my last word ending in a squeak as the roach I'd smashed began waving its spindly legs. Its body snapped into place and it began waving its antenna.

Oh my word. "Zombie roach." I was going to be sick.

"Zatar wants me," he said, his voice ending in a dry cough as a new flurry of roaches pattered across the floor. "Help me."

I stood, stunned. "You're calling up dead things. I stared so hard my eyes dried out as the coffee table in the living room began to splinter and crack. "It's trying to move!" A woolen sock flip flopped on the carpet next to the bookcase.

Anything that was ever alive or could be alive was starting to move.

"I am a harbinger of death."

I swallowed the lump in my throat, and resisted the urge to say *yes, you are.*

I blinked, still not quite able to believe it. "You're calling these things back to life."

"Help me." My father clutched the wall, eyes wild.

"Did you send a dreg after me?" I demanded.

"No. Of course not." He shook his head. "Zatar is building an army."

That demon? That lizard with an angel's face? "For what?"

My dad hacked out a cough, and the entire bookcase shuddered. "The final revolution."

Oh no.

Why couldn't this be a simple case of a semi-demonic father? Oh who was I kidding? I didn't even know how to solve that and now we were talking about a revolution in hell?

My father's haunted eyes fixed on me. "He's killed the slayers. Now he's coming."

I stared at the bloody curses on the wall. "Aw, hell." This time last year, I was a preschool teacher in Atlanta. Now I had to take out the Earl of Hades. It didn't add up.

"I can't do this by myself," I said, overwhelmed and more than a little scared. I didn't think adding a griffin, a hunter and a few dozen biker witches would help, either.

"You must," my Dad insisted.

I took a deep breath. "What does Zatar want? Besides you?"

He shook his head.

I knew he was afraid to use his voice, and with good reason, but he had to help me out here.

"Do you know?" I asked.

"Save me," he said, struggling over every word. "We can stop Zatar together."

"Like a father-daughter kick-butt team?"

He grit his teeth.

"How do I help you?" I asked.

He shook his head. "Just do."

"Okay." I could figure this out. I'd solve this. Somehow. "Hang tight. I will help you."

I couldn't fail. I refused to let this Zatar have my dad. Something big was going down. "He's not going to use you."

It tore me up to think this may be the only version of my father that I'd ever meet.

"After this is all over, you're going to take me out for ice cream." At least that's what I thought dads and daughters did. I wanted to have a real conversation with him, get to know him—and myself. The alternative was unthinkable.

Chapter Twelve

So what do you do when Zatar the demon is after your dad?

Plan. At least that was my approach. I needed to come up with a strategy, a way to beat Zatar that wouldn't hurt, kill or (God forbid) damn my dad. Luckily, I had a demon-slaying expert out on the front lawn.

I burst out of the house. "Max!"

My eyes burned with the sudden change from my dad's darkened house to daylight. No matter. I took the steps two at a time, eager to find Max and to get the heck out of that creep show my dad called a house.

I slowed my pace as the witches drew their spell jars. Squinting, I tried to make out faces in the throng of biker witches forming a semi-circle around the house.

"Hold your fire," I said. "It's just me." I hoped.

Braced for attackers, I turned. The blue door hung open. To my relief, nothing stirred inside. Well, except for the straw doormat.

It flopped out onto the front porch and shuffled sideways until it collided with a flowerpot full of brown hydrangeas.

"It's just a zombie doormat," I said.

Nothing to see here.

The biker witches recoiled as a unit.

Tell me about it. I'd sure feel better once we'd put a few miles between us and this place.

I half wondered if the hydrangeas would come back to life. Scratch that. I didn't want to know.

A large winged griffin swooped overhead, his red, purple and green feathers bright against the blue sky. Dimitri. The man was hard to miss. My eyes adjusted and I cringed as I saw another winged beast in the distance. Flappy. And he had a small knobby-headed passenger. Cripes. If I told Pirate once, I told him a hundred times—no riding the dragon.

I reached the edge of the wards and shuddered as I pushed through the warm, soupy barrier. From this side, it tasted stale and dead. I rubbed at my lips with the back of my hand. Yuk.

Grandma spared me any sympathy. She shoved my demon slayer utility belt against my chest. "What happened to you in there? Did you see Xavier?"

I hitched the belt around my waist, the familiar weight of it soothing my frayed nerves. "Dad's in real bad shape," I said, glancing back at the house. "Where's Max?"

She rolled her eyes. "Gone."

A sliver of panic stabbed me. "What do you mean gone?"

"He muttered something about unfinished business and took off."

For heaven's sake, "we're supposed to be following him." We needed to know what the dreg was supposed to do. "You didn't stop him?"

"And leave you alone in there?" she asked. "No. Besides, you ever tried to stop Max from doing something?"

"Yes." And I expected Grandma to know a few more dirty tricks.

I rubbed at the dull ache forming along the bridge of my nose. *Not now.* I needed something to go right. If history was any indication, Max tended to create more problems than he solved.

If only he hadn't eaten the dreg.

Grandma said what I'd been thinking. "I'll bet whatever was in that dreg compelled him."

"Yes, but where?"

"That's the million-dollar question, isn't it?"

A small part of me was relieved that the attack in the desert hadn't come from my dad. Of course now it likely came from Zatar, the Earl of Hades.

Pirate jumped up against my leg. I scooped him up. "The prodigal dog returns."

He wriggled against my stomach. "I watched Max drive away."

Hope surged in my chest. "Did you see where he went?

"Naw. I was too busy trying to teach Flappy to roll over."

"In the air?" I lifted him to face me. "Were you even using a harness?"

He tilted his head. "Aw, you know that messes up my fur. Besides, Flappy and I were real careful."

"Flappy." I used my sternest voice. The dragon was trying to hide behind a tree. It didn't work. "You both know better."

"Snurfle," the dragon whined.

Yeah, that had better be dragon for I'm-dreadfully-sorry-I'll-never-do-it-again-and-by-the-way-lavendar-hair-looks-ravishing-on-you.

I let Pirate down and he ran straight to Flappy. I didn't know what I was going to do with those two.

Grandma wrapped an arm around my shoulders. "Come here." She led me down the sidewalk, away from everyone else. "Frankly Lizzie, Max is expendable. We were more worried about you. That house is alive. I can almost see it breathing. After you closed the door, I got the sick feeling I'd never see you again."

"I'm fine," I said, pretending I didn't know exactly what she meant. "Do you know anything about a demon named Zatar?"

She considered it. "No."

"Then we do need Max," I said. Sure I could Google it, but I was willing to bet Max knew things that weren't on any research sites.

Grandma swore under her breath. Evidently she was thinking the same thing. "He'll turn up."

"I hope," I said. "Maybe he'll lead us to whatever sent the dreg."

Grandma crossed her arms over her chest. "Because we need another enemy besides the demon who is after your dad." She gave me a long look. "If we're going to be facing down a demon of that caliber, we need to hunker down and prepare. I'll also put in a call to Rachmort."

She pulled out her cell phone and hit a button. "Damn," she said, phone to her ear, "voicemail."

My mentor had me worried. "He usually answers his phone."

"Unless he can't catch a signal. I doubt Sprint has towers in Purgatory."

Grandma pressed a button and left a message for him to call us back right away.

"Are you sure he's in purgatory right now?" I asked. "He spends half the year in Boca Raton."

"Only the winters," Grandma said. "Sometimes fall."

I hoped he wasn't in trouble. Rachmort trained demon slayers, but he also worked with the semi-damned creatures trapped between heaven and hell. He worked for the Department of Intramagical Matters in the Lost Souls Outreach Program, which was kind of like a supernatural Peace Corps. They didn't have a lot of necromancers, so Rachmort was up to his knees in spirits.

"Come on," I said, heading back.

The witches were watching us. They knew something was up. I glanced back at the house. "I used to think dead was dead."

Grandma grunted. "You also thought dogs couldn't talk."

"And fairies were cute."

"And hell was made up," Grandma added.

Boy did I wish that last one were true.

Speaking of mythical beings... "Did anyone see where Dimitri flew?" He should have shifted back by now, and found his clothes. Dimitri wasn't the type to fiddle around.

I walked past Grandma and kept going, through the throng of bikers. "Frieda, have you seen Dimitri?"

She popped a pink bubble and cocked a thumb to a grouping of holly bushes a few houses down. "He ran into another griffin."

"Lovely. We're trying to ward off the ultimate evil and he's socializing."

But I knew the truth. Dimitri was needed elsewhere. It was just a matter of time. My heart sank as he emerged from behind the cover of the foliage, his face deliberately blank.

He was holding back again, probably because he didn't want to overwhelm me with everything else that was going on.

I shot him a look that let him know we'd be having a long talk—sooner rather than later.

"Come on," Grandma said, "Bob's found us a place to stay. We'll loosen our boots and I can work up that tracking spell."

"Spectacular. Where are we going?"

"Someplace off the beaten path. His brother owns it."

Okay, that was good for any kind of explosive spells the Red Skulls wanted to mix up. And we wouldn't have to worry about innocent bystanders if something attacked.

"What does Bob's brother do?" I asked.

Please tell me he's a banshee hunter, or a dreg exterminator. I'd even take a voodoo mambo at this point.

Grandma just winked and hummed "I Got You, Babe" as she headed for her bike.

"You?" I called after her. "Sonny and Cher?"

Things were about to get weird fast. And in this world, that was saying something.

Chapter Thirteen

We drove up Highway 14 until the city gave way to monstrous hills that jutted straight up out of the desert plains. Scraggly plants clumped over parched soil, like nature going bald. Pockets of housing developments in earthy colors blended with the desert and scrub.

You're not in Atlanta anymore.

I'd grown up with green—lush fields, magnolia trees and even highway overpasses dripping with bright pink flowers. This place reminded me of an alien landscape.

As we climbed higher and higher, the houses gave way to hot scrub forests, Joshua trees and the occasional scraggly pine. The sun beat harder here. I felt it warm on my shoulders and back.

Max should have been behind me on the bike. Instead, he'd taken off. I wondered exactly where he'd gone, and if he'd had a choice.

We rumbled up the narrow road, climbing a never-ending series of hills, which was an adventure in itself since Grandma and the witches liked to do wheelies at the top. My hair tangled out in front of me as we thundered higher and higher.

Betty Two Sticks shot out ahead, with Bob in her sidecar. He pumped his arm up and down, signaling a hairpin turn down a dirt path.

That sounded about right.

We pulled off the main road in a place where two golden-red sandstone formations slanted out at odd angles from the side of the road. If you didn't know where to turn, you'd miss it entirely.

Low brush in scraggly gold and green clashed with the deep blue sky. We bumped over a country road for at least five miles. Dog-eared plants twisted seven feet tall in places, white flowers scattered among their sage green leaves. Dust tickled my nose and I was glad Pirate had opted to ride with Dimitri. At least he'd be farther off the ground.

The scrub gave way to green vegetable fields, held back by a series of colorful fences. Red, yellow, blue—somebody had a thing for primary colors. An immense sunflower made from recycled scraps of metal dominated the last field. Old pie pans hung from its petals, clanking in the breeze.

The road ended at a tall gate made up of round logs with the tree bark still attached.

Hippie graffiti ebbed and curled across the rough wood. A huge sun shone from the top, over daisies, polka-dot peace signs, rainbows and eyes with long curled lashes. Birds swooped back and forth. Fish curled around each other like yin and yang. There was even a smiling red skull. Coincidence? I didn't think so.

Wound around two naked mermaids and a sea turtle, bright orange lettering announced our arrival at the Aquarius Ranch.

Why did I get the feeling it should have been called Time Warp?

Betty Two Sticks pulled up to the edge of the gate and Bob grabbed hold of a large hemp rope. He yanked it, ringing a dented cowbell.

These people and their cowbells. I smoothed my

lavender hair away from my forehead and back under my helmet. At least I'd fit in here.

Henna-dyed fingers reached around the gate.

"Cowboy Neal?" Grandma gave a whoop. "That you?"

A skinny gray-haired guy in purple sunglasses ducked his head out and waved like a wild man. He swung the gate open and gestured us in, a crazy grin plastered on his face.

Dimitri and I exchanged glances. "This is a first." I'd never seen the witches so welcome anywhere.

We eased our bikes down a white gravel road flanked by vibrant orange flowers while Cowboy Neal bolted the gate behind us. He gave Sidecar Bob a knuckle bump and a big bear hug before sliding onto the back of Grandma's bike.

"What the…?" I shot up in my seat as the hippie patted Grandma on the rear. Then he twined his arms way too comfortably around her waist. I waited (okay, rooted) for her to break his bony little arm. Instead Grandma took off down the road, fishtailing her back tire and showing off.

Oh help me Rhonda.

My gut churned with uncertainty. This had better not be what I thought it was.

We drove past a brightly painted pavilion and a half dozen rusting VW vans before coming to a stop near a red stucco cabin. Sunflowers tilted in the breeze and several half-barrel planter pots overflowed with green leafy plants.

I about fell off my bike when I saw just what kind of plants.

Flat serrated leaves reached like fingers from thin stalks. They grew in clumps like my schefflera plant back home. Only this was pot, hemp, cannabis.

"I hope they're growing that for medicinal

purposes." I'd tried to stage whisper, but it came out as more of a shout.

Dimitri just laughed as he unhooked Pirate.

Yeah, I'll bet he wouldn't think it was so funny if this was his grandma's place.

Pirate's legs were already moving before Dimitri set him down next to the field.

"Geronimo!" My dog dove into a clump of orange poppies, leaping over tufts of flowers. Pirate loved to run. Unlike me, he didn't even have to know where he was going.

Meanwhile, this Neal guy had his arm wrapped around my Grandma as if they were at the junior prom. He stood on the porch of the cabin, a firm grip on her as he gave half-hugs and friendly greetings to the rest of the witches.

Oy vey.

Dimitri practically dragged me up the walk.

"Go on inside." The old man shepherded the witches into the low-slung building. "I've got a whole pot of avocado soup in the ice box and ginger tea bags under the counter. Bob will show you." He high fived his brother, still not letting go of Grandma.

I dug my hands into my pocket, my fists making lumps in my leather pants. "You see how he's manhandling her?"

"Disgraceful," Dimitri said, wrapping an arm around me.

Yeah, that wasn't going to work. "It's not the same. She's..."

Grandma.

Of course when Neal saw me, he rushed straight over, dug my right hand out and shook it with both of his.

Jerk.

"Hello," he said, wrapping me in a huge bear hug,

strands of wiry hair tickling my cheek. He smelled like mint and earth. He probably smelled like marijuana too. I didn't know because I'd never smelled any before, but I'd be willing to bet he had it all over him.

After way too long, Neal pulled away. His hazel eyes shone with an inner warmth and confidence. "Welcome, Lizzie. You don't know how wonderful it is to have you and the rest of your group here." He spared a wink for Grandma.

I was ready to give him a shot until he did that.

Okay, no I wasn't.

But the old hippie couldn't take a hint. "Tripping 'do," he said, reaching to touch the lavender hair at my shoulder.

"You can't be serious," I said, stepping back, nearly bumping into Frieda.

"Dimitri," my overly friendly griffin said, moving in between us as Neal pumped Dimitri's hand up and down.

"Isn't Neal dreamy?" Frieda whispered into my ear, passing us by.

"Oh, go eat green soup."

Truly, the man was fondling my Grandma. He could be the pope's brother and I wouldn't like him.

Besides, we had important work to do. Max was missing. We had killer beasts on our tail. I couldn't let Grandma get distracted.

Decision made. We'd be out of here faster than Neal could say Woodstock.

"Thanks for the welcome," I said, "but we need to go. Now."

"Oh, we're staying." Grandma nudged mister grabby with her hip.

"Lizzie's right," Dimitri said. "We need to track a demon by way of a demon hunter. As much as we'd enjoy your company, we can't guarantee your safety,

Neal."

It wasn't necessarily the *goodbye and good riddance* I'd been shooting for, but it was true. So far, when we'd had evil creatures ambushing us, we'd stayed in enchanted hotels or in hideouts far, far away from innocent people. Yes, this was partly about getting away from annoying Neal, but it was also about keeping him or any of his people from getting caught up in the trouble we'd brought with us.

"I'm in charge of this gang," Grandma said, through gritted teeth. "And I say we stay."

"I'm in charge of this mission," I countered.

Neal didn't look convinced. Neither did Grandma.

Okay, fine. "If a rogue demon hunter isn't dangerous enough for you," I added, "you should know we're being chased by banshees."

Neal didn't even flinch. He nodded, earnest to a fault. "My brother Bob explained all that to me."

Of course he did. I threw my arms up. I couldn't help it.

"Lizzie…" Grandma warned.

"I'm giving him fair warning," I said, ignoring Frieda as she popped her head out the door of the cabin.

Neal stood firm. "I know all about demons and banshees." He ran a hand down Grandma's back. "Not to mention this young lady's powers."

Was Grandma blushing?

I needed to learn some spells. Then I could thwack Neal with a jelly jar.

"It's exactly why you must stay here," he concluded.

"Wrong answer." This man should be a politician. He was taking the truth and turning it sideways.

"This commune has been soaked in love since 1962." He zapped Grandma a heated look. "I can't think of anything more powerful."

Just shoot me now.

Time to bring out the big guns. Bob might have briefed him on the bad guys, but what about the creatures?

"You see that?" I asked, pointing to Flappy, who had stopped flying majestically and was instead chasing Pirate across the field like an overgrown ostrich.

Neal shaded his eyes with his head and craned his neck at the field. "See what?"

"Neal isn't magical, Lizzie," Grandma said, running a hand along his chest. "He's something else entirely."

Okay. Code Red.

"Dimitri?" I needed backup here.

He shrugged. "We need to track Max before the trail goes cold. Neal is willing to lend us his support, his land."

I gaped at him. "Not you, too."

But Dimitri didn't back down. "He seems to understand the risks, Lizzie."

Did he? Well, this should put a twist in old Neal's boxers. "I have a zombie rope." I untied the jar and presented it to him.

Ha!

Naturally, the rope was asleep.

Neal gave me the kind of smile you save for small children and puppies.

Hells bells. I jostled the bottom of the jar.

"It really is alive," I insisted.

"Of course it is." He started toward the field. "Follow me," he said, raising his voice to be heard by everyone. "We only ask that you live by two rules while you try us out: love and tolerance. That's how we flow here. We are the Rucksack Wanderers and we're thankful to have you."

I sighed, knowing I was reaching now. "Have the Rucksack Wanderers even voted on this?" Maybe some of them would be a bit touchier about demons, banshees and zombie ropes.

Come to think of it—where was the rest of the commune?

We trudged through the poppies, their prickly fronds grabbing at my ankles.

"Er, where are the other Wanderers?" I asked.

Neal threw out his arms. "Why, wandering of course."

"Since when?"

"The last one left in 1972," he said, turning to walk backwards, facing us. "Until they return, it's just me and Rain. She'd be here, but she needs to weave her purple rocks into the fields by sundown."

No wonder he didn't think my zombie rope was weird.

"I've aired out the buses," he said, stopping in front of a series of school buses parked near the woods. "There's fresh bedding and lanterns. And I dug you a new outhouse." He trudged ten feet into the woods. "Right here behind this tree."

This was definitely going to be a short stay.

"Come on." Pirate zigzagged between us. "Let's get the red bus. It has a dragon painted on the side." He ran a circle around the red bus. "It has a lemon and a star and a round thing and I don't know what that squiggle is…"

I put a foot on the bottom step and the whole bus shifted.

"Can I room with Flappy?"

I didn't have the heart to tell him they didn't make buses big enough for dragons. "You're with me."

The inside of the bus was stuffy, but it seemed to hold everything we needed. I pushed back a gauzy embroidered curtain at the top of the steps. They'd removed the seats. A platform in the back held a large mattress covered in tie-dyed sheets and colorful homemade quilts. Red and silver lanterns hung from hooks in the ceiling and pillows lined the walls. A small metal table had been welded into the wall behind the driver's seat. Four homemade stools clustered around it.

Not bad.

Evidently, some of the buses had stereos. "Black Magic Woman" blared across the field, the low beats vibrating the metal walls.

Pirate dashed from the front of the long aisle to the back and up front again. He skidded to a stop just below my left knee. "Can Flappy spend the night?"

A dragon? In a bus? "You can help him build a nest outside."

Pirate scratched is belly with his back leg. "A nest? Like for a bird? Flappy's not a bird."

"See? Look." Outside the bus window, we could already see the dragon hauling broken tree limbs from the forest.

"Okay, Flappy," Pirate hollered, dashing past me and down the stairs. "We can build it here at the back. I'll go get you Lizzie's sheets."

"Pirate," I warned.

"I mean some nice, soft grass."

Good luck with that.

I held the curtain back as Dimitri took the bus steps two at a time. He'd rolled his sleeves up to reveal his muscled forearms.

The bus lurched under his weight. "I just talked to your Grandma. She's going to get a tracking spell going."

"What about Neal?"

He shot me a heated look. "Give the man a chance,

Lizzie. Besides, your grandma has a job for us."

"Are you sure she's not trying to get rid of us?"

A smile touched his lips. "I don't think your grandma could even make this up. We need to locate a three-pronged stick from a tree that leans to the north."

Good point.

I leaned into him and felt his arms close around me. "I'm glad you're here."

His arms tightened. "Where else would I be?"

Well it seemed like he had griffins hounding him, if the one in the desert was any indication. "Nowhere." I didn't feel like fighting. Not when I was about to go on a nature walk with a drool-worthy griffin.

Not quite a real date, but I'd take what I could get at this point.

The sun blazed in the west as Dimitri and I headed for the woods, passing Pirate and Flappy on the way. We still had a few hours before sunset. So far, the dragon had managed to drag four logs into a haphazard frame. Pirate had his back to the whole thing and was busy kicking grass into it while sniffing whatever it was dogs sniff.

"Remember," I said as I passed him, "don't go into the bus for nest supplies."

Pirate's head shot up. "Can we use the tires?"

"No."

His ears fell.

Poor doggie. I didn't have the heart to tell him that he'd have a hard time using a tire jack.

Instead, I opted for logic. "Dragons have gotten along for centuries without bus tires."

Pirate glanced at Flappy, who had taken a break and was busy gnawing at the end of a log. "Yeah, well dogs used to get along without Pup-per-roni Bites, but that's not a good idea, either."

We left Pirate and Flappy to earn the nest building

merit badge and walked deeper into the woods, until even the sounds of the biker witches were drowned out by the natural sounds of the forest.

Dimitri held back a sprawling evergreen as I slipped past. "Lizzie, I know you wish you could to control everything."

"Such as?"

"Biker witches, banshees and demons." He let the branch fall back behind us.

I let out an unladylike snort. "You see how that's working out."

"You might want to lay off Neal."

I stopped and turned around to face him. "Would you stand by and let an old hippie hit on your grandma?" I asked, hands on my hips.

"If it made her happy, then yes."

"Well, you're a better man than I am."

He leaned close. "I hope so."

It would have been so easy to let him kiss me. But I had a valid argument when it came to Neal. "He's a distraction and we just met him."

"He's Bob's brother."

"He could be a demon spy for all I know."

Dimitri moved away. "He's not. And it's obvious your grandma knows him very well."

"Ick. Thanks for that mental image."

We began walking again.

"We're here to find Max and save your dad from a demon, not to decide who your grandma spends time with."

Touché. "Speaking of how we spend our time, what was going on with you and that griffin?"

"I already told you," he said, shutting me down.

"I heard there was one outside my dad's house too."

He kept walking.

"Pirate says he gave you something."

"Look, Lizzie," he said, turning. "I explained before. It's griffin business. You don't need to worry about it. What is that demon-slayer truth of yours? *Accept the Universe.*"

"That doesn't apply to demon-slayer dating, so you might as well tell me and get it out of the way."

"Or else you'll keep hounding me?" he asked, resigned.

"Like Pirate teaching tricks."

"All right," he relented. Dimitri narrowed the space between us. "He gifted me with weaponry."

I felt my eyes widen.

"Does this look familiar?" He hitched one leg against the tree and drew a long bronze knife from a holster in his boot. The thing was ancient, with strange carvings and green gemstones wrapped around the hilt. The polished blade gleamed razor sharp.

"Heck, yes. It looks like the one you had when I first met you." He'd dashed into a possessed biker bar in a blaze of glory and left me tied to a walnut tree.

"That one I lost to a demon. This is another, almost as old and equally blessed."

"Oh sure." That made sense. "Why?"

An intense expression passed over his features, and was gone as soon as I saw it. "Griffin politics. He's trying to gain my favor."

"And the griffin in the desert?"

"He put his armies at my disposal."

"Of course."

Dimitri towered over me, brave strong—and no doubt hiding something. "Lizzie, I'm here. I'm on your side one hundred percent. Now you have to allow me to conduct my clan's business as I see fit. We are at a crossroads. Alliances are necessary. It is our way."

We'd left his family in a bad position. I knew that. Most griffin clans had hundreds of members, made up of extended families, loyal to the death. Dimitri's clan was down to him and his two sisters.

I'd watched enough *Survivor* to know what happens when one group gets too small.

"Okay. Fine," I said—which was a lie because it wasn't fine by a long shot. It burned me that he didn't trust me with this. We both knew he had another place to be, another life entirely.

Refusing to talk about it didn't change things.

Even so, there was no way to force him. The more I pushed, the less he'd tell.

It felt like a giant grinding hole between us.

I wiped at a trickle of sweat on my back. "Let's just find a three-pronged stick from a tree that leans to the north."

It turned out that was the easy part. We spotted one halfway up a beat-up pine. Thanks to my kick-ass demon slayer powers, I didn't have to climb, which was good because the thing looked scraggly, like it would break. And I did *not* want to be heavy enough to break a tree. Not in front of my boyfriend at least.

I let my power flow through me and as quick as you can say "think light," I levitated up and used Dimitri's knife to help break it off.

We brought it back to Grandma, and I was thankful to see her outside of a psychedelic yellow school bus—alone.

Neal sat with a guitar by the main building, doing a decent version of "Bad Moon Rising" with biker witches sprawled out on the ground around him.

Grandma hurried toward us. "You find it?"

I held up our prized stick.

"Now that's a beaut," she said, ushering us over to a flattened circle of dirt behind her bus.

"Flappy finally learn how to sit?" It was about the size of a dragon tush.

"No. But he knows how to eat an entire jar of wolf spiders. I was saving those."

"Where are they now?" I asked, doing a quick sweep of the strawberry field across the road from us for my dog and his dragon.

"Playing in the poppies. I gave them two thermoses of water and told them to make a thousand mud pies for my spell."

"With just two thermoses—"

"Doesn't matter. They'll be busy until next Tuesday. And they like to help."

Good plan. "You'd better actually need this stick," I said with a newfound suspicion for her motives.

"Ohh…that's nice," she said, taking it from me and weighing it with both hands.

Yes, I had to admit it was a lovely stick. "What exactly are we doing here?"

"Luckily, I found some spiders on my bus."

I shuddered.

She pointed to the center of the circle. "I've got dirt from the last spot we saw Max. Mixed that with some muddy water I found at that old prison."

"You were collecting water?"

She winked. "Aren't you glad I did? Besides, you were too busy to do it."

I can honestly say I never would have thought to drain water from a demonic prison. The water and the dirt made a nasty looking sludge.

Grandma clucked her tongue in approval as she placed the piece of wood in the center of the circle. "Add the spiders," she mused to herself, shaking a baggy full of bubble-butted spiders out onto the wood. As the smart spiders began to escape, Grandma placed five mirrored crystals around the clearing.

My cell phone vibrated in my back pocket as "Electric Avenue" blared across the field.

Hillary.

I reached behind me and clicked it to voicemail.

"You really should call her," Grandma mused.

"What? And tell her I'm helping work up a spell to find a missing half-demon at a hippie commune?" My adoptive mother's version of flower power consisted of her heirloom roses. She thought her milk delivery man was a beatnik because he drank bubble tea.

Grandma stood, admiring her handiwork. "Beautiful." She glanced up at me. "Now take off your shirt."

"I like this spell." Dimitri grinned.

Not that I wasn't all for spells, as well as inappropriate flashing of skin to Dimitri but, "Why?"

Couldn't Grandma have a spell that didn't involve dead things, insects or semi-nudity?

Grandma huffed as if I was the one causing trouble. "You question everything."

"It's kept me alive," I said.

Grandma shot me The Look. "Your shirt touched Max. I need something for the Bloodhound Spell to track. Unless you'd rather use your pants."

"Shirt is okay," I said, reaching for the zipper on the side of my bustier while my mind scrambled to think of anything else Max had touched that wasn't bolted down to my bike.

I slipped the silken garment over my head. I was probably going to regret this.

At least I was wearing a nice bra.

And, yes, I know a bustier is technically a bra too, but what can I say, I've never been able to wear one without, well, added insurance.

"Here." I handed it over. "Use it well." Or this wouldn't be happening again.

She inspected it. "You should be wearing leather anyway."

"Yes, well now that you have it, you want to tell me what you plan to do with it?" I glanced back at Dimitri, to confirm just how much Grandma was demanding from me. Naturally he was completely distracted by my pink bra.

I didn't miss the way his eyes trailed over me. In fact, I couldn't wait to explore that thought further once we made it back to our bus.

Grandma spread my lavender bustier over the three-pronged stick and sprinkled the entire thing with an herb mixture that smelled like smoked wood and cinnamon.

"*Locos veloxio*," she chanted, low under her breath.

Okay, maybe I didn't mind this spell too much.

"*Locos veloxio*." She raised her hands to the sky.

Nearly a year ago, I would have worried, but in that time, I'd seen for myself how Grandma's spells made a difference. Sure it was my only shirt, but I trusted her. She'd use it right. She'd track Max.

She pulled out a pack of matches from her back pocket.

I started for her. "Heavens to—"

Dimitri's hand clamped down on my arm. "Lizzie, you can't interrupt."

"She's going to torch my shirt!"

"Here," he said, starting to take off his.

"I don't want it," I fired back, and instantly regretted it as his abs disappeared back under the black T-shirt.

God bless America. I couldn't win.

Grandma held the flame over the last decent thing left in my wardrobe. "Don't worry, Lizzie. This is going to work."

"I think it just did," Dimitri said, pointing to a figure running headlong across the strawberry field.

Holy heck. "Max!"

Chapter Fourteen

Grandma dropped the match.

"Hey!" I leapt over the crystal barrier and stomped at the smoke curling from my only nice top. The three-pronged stick snapped under my boot, and I tried not to think of the spiders Grandma had added to the mix as I mashed the silk bustier into the dirt and slime and devil knew what.

Was it too much to ask to get through one mission—just one—fully clothed?

"Lizzie, stop!" Grandma charged over the barrier just as the entire mess gave a loud pop and belched blue fumes. "Your shoe's on fire!"

Silver flames erupted and I barely got my foot out before my boot—and my shirt—ignited like a fourth of July smoke bomb gone wrong.

The silver wall blasted as high as my head and shimmered, forming a mirror. The flickering surface showed Max high-tailing it across a strawberry field.

"Don't wreck it," Grandma frantically re-positioned the crystals I'd knocked over.

"We don't need it," I shot back. And it almost toasted me.

Heart hammering, I whirled around, hands on my hips my pink Victoria's Secret Angel bra on display for the whole flipping camp.

Max ran straight for us as if chased by the devil himself. "What the heck is he doing?"

"I don't see anyone behind him." Dimitri handed me his shirt. This time I took it.

Grandma scanned the sky. "No banshees."

"Or dregs," I said, with rising concern. Dimitri's shirt felt warm as I slipped it over my head.

Max burst into camp. "Get down, get down!" He whirled me around by the shirt sleeve as I was still putting the thing on. That's when I noticed the tiny blonde on his tail.

Dimitri shoved me into the dirt as a blast of heat rocketed over us.

Max sprawled on the ground next to me. "She's going to kill us."

"What did you do?" I demanded.

But he was already up and running again.

I chased him because what the frick was I supposed to do? Spindly plants tore at my bare foot as I thundered after Max, with one boot on, one boot gone.

He dove behind a yellow rainbow van as another blast of heat nearly fried us.

I shoved a clump of hair out of my face. "Why is she trying to kill us?"

"She's a pissed off demon slayer." He drew a red, churning switch star out of his belt. His hunter weapons were useless, though. He couldn't throw them. He had to get close. "Damn." He slammed the star into the side of the bus.

I ducked. Sparks flew as it churned into the metal.

Max drew another star. "I wish I had a gun."

I grabbed his arm. "Cut it out. You're screwing up our cover. Besides, I'm the last of the demon slayers."

"Oh yeah?" Max asked, eyes wide, his hair spiking all over the place.

I chanced a look and saw a petite blonde stalking

toward our side of the bus. She couldn't have been any older than me, with a pixie face and Marilyn Monroe hair tied up in a teal scarf. She wore a tailored white wrap-around shirt, flowered Capri pants and yow— four switch stars on her turquoise studded belt. She held a fifth star in her hot little hand.

Shock zinged through me.

"She's a demon slayer."

"Told you," Max drawled.

Hells bells. Only demon slayers could touch, much less carry switch stars for any length of time. She had five, same as me. They were pink and rounded, the same as mine.

"She should be on our side," I said, my voice about two octaves higher.

This is *not* how I envisioned a demon slayer reunion.

Max moved quickly down the side of the bus. "Yeah well it's the dreg. Roxie is usually the life of the party."

I snuck another glance around the front of the bus. She glared at me, cold and calculating. She was ten feet away. Tops. And drawing back to fire. "What do you mean?"

Max gave a low whistle. "You should have seen her sing from the top of a table in the Tic-Tac Club," he said, his voice low and husky, "unbelievable."

"Max!"

The star slammed into the other side of the bus, rattling the widows—and us.

Max drew a bowie knife from the back of his pants, holding it as he crouched low. "I had to find her. I was out of my mind. And not because she's the best fuck I've had in the last hundred years." He swallowed. "As soon as I saw her, the dreg flew up my throat and into her. Straight through her skin."

My insides ached, remembering the pain.

Max ducked his head around the side of the bus and jerked back as a switch star screamed past. "The dreg compels you to kill the person that gave it to you. Then you have an insane urge to find another slayer and it goes on."

Wait. When I had the dreg, I hadn't set out to kill anyone. Of course I'd kept it in a jar at the time. Still, "You didn't want to kill me after I gave it to you."

"No offense, but you're different. So am I."

No kidding.

"Come on," he hissed.

I followed, lopsided on one bare foot as we moved behind a pink bus closer to the woods.

"So she's trying to kill you because you gave it to her?" I asked.

He grinned. "She's been trying to kill me since Prohibition."

I didn't doubt it.

He shook his head. "Damn, she is hot."

"Yeah, well, she's trying to murder us." I could sense her drawing closer.

"Hey," I called out to her as she put a bus between herself and the biker witches. Smart slayer. Knowing the Red Skulls, they'd look for any chance to take a pot shot. "Put the weapon down," I said, "let's talk."

"Not a chance," she said, fire in her eyes, her white blond hair blowing back with a sudden gust of wind. "I'm going to axe him."

I glanced back at Max. "You know what? Go ahead."

"Thanks," Max muttered as I crouched behind him.

"You asked for it," I reminded him.

My emerald necklace hummed against my neck.

Oh who was I kidding? I was the only one who could face off against a demon slayer.

It was such a waste—a stupid, senseless waste. I tugged off my boot and tossed it away.

"Run. Hide," I hissed to Max. "If I don't make it, you don't have a chance." Not against demon-slayer weapons. She could wipe out the whole camp.

Sacrifice yourself.

I jumped out, firing.

Grandma had run to get the witches, hopefully to get them out of the way. Dimitri looked ready to jump in between us and Max stared in horror.

I shot low, hoping to clip her in the knee. She leaped in the air as my star streaked under her.

Yow.

Then she fired straight at my head. I ducked as the star slammed into the bus behind me. It forced me to miss my own star as it boomeranged toward me, screeching against the bus and whirling out into the night.

Holy Hades. I was down a weapon, I realized, as hers sailed back.

The crowd surged around us, but luckily not behind us. Dimitri looked ready to blow a gasket. I just hoped he didn't do anything stupid, or heroic—one in the same at this point. He wasn't a demon slayer. He couldn't block our weapons. He couldn't save me. I had to do this by myself.

I'd save both of us, all of us—somehow.

She stiffened, crying out as pain wracked through her body. I could see the dreg pulsing through her.

The pain was excruciating. I knew first-hand.

Is that what would have happened if Dimitri hadn't saved me?

The emerald grew hot on my neck, its bronze chain snaking down. I always hated this part. It felt wrong and creepy and it usually meant I was in trouble.

Nuts.

The emerald and bronze wound around my left side to form a barrier directly over my heart.

Oh geez.

She launched another switch star straight at my head.

I watched it—every curve of the blades as it sawed through the air, straight for my neck. I drew my own switch star, fingers white in the handle and watched my arm release it in a perfect arc. The stars collided on the field between us, sizzling and crackling as they fell down dead.

Three left.

This was ridiculous. I didn't want to kill one of the last of our kind. There had to be better way.

The demon slayer drew again. She fired, I fired. Again, our stars collided over the field. Two left.

My heart shoved against my chest. I needed my weapons. I couldn't let her destroy my weapons.

She fired again.

I released again. We lost our weapons, sizzling and burning, tangled together smoking in the scrub brush and dirt.

One left. She fired again. I had to stop this.

Instead of firing back, I made a mad dash for the pink bus. I could feel the switch star whistling behind me as my bare feet dug into the dirt. If I could get behind the bus, maybe I could talk to her, reason with her while she tore it apart.

But I wasn't fast enough to outrun a switch star.

It shrieked closer and I turned as it bore down on me, twisting blades and tearing metal. I fired, catching it an arm's length from my head. Energy dropped on me like a blanket of electricity as the switch stars sparked and burned each other out.

She drew again as I made it behind Grandma's bus. I forced the world back into focus as I clutched the cold metal side.

A switch star tore into the side of a bus with an inhuman screech. I listened to it rip through the metal side before soaring back to her.

I ducked my head around as she caught it, ready to fire again.

She stalked toward me, switch star drawn. Cripes.

I was out of weapons.

Witches scattered behind her. Dimitri began to shift. Oh no.

He'd better not try to save me.

I ducked behind the bus. Back flat against the cold metal, aware of her every step crunching the sage grass as she drew near enough to be very, very lethal.

Okay, think, think, *think.*

What could I use as a weapon?

A hand slammed around the bus, switch star churning as it bore down on me.

I screamed.

Energy rocked through me, sizzling down my spine and driving me to the ground. My arms gave out. My legs wouldn't work. I lay there with my face in the dirt, amazed I was even alive.

Pain seared my chest.

I should be dead. I should be torn open.

Rolling onto my back, I lay weak, my limbs refusing to obey me. The bronze plate throbbed over my heart as I fought for breath.

Leave it to Dimitri. His necklace, with its protective magic, had saved me. At least for now.

I tried to move my arm, somehow find a star, but I could barely move.

Tears welled in my eyes. Frick. I wasn't a crier. I was a slayer. I was just so hurt and tired and frustrated. This was wrong, so wrong.

The other slayer stood above me. I stared right into

her blue eyes, the picture shifting through my tears. "You're not a killer," I told her, praying no one got close enough to see what might happen to me.

"I'm not," she said, regret in her voice as she drew a star. "But you're not letting me kill Max. And you're going to die anyway. We all are."

I tried to sit up, but my body wouldn't move. "You're stronger than the compulsion," I insisted. "You're a demon slayer." She had to understand. "If you kill me, we'll all be weaker. We'll never defeat this."

She shook her head, her pain on display. "We can't defeat it. It's over. After this, I'll infect my sister." Her voice quivered. "I know where she is." Her hand shook, still holding the star, ready to fire. "Mags will kill me. Then she'll die."

No. We had to fight. "We can stop the one who started this, and the dreg will die. You *can* save your sister." And yourself.

"Stay back," she ordered as the crowd approached behind her. Then to me, she asked, desperate, "How do you know?"

"I survived the dreg. You and your sister can too," I added, hoping I was right.

The weakness I felt had turned into an intense, knife-like throbbing. It was as if my entire body had lost circulation and was now coming back.

A massive griffin swooped overhead. Dimitri. His immense lion's claws gleamed against the setting sun as he prepared to dive.

Don't. I lifted my hand.

Please. He couldn't stop her. I could.

She saw. "Touch me and the slayer dies!"

Dimitri dove low on colorful wings, his claws scraping the air inches from her head as he took to the air once more.

"How did you survive the dreg?" She demanded. "You should be mad with the compulsion."

I tried to sit up, my arms screaming in protest. "I was made, not born," I said through gritted teeth.

She stared at me for a long moment. "So you're the one."

Chapter Fifteen

She holstered her star and held out a hand. "Roxie."

I took it, still on the ground, giving her the limpest handshake in history. "Lizzie." I grunted as I sat up. "Thanks for not killing me."

She stared at me. "The day's not over yet."

Oh lordy.

She stood over me, tense. "I'm fighting this as hard as I can. I don't know how long I can last."

"Let's figure this out," I said, staggering to my feet.

"Lizzie!" Pirate ran at me so fast he smacked up against my shin. He bounced off, scrambled to his feet and leapt up against my leg, his claws scratching.

"Lizzie! I was trying to get to you and Bob held me down and I couldn't get out of his lap and I saw you needed me" —he didn't even pause when I scooped him up under the tummy— "I barked and then I barked and I barked." He twisted around to face me. "Are you okay because you don't look so good."

I nuzzled against his warm doggie neck, keeping an eye on Roxie the entire time. "I'm just fine." For now. I wasn't about to let my guard down around a demon slayer with a death wish.

Dimitri landed a short distance away and began to shift. Feathers in blue, green and purple folded over on themselves. He fairly shimmered as his lion's body morphed to reveal a broad, muscled back, lean legs and oh my word we were going to have a naked griffin on our hands in a couple of minutes.

Make that an angry, naked griffin.

I knew Dimitri would be pissed. He got that way when people shot at me.

On this occasion, however, we needed to use some restraint. I'd finally gotten Roxie talking instead of attacking. We had to keep her engaged, learn what she knew and figure out what in bloody Hades we were going to do next.

Grandma pushed through the advancing crowd of biker witches, a red jar in her hand.

It was a death spell. She marched up to Roxie, chin thrust up and fire in her eyes. "Give me one good reason why I don't bust a cap in your ass right now."

Roxie drew a switch star.

"Stop it," I said. Needles of pain shot down my legs as I forced them to start working. Crab walking, I inserted myself between them. "Cut it out." The weight of Pirate got to be too much and I set him down.

"I need a minute!" I said to Grandma, to Neal who had somehow produced a shotgun (what about hippies and peace?), to the witches who had gathered behind Grandma, jelly jars ready to fire.

"The fight is over. We're talking now." I sure hoped Roxie didn't recognize the jars as weapons or our tête-à-tête could be finished before it started.

Even my fingertips tingled. Wincing, I pointed to the chewed up wreck behind me.

"Give us five minutes in this bus," I said, knowing they'd give me about two.

Frieda chewed her gum. "Yeah, uh, that's my bus and you ripped the side out."

"Use mine," Grandma said, watching us with cold calculation. She knew that I needed time with Roxie.

She wasn't happy about it, but she understood.

"Explain it to Dimitri," I said, limping toward Grandma's bus, happy for once to give someone else an impossible job.

My legs had turned to rubber. I hoped I wouldn't trip over a clump of scrub, or fall in a hole. A demon slayer has to keep up appearances.

Roxie fell into step next to me. "You have some strange friends."

I sized her up. "And even stranger enemies."

Danged if she didn't look like a 1950s Hollywood starlet, or a Banana Republic model. Not bad for a girl who had to be at least 112 years old.

What was she anyway?

It bothered me to no end that figuring it out wasn't even on my top-ten list of things to do today.

So you're some kind of supernatural creature. So what? We have work to do.

Grandma's yellow school bus shifted as we climbed the stairs. Privacy, at last. I wrinkled my nose at the smell—dust, mildew and spiced orange incense.

If Grandma thought her Wild Ass Gertie's Citrus Combustion sticks were covering anything up, she needed to re-tool her sniffer. I held a blue and yellow tie-dyed curtain back for Roxie.

She paused. A furrow creased the perfectly smooth skin between her eyebrows. And dang, that woman had the longest, thickest eyelashes I'd ever seen. "You first," she said, peering into the bus, switch star drawn.

Yes, I supposed it could be a dusty, orange-scented trap, although I didn't know where a bad guy would hide in this mess.

Grandma had unpacked her essentials, which meant, well—everything. The small table at the front of the bus held a goat's skull, a twelve-pack of mouse traps and an empty, obviously used ten-gallon aquarium. A menagerie of pink and red candles burned in every space that remained.

There was no way Grandma had fit more than her goat's head and a few dozen spell jars onto a Harley. She had to have gotten at least some of this from the other witches, and most of it from Neal.

I whistled under my breath.

There was no denying those two had a history. It was written in black sharpie all over the beat-up cardboard boxes crowding the bus, and every chair at the table.

Cauldrons, vats and kettles
Dried turtle innards (miscellaneous)
Pelts, skulls and toothy ingredients

My ankle brushed a stack of jars under the table. They clattered against each other, but dang, you couldn't take a step in here without running into random jars or boxes.

Anti-Mephistophelian experiments, caustic
Anti-Mephistophelian experiments, benign
John Wayne DVDs

A flicker of dread sparked in my stomach. She'd even mashed the bed full of boxes.

Grandma had *better* be sleeping in her own bed tonight.

I shivered at the thought of her with that annoying hippie. We'd deal with that later.

Roxie took in the mess around us, her eyes flickering back to me.

"Don't ask," I said.

She gave me a mocking smile. "Believe me, I have better things to do." She looked me up and down. "You're the made slayer," she stated.

"Yes." What about it?

"How?"

I shook my head. "I don't know."

I didn't even know I was a slayer until this past summer. I'd come a long way since then, but our little party in the yard showed me how much farther I had to go. Roxie would make a good mentor, if she didn't kill me first.

Neither one of us was willing to take our eyes off the other. Still, I let her move, get comfortable.

Roxie used the opportunity to circle back around me and take the spot nearest to the door. A wave of claustrophobia hit me and I fought it down, ignoring the way the boxes seemed to crowd closer. The incense burned sweeter. The air itself felt heavier. I'd give her the exit. If that's what it took to get her talking, I could handle it.

"How do we save my sister?"

"Have you ever heard of a demon named Zatar? I think he's behind the dregs." And a lot of other things.

She tapped a finger against the switch stars at her belt. "That bastard took Rachmort too."

I about fell over. "The Earl of Hades has my mentor?"

"Mine too," she said defensively. "I thought Zatar wanted him out of the way because he's been freeing black souls. Now I'm wondering if it has something to do with us."

"You trained with him?" I asked.

She nodded. "He was like a father to me." Her wistful smile turned to a frown. "Then, thirty years ago, the dreg attacks started. It was awful. All of a sudden, demon slayers started turning on each other. No one was safe." The regret and sorrow in her voice shook me. "So many were killed," she said quietly. "The only way to save our race was to give up our powers," she gave a small laugh, "which is impossible."

Oh yeah? She should ask my mom about that. The

knowledge stung. Her betrayal was complete. My mother didn't just foist off her responsibilities, she'd given me a death sentence.

Roxie's eyes held the pain of the memory. "My family faked my death and my sister's as well. They claimed we turned on each other," she shivered, "killed each other. It was a believable story."

"Then you hid from the other slayers."

"Rachmort too," Roxie said, her voice dripping with regret, "nobody could know we were alive."

"So Rachmort really did believe it when he told me I was the last of my kind."

"He thinks that. The rest of us are in hiding, even from the people who could help us. It's the only way to stay completely safe."

"How many others survived?" I asked. I had to know.

"In the years since, I've learned of only four other slayers." She gave me a once over. "And then you."

"We could save Rachmort." We owed it to him.

Roxie balked. "Never. He's on his own. Just like we are."

No. "Consider this. What if it's time to unite again? What if Rachmort can bring the others out of hiding?"

He'd dedicated his life to training slayers and saving lost souls—which, at times, could be one and the same. The other slayers would have to see how much trouble he was in. Rachmort had been taken by a demon that, according to my dad's books, had sixty-six legions of dark angels.

"No," Roxie said. "It's impossible."

"Why?" I challenged, stomach churning, "Do you think he's in hell?" Because I had some experience with Hades. Not that I was in any hurry to re-live it.

Roxie looked as wretched as I felt. "Last I heard, he was in purgatory. Zatar hadn't had a chance to move him yet."

"Purgatory," I said, trying to work up a plan. Okay. "We can do that, right?"

She stepped backward, colliding with a box. She kicked it away. "Are you nuts?"

I didn't hear her offering up any better plan. "We've got to do something." Rachmort had never left us hanging.

"We survive," she snarled. "Or we die so that the others can live."

Geez. You could play a drinking game to this woman. Take a shot every time she wants to off somebody.

"Fine. At least let me contact the other slayers." They could choose, as she had.

"No," she snapped. "They stay hidden. If I die, I die. I'm not going to compromise the entire demon-slayer race."

"We're not compromising them. We're rescuing them. We're allowing them to actually be who they were born to be."

It was the only way. I could set this right. I could save my dad, my mentor and the last of the demon slayers.

Roxie watched me with disdain and a smidge of hope. "You think we can do this." She shook her head. "I can't stop thinking about Max. I want to kill him. It would feel so good to fire a switch star through his heart." Her breathing deepened. "I want to. I want his blood. I want –"

"Control it," I snapped before she talked herself into slicing up Max. "Stand up to it. This is not the natural order of things."

If she didn't fight this, we were looking at damnation, destruction and death. "This might well be the most horrific thing we ever have to face, but it's *not* impossible." I refused to believe it could be.

I may not be able to control my dog or what the biker witches did or Dimitri's need to run around and keep griffin secrets, but demon slaying was my destiny. I'd been given this power for a reason.

Roxie rested a hand on her chest and bowed her head, taking her eyes off me for the first time since we'd met. "You don't have a dreg in you. I do." Her voice cracked. "I can feel it. I don't know how long I can control it."

"You're a demon slayer," I said, wishing I could reach out to her, knowing she wouldn't welcome it. "You can't choose to do this. You simply have to do it." For the first time, I truly understood what the last demon slayer Truth meant. "Sacrifice yourself." It wasn't about what you thought you could do or what you wanted to do. It wasn't about us at all.

She took a ragged breath and nodded.

I grabbed two of my grandma's all-purpose spell jars. She'd never miss them.

"Come on," I said, brushing past Roxie, "let's go find Zatar."

† † †

Instead we found Dimitri. And I was right—he was hacked off. He stood at the door of the bus. Shadows played over his wide shoulders and a fine sheen of sweat coated his chest. He'd found his jeans. I still had his shirt. Two other griffins flanked him, wearing equally pissy expressions.

I paused at the top step, not exactly thrilled to have my back to Roxie. "What is this, the greeting committee?"

"Fuck yeah." Dimitri rushed to me, kissing the living daylights out of me as he pulled me from the bus. Gee, I hoped his friends had my back because whoo-ya, the man could kiss. I gave in for a moment, just a moment and sank into the pleasure of it.

I arched beneath his mouth, reveling in his strength and how easy it was to get to him. I slid my fingernails up his back and felt him shiver.

Dimitri pulled away far too soon. "My god, Lizzie, I thought I lost you."

He was looking down at me as if I was the most precious thing he'd ever found and it took everything I had to remember that we were standing in a hippie field full of curious biker witches, not to mention Dimitri's two new friends.

"I'm fine." I glanced behind me. "Roxie's fine." For now. "What's going on?"

He kept me close, which felt good. Frankly, I was still a little shaky from the kiss.

The griffin at the right gave a short bow. It was then I noticed he had a golden wreath woven through his thick black hair. "I am Thereos, Prince of the Aries Clan."

"Say!" Neal sidled up next to him. "We could use some crop dusters."

The prince balked. "I am here to bring tribute. Weapons. Please, Dimitri of Helios," he said, eyes on my man, "we must speak alone. I will not negotiate here."

Tension rippled through Dimitri as his arm tightened around me. He gave a slight bow. "I understand, Prince Thereos. I look forward to our meeting. However, we are in the middle of a crisis right now."

"So am I!" The other griffin nearly shouted. His companion drew a bronze sword.

Sweet mother. What did these two need?

"Your meeting is important as well," I said more to

Dimitri than to anyone else.

He nodded, angry, tired and torn.

"Do it," I said, slipping away. "If you need to convene with these griffins, do it now. I'll wait for you."

Roxie's hand twitched over the switch star at her belt.

She didn't have much time. "Go," I said to Dimitri. "I'll be here."

What I said was mostly true. If it was meant to be, I'd be here. If not, I'd return to him.

There was no way I was taking him on a mission to find Zatar if it would cost him with the griffins. These people were seeking him out. They were talking about negotiations, weapons, war.

Yes, Dimitri loved me, and I loved him too but I wasn't about to let him lose everything he'd spent a lifetime building just to stand outside my dad's house while Roxie and I tried to find a way to beat Zatar.

Dimitri couldn't enter. He couldn't help me with this. Rather, I could help him. I'd give him his old life back.

And then, soon, he could choose.

"I'll make it fast," he said, his expression softening as he bent to kiss me on the forehead. He brushed a lock of hair away from my forehead and tucked it behind my ear. "You are everything to me," he said, with a ferocity that shot straight to my toes.

"I know." I hoped he could read on my face that he was my world too. "I love you," I said, hoping he could forgive me for what I was about to do.

Chapter Sixteen

I found my last switch star—the only one that wasn't ruined—gleaming next to the pink bus. I sheathed it, bracing myself as the emerald necklace began the slow transformation back into jewelry.

Groups of biker witches wandered the battle site, murmuring over the destruction. Grandma hunched over her ruined fire, working up another spell. And Pirate? Well, he was teaching Flappy how to fetch grasshoppers. Naturally, Flappy was doing more eating than fetching.

Guilt clawed at me as I watched Dimitri walk out into the scrub forest with the griffins. He'd gone with them because he trusted me to wait. I chewed at my lip, holding back until I was sure they'd begun their business. Then, I left.

Roxie followed in my wake. "You're cold," she chuckled as I motioned for Pirate and Flappy.

"You don't know a thing about me."

"Back at you," she said, bringing her fingers up to her mouth and letting out a shrill whistle. As if on command, a huge white horse trotted out from the shadows near the front gate. Big as a Clydesdale, it whinnied and pranced, stomping the ground with saucer-like hooves.

What the... "I'm not getting on that thing."

"I didn't ask you." She climbed onto its bare back.

"Right." And while I had her, "you're not human, are you?"

She gave me a superior look.

"Yeah, okay," I said, wishing I could hop on my Harley. "I don't want to know."

My bike was too loud for sneaking out of the compound.

Flappy tottered up to me, two tons of power with a lolling tongue and bad breath.

"Hey buddy," I rubbed him under the chin, "you think you can help me out?"

"Snarfle!" He licked at me like an overly friendly Labrador. I managed to dodge his first swipe, only to be caught on the bicep by the sideways-lick.

Ew. I tried to ignore the warm dragon spit on my arm and the fact that he'd just been eating grasshoppers. I took hold of his neck ridges and hoisted myself up on his back.

Pirate tried to jump up after me. "You said no riding the dragon."

"It's an emergency." No way I'd be doing it otherwise.

Flappy smelled like a lizard and he would not stop dancing around. It was like a herky-jerky carnival ride. I was going to get dragon-sick in a second.

Roxie sat on her glorious steed, gloating.

"Wait!" Neal dashed toward us, skinny legs pumping, his ponytail flying out behind him.

Oh lord. Flappy began beating his wings, itching to go. I knew the feeling.

"Here." Neal shoved a pair of hippie-looking cork-soled Birkenstocks at me.

What was this? Some sort of a joke? I held the shoes by their buckled sandal straps. "You can tell Grandma—"

Neal seemed way too pleased with himself. "She's going to find you if you don't go now." He winked. "I don't even need to open the gate, do I?"

"You mean you're just going to let me sneak out of here."

"Everybody's gotta wander," he called. "Just remember to eat organic and take care of your feet."

Hands down this was the weirdest place I'd ever been.

"Ready?" I asked Roxie. She'd donned a steel battle helmet that covered her head and the entire top of her face. A golden eye plate formed a medieval-style Batman mask, and wound around the side of the helmet to form stiff gold wings.

Okay, then.

I slipped on the Birkenstocks and—other than looking completely ridiculous next to my black leather pants—they did feel good. "Try to keep up." I nudged Flappy with my heels and he started running, his head bobbing up and down like a giant bird.

Roxie galloped past us on her white stallion. It had to be enchanted or mythical or—oh my. The beast lifted up into the air and began to fly.

Impossible. It had no wings.

Then again, who was I to judge?

It let out a satisfied burst of flame from its nose as it climbed higher and higher.

My dragon was still running like an overgrown ostrich. "Flappy, fly! Up!" I hoped I wasn't too heavy for him. "Fly!"

With a stumble, a bump and a small burst of flame, Flappy took to the sky.

"G-g-g-ood dragon!" It felt like we were riding on rails.

"Snurgle!" Flappy wriggled and tried to lick me.

"Eyes on the s-s-sky!" I begged as he started to veer

sideways.

I set Flappy on a course for my dad's house. This was nothing like riding a griffin. In fact, it was the difference between hitching myself to a rocket versus a souped up go-kart with four flat tires.

Where Dimitri's massive wings would beat in a steady rhythm of cool air on my legs, Flappy's veiny wings fluttered hummingbird-style.

At least we were airborne.

I resisted the urge to pat the dragon on the neck, lest he try to kiss me again.

Instead, I kept my eyes on the city below and wondered what had happened to my dad since our last visit, and what we would find when we visited him this time.

Roxie kept pace next to us, following my lead. Her horse galloped on air as if it were dashing head long across a prairie. It snorted fire every few minutes.

And I still couldn't get over Roxie's Norse battle helmet.

What was she?

Besides trouble.

†††

My dad's house looked even more desolate at night. His bare front lawn hung in shadows. The windows lay dark. A lone streetlight sputtered. The other two on the block had burned out entirely.

Just a little creepy.

I tried to shake it off but couldn't. A sense of foreboding clung to me.

Flappy skidded to a stop, clipping several streetlamps and a fire hydrant. Roxie landed in the middle of the street.

I slid off the dragon, my stomach flip-flopping. "Good job, Flappy." I forgot to duck and he caught me with a lick upside the head.

Great.

For kicks and grins, I said, "sit."

The dragon flapped its wings and yowled.

That's what I thought.

Roxie stared at the wreck of a house as she tied her horse to one of the broken street lights. "I wonder what the neighbors think."

I ran my hand along Flappy's snout, trying to avoid his sharp snaggletooth as well as his tongue. "I don't think anybody sees this place anymore."

She winced. "Your dad must be a piece of work."

Her comment pricked at me. As far as I could tell, my dad wasn't guilty of anything worse than some bad decisions. Roxie should know better than anyone how a demon could take over.

"Nobody chooses to be this way," I reminded her.

Her hand wandered to the switch star at her belt. "I just hope to hell it lets me in."

I ignored the growing lump in my throat. "It will," I said, loosening my utility belt.

Last time, I was the only one who could make it past the wards. One look at my dad told me he'd been too weak to maintain them, so someone else wanted me in there. I was betting on Zatar.

The demon would love it if I brought another slayer to the party.

I walked up to where the wards began. Eyes half closed, I stuck my hand in. Heat seared my arm as the ward threw me backward. I could feel every molar in my mouth as I landed hard on the ground.

Roxie stood over me, not bothering to help me up. "You said you could get in."

"I can," I said, climbing to my feet. "The wards won't open for demon slayer weapons." I stood for a moment, gathering the scattered bits of my brain. "I had to try. You'd better as well."

Sometimes wards weakened. Too bad this one had gotten stronger, at least when it came to me.

Roxie hesitated on the sidewalk. Smart girl. Still, I knew she'd try the wards. She wasn't a coward. I looped my switch star belt around Flappy's neck and shoved my Maglite and GPS into my back pocket.

When the wards blew Roxie back onto her Capri-covered tush, I held out my hand for her weapon. She stalked over to me, shaky on her feet, not happy about giving up her last switch star.

"If I can't recover, I have to end it. I don't know how I'm going to kill myself without switch stars," she seethed.

"Would it make you feel better if I told you I was getting closer and closer to wanting to kill you myself?"

She gave me a look that could have peeled paint.

"I brought some magic for you," I said, handing her an all-purpose jar. They wouldn't slow down a demon, but they could come in handy.

She held it with two fingers. "What kind of a demon slayer are you?"

Wasn't that the million-dollar question? "I'm the kind who's going to get us out of this alive."

By skill, luck or unusual weapons.

"This is a disaster," she said, still coming to grips with the biker-witch way of doing things.

"It's the best we can do." I checked one last time to make sure my utility belt was firmly looped over Flappy and then dug into a side pocket for a pinch of Grandma's locking powder. "This won't hurt, Flappy," I said, sprinkling it over my belt and his neck. "It just keeps it on tighter."

Flappy sneezed.

Roxie gripped her switch star belt, not ready to give it up. "I don't want to be taken by a demon. Do you know what they do to slayers?"

"No," I said. "Keep it to yourself." I couldn't afford to lose my nerve. "This brand of magic has saved my skin more than once. Besides, if there was a demon in that house, we'd feel it."

"Zatar could appear in an instant."

Didn't I know it.

I kept my mouth closed as I walked through the thick, warm ward. It tasted like rot and death, as it had before. Only this time, I detected a faint trace of sulfur as well.

Jesus, Mary, Joseph and the mule. I cringed. Something nasty had been this way.

Roxie held back.

"Come on," I said, making my way up the twisting front walk, keeping an eye out for zombie doormats.

Tension rolled off my reluctant partner. Finally, she looped her belt over her horse.

Good slayer.

Gripping Grandma's magic jar, I made my way to the darkened front door. Even from the front porch, I could smell the coppery tinge of blood.

You can do this.

I stepped over the threshold and clicked on my Maglite.

Roxie hurried up behind me, as if she didn't want me leaving her alone in the barren front yard. "It's too quiet," she whispered.

"I know," I said in my normal voice.

Whatever was in there knew we were coming.

I found a light switch and tried it. Nothing.

The walls groaned and shifted as my pool of light filtered across the dirty carpet to the walls with their bloody scrawl. *Subvenio arranagnato Zatar unum levis letum.* Was it a warning, a threat…or promise?

Roxie sucked in a breath. "He's calling the demon."

I froze. "What?" I didn't hear anything.

She pointed to the wall. "*Subvenio arranagnato Zatar unum levis letum,*" she whispered.

I traced my flashlight over the gruesome letters. "I don't speak Latin."

"It's not Latin. It's Harken, the language of the other worlds."

More things to learn. It was one of the most frustrating parts of the job because I liked to know everything going in. And then I liked to plan it, map it or file it...or at the very least type it out.

"I didn't do the academic side of training," I said to Roxie. Just the killing part. "What do you mean he's calling a demon?"

She shook her head, the faint light bathing her face in shadows. "He's helping it."

My heart thudded against my chest. Heaven save us if that were true.

But it didn't make any sense. Why would my dad be in league with a demon if he was trying to escape it? He'd called me, begged me, to find a way for him to be free.

"I'll say one thing for him. He gets around," Roxie murmured, as she followed the word *Zatar*, scrawled in blood on the side of an oak bookcase, the ceiling above us to the front door that clicked closed on its own.

"Dad?" I stepped over the books cluttering the room, trying to ignore the dark power radiating from the cracked and worn volumes.

There was no answer.

I didn't appreciate the way Roxie had barged into my life but I had to be thankful that I now had someone—an experienced slayer—who could help me figure out what was happening to my dad.

Roxie struck a match. The sizzle of it filled the

room, along with the heady scent of sulfur. "Look at this," she said, excited.

She lit a fat red candle, similar to one of Grandma's ritual candles.

"Are you so sure that's a good idea?" I asked.

"You can't draw power with just one." She positioned the candle on a low table and opened a medieval looking volume. The cover was carved wood, painted in grotesque images of hell.

"Can we look at these?" I asked, still reluctant to spend too much time with the books.

"We can if we're careful. If you start to enjoy it or lose yourself in a book, get out right away."

Got it. "There's a picture of Zatar somewhere around here," I said, shining my pool of light over endless books. My eye caught a red leather-bound volume with the name Evangeline embossed in gold lettering on a black background. Tiny golden clover flowers, and holy heavens, switch stars formed a border.

"Look at this. This is from a demon slayer," I said, taking it and opening it in the light from Roxie's candle.

"It looks like a diary," she said, as we examined the stained pages. Precise notes, written in vintage script detailed imp sightings, water nymphs in freshly dug wells and whether or not the Pony Express had been infiltrated by valkyries.

Roxie sniffed at that last one. "As if they'd let women ride."

I ran my fingers over the precisely written notes. It was basically an 1800s version of my own Dangerous Book for Demon Slayers.

Roxie shook her head. "It's even indexed, by hand."

Well, sure—that made complete sense. I indexed my hand-written notes too. This Evangeline was a smart cookie.

A low moan echoed from the back of the house. The hairs on my arms stood on end as a chill ran through me.

I handed the diary to Roxie. "Keep this. See what else you run across. I'm going to find my dad."

My breath hitched as I moved into the next room, a small kitchen. The linoleum was gritty under my feet. Bloody messages trailed up the country wallpaper. They called for Zatar.

Oh no, Dad.

Sweat slicked my palms.

Where was he?

The walls groaned and shifted. I could taste the rotten fear of this place.

The zombie crow skittered across the counter toward me.

"Caw!"

"Go away," I said under my breath.

"Caw!" Its milky white eyes followed me.

There were no doors in this part of the house, no way to escape. It was like walking farther and farther into the mouth of the whale. And the sadistic thing was ready to swallow me whole.

"Lizzie." His voice barely carried from the next room.

A small flood of cockroaches skittered out from under the door. "Lizzie?"

"Dad?" My hand traced down to where my switch stars used to be. "I'm coming. Hold on."

Steady does it.

I cracked open the door. Dad lay sprawled on the floor next to a makeshift altar. His chest heaved, and his breath came in small pants.

This did not look good. For one thing, I could smell the sulfur. For another, Dad looked...off.

I stopped. Every stick of furniture in the room had been shoved aside to make room for the hideous altar.

It had been cobbled together with rough stones, masonry and animal bones. At least I hoped they were animal bones. Fluid oozed from cracks in the stone and fire had blackened one entire side of the structure. A bronze bowl at the top held a low-burning flame.

Holy hoodoo.

"Whatcha doing?" I tried to sound casual, but it came out more than a little panicked. Hells bells— what was he trying to pull?

This was starting to look like a Zatar love fest.

He's been helping the demon.

Or had he just been trying to survive?

Dad wore a pair of blue striped pajama pants. Strange symbols snaked over his chest and arms. I tried to make them out, but they were nothing I'd ever seen before. As I drew closer, I realized they were sliced into his chest. Blood dried crisp on the edges of the wounds.

Over his heart, I saw a twisted sickle.

Dad followed my gaze. "The name of the demon," he said, tears in his eyes.

"Did you put it there?" I asked breathlessly.

He shook his head hard and mouthed, "No."

"We can fix this," I said, feeling like scum. I didn't know what to do. I didn't even want to know this stuff, much less stand there unarmed at the altar of Zatar. "I have to get you out of here." Maybe if he got out of this house, away from the altar and the dead things, we could fix him.

We could at least wash this junk off his chest. Then maybe Roxie would know what to do.

Dad seemed to be thinking the same thing. He reached a hand up to me.

"Can you stand?" I asked, moving behind him,

trying to lift him off the wall. He was heavier than he looked, a dead weight.

"You came back," he said, patting me faintly on the arm. A half run-over chipmunk clambered out from under the mattress.

"Of course I came back," I said, lifting him. "Help me, okay? We've got to get out of here."

He nodded his head weakly.

I felt the power building in the room. We were ticking somebody off. And if they noticed Dad standing, they were really going to feel it once I got him moving.

"Hurry," I urged, as he wobbled on his feet.

"Lizzie," he said, his breath pained.

The mattress shuffled against the wall.

"Don't talk," I said, leaning back so I could see his face. He looked so much older than when I'd first seen him. He held on to my arm, then reached out to me with the other hand, as if we were meeting for the first time.

"What?" I asked, taking his hand in mine. It was a comfortable gesture, familiar and yet as soon as his fingers closed around mine, I sensed a change in him.

Power surged through the room, shaking the walls.

"Dad!" I tried to pull away, but his hand locked around mine.

He gasped for breath, groaning under an unseen weight. "Don't let go, Lizzie. Don't ever let me go."

I gasped as the floor cracked under our feet. Red light churned underneath.

"Jump!" I hollered as a portal opened directly below us.

It was too late. Dad fell.

He clutched me tightly, and I didn't let go as the churning mass swallowed us whole.

Chapter Seventeen

The portal spit us out between two trash bins overflowing with old beer cans, fast-food wrappers and muck. The air was damp and smelled like rot and urine.

"Stay here," I said, helping my dad brace himself against a cold brick wall. Sirens blared in the distance. The silver portal snapped shut, abandoning us in a narrow alley.

"God, I hope Roxie knows where we went." Because I didn't have a clue.

The vortex had a powerful suction. I'd lost the Maglite, my grandma's jar, even my ponytail holder. Tucking my hair behind my ears, I pulled the phone out of my back pocket and took a look at the GPS.

Error.

Yeah, I needed a $200 phone to tell me that.

The GPS had been a long shot at best. Still, I needed to figure out where we were.

To our left, past a teetering pile of boxes, I could see figures in the street. We'd risk that in a minute, once Dad had a chance to rest.

To our right, the alley ended in a brick wall covered with drab gray notices.

Need an escape? Haunt Jamaica! Call Millennium Travel!

Not in a million years.

2 for 1 tacos at Taco Bell

Pirate would like that.

EZ Soul Counseling: Clean up your eternal credit score

My stomach tingled. "Dad, I think we're in trouble."

He stood with a groan.

"No," I said, backtracking toward him. "Don't move." I didn't want him to panic. I was close enough to it myself.

He looked awful. "You're weak," I said, feeling his forehead. "You were just at the altar of a demon."

He rubbed at his eyes. "At least I was still at home."

Now we were in some kind of supernatural slum.

"I feel better," he said, testing his arms.

"No, you don't." I really didn't want him to come out from between the trashcans and see this.

He blinked, orienting himself. "I do. I feel stronger. It must be something in the air here."

"You've got to be kidding," I said, watching black clouds billow over dank gray skies.

The zombie rope's jar bumped against my leg. Naturally I didn't lose *him*.

I tipped the jar to get a better look and he slid sideways into the lid. "What is this thing anyway?" I asked dad.

He shrugged. "A simple compulsion spell," he answered. "My mom used to give them to me when I first started driving." He softened at the memory. "They helped me find my way home."

I watched as the zombie rope coiled along the bottom of the jar. "This one seems to have taken on a life of its own."

Dad watched. "It was only supposed to help you to Pasadena."

"What do you think, buddy?"

He stood on end and sniffed his nub at the air, the gray silent type. If I wasn't mistaken, he seemed perkier too.

What was it with this place?

Something clanged out on the street. I handed the zombie rope to my dad. "You guys stay here." I'd check it out. I grabbed a trashcan lid along the way. At least they had metal ones here. I also picked up a nice-sized rock. I could only imagine what my dad must think. Here was his demon-slayer daughter in Birkenstocks and torn leather pants, swimming in a black T-shirt and carrying urban cavewoman weapons.

What can I say? I was in it for the glory.

I certainly wasn't in it for the clothes.

The alley opened up on a city street swirling with debris. There wasn't a car in sight. Instead, people with grayish skin wandered up and down. A trashcan had toppled on its side, spilling empty cups and even more wrappers.

Nobody seemed to care. These people were like empty shells. They bumped against street lights, unused parking meters and even each other with barely a nod of recognition.

There were no birds, no plants, nothing but gray streets, stone buildings and an eerie quiet. Compared to this, our brick alley seemed positively cheery.

My mouth went dry and my palms started to sweat. "This isn't cold enough to be hell," I said to myself, trying to look on the bright side.

"It's purgatory," my dad said.

Shock rocketed through me. "What?"

I had the sudden urge to run back to where our portal had been. Operative word being *had*. Our exit was long gone. And I sure didn't know how to summon another portal—or get us out of here.

Skill #673 that I wish I knew—portal manipulation.

Rachmort spent six months out of the year in purgatory, ministering to lost souls, but he never told me how to get in—or out.

I tapped my rock against my trashcan shield, nervous. I should have asked Rachmort how to summon a portal. Yet another thing I planned to change.

Dad raised himself up off the wall and came to stand next to me, stronger and more balanced than he'd been since I saw him in the wall of fire. I checked his skin tone, then mine. Both were pink as a baby's butt. "You look…good," I told him.

That should have been welcome news, but it wasn't. This was wrong.

From the moment I'd first seen him, my dad had been hunched over, defeated. Now he stood erect, his shoulders back. There wasn't any rational explanation I could think of for the return of his glossy black hair or smooth complexion.

A trickle of fear slid down my back. "Why are you better here?"

"Angelic good luck?" he ventured.

Oh lovely, a sense of humor too.

Speaking of angels… "What does being an angel mean? I've never met one." Or if I had, I'd never realized it. Was it his full-time job? Had he followed people around as a guardian? Did anything pass to me?

His humor disappeared. "It's complicated, Lizzie. Too sensitive to discuss in the open."

It wasn't the answer I wanted to hear, but I'd let it go for now.

"We will talk about it," he said, his expression earnest. "I'll explain everything. I promise."

If we made it out of here. "Okay," I said. "I understand." I didn't want to rush it, if for no other reason than this was a chance to truly get to know my dad.

We would have time, because I would get us out of here.

He still looked weak, but he wasn't as afraid as he should have been.

I stared at him as the realization crept over me. "You've been here before."

He didn't bother denying it. "Come on," he said, groaning as he stepped out of the alley. "I'll take you for a coffee."

Oh, no, no, no. This was wrong. "I don't want to have coffee in purgatory."

"Ice cream?" he offered.

"No," I snapped.

"It's vanilla," he said, trying to tempt me.

"Why?" I asked slowly.

"All ice cream in purgatory is vanilla."

Naturally.

He held his hand out toward me, and even if my hands weren't full of makeshift weapons, I still wouldn't have summoned up the nerve to take it.

"Be a sport, Lizzie," he coaxed. "I never got to take you out for ice cream. It'll be a nice father-daughter moment."

Okay I admit I'd had fantasies about my real dad taking me out for a chocolate dip cone, but not in the dark realm between heaven and hell.

I watched the gray-toned people ambling behind him. "Why are you trying to pretend this is normal? This," I said, waving my rock at the gray bleak world in front of us, "is not normal."

He sighed. "Sorry. I just want to be a dad."

Ouch. He had the guilt part down right.

"My apologies if I don't want to sit around licking dip cones, but in case you haven't noticed, we're in trouble here. We're trapped in purgatory and my weapons are gone and meanwhile someone up there is killing demon slayers and Zatar wants your soul and all I want to do is get us the frick out of here." I paused to catch my breath. "Now."

He winced. "I might be able to get out on my own power with a couple of days' rest. Not you."

Of course.

"But, Lizzie, I'll stay here. I'll protect you. With each passing minute, I'm more myself."

"Um-hum. Yeah. It's a bad sign when you get stronger the closer you get to hell."

He didn't deny it.

"It's not as if you're getting distance from Zatar. If anything, he's closer." It was wrong. It was utterly and frighteningly wrong. I pointed my trash can lid at him for emphasis. "I'm leaving."

"Not without a portal."

"Cripes."

Rachmort would know how to get out of here. Roxie said he'd been taken to purgatory. "Do you know where Rachmort might be?"

Dad nodded. "Zatar has him at his compound."

"Lovely. So your buddy's got him." That demon was really starting to tick me off. "We'll rescue Rachmort and kill Zatar." We might as well be efficient.

"He's not my buddy," Dad snapped like, well, a dad. "Zatar is building his strength by preying on slayers and lesser angels."

"Fine," I groused.

"Fine," Dad replied. "You should be glad Zatar can't get a read on me down here. I can actually help." He turned and started walking down the street, into the gray city. "Let's go find some real weapons."

"That's what I'm talking about," I said, right behind

him. "Where are we going?"

"I know a guy. He's not far."

Dad waited for me to catch up, then put his hand on my back as he led me down the narrow walk. It was the same as any other main street except half the people didn't seem to be going anywhere. They walked, eyes straight ahead.

"These are lost souls, aren't they?" I asked.

"Yes."

It was creepy. And sad.

We passed several shuttered businesses, a few open ones.

Fast food seemed to be the most popular. Leave it to Taco Bell to find markets in other dimensions.

"Okay," I said, giving in to the need to plan, "after we get our weapons, how do we find Rachmort?"

"Keep your voice down." My dad gave me a guarded look. "He's in Zatar's compound. I can take us there."

"No kidding." That was good news, but how did my dad know so much?

His mouth quirked, as if he could tell what I was thinking. "There are advantages to being tied to a demon. You learn things."

Score one for Dad.

We stopped at a crosswalk and Dad pushed the *walk* button. He realized too late what he'd done. "Sorry," he said, as we started up again. "Habit."

"So are these souls doing penance?" I asked.

"Some," he said. "Others will stay for eternity."

"Ouch."

"It's better than hell."

Good point.

I waved at the guy behind the Toasty Almonds cart. At least you could get roasted nuts down here.

Dad saw me pause. "Would you like some?"

"No." Go figure. This place didn't give me an appetite.

"We can eat by the fountain." He pointed down the street to what looked to be a park. An expanse of gray grass featured black benches and a dry, gray stone fountain with an immense gargoyle in the middle.

Festive.

I understood Dad's need to be, well—a dad, but we didn't have time for bonding in the netherworld. "Let's keep moving. How much farther?"

"Right down this way." He led us across one street and then parallel to the next block to a drab storefront with a spray painted sign over the door. Rae Rae's Re-Usables.

Dad opened the creaky, dirty door. "Down here, we barter for supplies."

"With what?" Even my World Visa card had its limits.

He touched the lavender hair on my shoulder. "Color is very valuable," he said, a note of apology in his voice. "Stay behind me."

We stepped inside a small shop lit by candles and a busted out part of the roof, now covered in makeshift glass and duct tape.

"How's it going Rae Rae?" Dad asked.

A freakishly tall woman slid out from behind a dingy curtain. She wore a brown and orange flowered dress and looked like a black Vin Diesel. Rae Rae wasn't fooling anybody. She didn't seem too worried about it.

"Doing fine, sugar," she said in a deep velvety voice. "Long time, no swap."

"You got me some more Luckies?" she asked, gliding into place behind the counter.

Dad hesitated. "Not this time. I have something better."

I stepped out from behind Dad and Rae Rae gasped. "Aunt Em, we are not in Kansas anymore. It's the mother lode!"

She slid from behind the counter and practically purred as she ran her French-manicured fingers through the ends of my hair.

"Doesn't fade," Dad said proudly.

She clucked. "Magic?"

"You could say that," I replied.

My dad stood over the counter. "We need two night crystals, a pair of razor cutters, neutralizers—"

"Cosmic or proton?" she asked, focused on my head.

Dad scratched his chin. "Better go for cosmic."

"You have any switch stars?" I ventured.

"Hell, no," she crooned.

It was worth asking.

Dad stared her down. "I also need demon dust," he said low under his breath.

Rae Rae whistled. "You could break into a demon's hold with all that."

Dad tilted his head. "Now why would I want to do that?"

"I have no idea," she said, hitching up a muscled, hairy leg and slipping a key out of her garter belt, "I don't want you telling me either."

She opened up the dingy glass case and pulled out a plain black box. As soon as she opened the lid, light streamed out like a Bahamas beach in July.

"Nice," Dad said as Rae Rae counted out two crystals and placed them each in a black leather bag.

I peered at the other objects in the case. There were more black boxes, some crystals and, "crayons?" Two stubby red crayons were lined up on black silk next to a broken green one and the tip of a yellow.

"A newbie, huh?" Rae Rae crooned. "Don't worry,

luv. I could tell by the hair."

"The portal strips color," Dad said. "If you keep it close enough to your body, you can sometimes get something through."

"Tell it. You'd be surprised what folks will trade for a fast-food fix," Rae Rae said.

"Is this a dryer sheet?" It was folded carefully next to two used and curling Snoopy stickers.

"There aren't any smells down here," Dad said, "except for the rotten ones. Dryer sheets are like gold."

"And out of your price range," Rae Rae added.

"We'll manage," I said, watching Dad test the weight of the crystals.

"I have Armstrong cutters. They'd slice through an ox." She shook out a brown paper bag. "You get two neutralizers. Oh, Marcus?" she called to the back.

The curtain shimmied and a few minutes later, a burly man placed two pistol-type weapons on the counter.

Dad ran a finger along the blade of the cutters. "Do you mind?" he asked, poised over the neutralizers.

Rae Rae shrugged.

Dad lifted the weapon and shot it into his hand.

"Dad!" I felt the energy whom-whom off him and through the room before he smiled and placed the weapon back on the counter.

"It's good magic," Rae Rae stated. "You know good magic don't come cheap."

Dad nodded. "What's it going to cost, Rae Rae? We need to keep moving."

"Fine," she said, her gaze wandering over me and stopping at my hair. "It will cost you the entire head."

"What?" I protested.

Dad was busy inspecting the other neutralizer. "Don't worry. She only means your hair."

Obviously Dad didn't have any experience raising

daughters.

"No," I said. It was bad enough my hair was purple. I was not going to shave my head for Rae Rae, the cross-dressing weapons broker.

"This is no time to debate, Lizzie," Dad said, his tone grave.

Actually, this was the perfect time to negotiate. And I knew who I wasn't taking to buy my next Harley. "I'll give you two inches," I told her.

Dad stormed over to me. "What she's giving us is worth at least eight," he hissed in my ear, loudly enough for Rae Rae and her sixteen closest relatives to hear.

He was the worst negotiator ever.

Rae Rae stilled. "Ten," she countered.

"Four," I hitched my chin, doing my best to look down at her.

She didn't take her eyes off me. "Eight."

"Lizzie," my dad pleaded.

"Not now." Heavens to Betsy. No wonder the man was about to lose his soul. He shouldn't be bargaining with a six-year-old much less a demon.

"Four is my final offer," I said. "Take it or we'll go to that other pawn shop Dad told me about."

Rae Rae frowned. "Who else you doing business with?"

"Nobody," Dad protested.

I believed him.

Good thing Rae Rae didn't. Her eyes narrowed. "Are you talking to Lenny? He can't give you what I'm giving you, sugar."

"And he stinks," I added, figuring it wouldn't be too far off. "Come on," I said. "Look at this." I tried to do my best impression of a shampoo commercial model. "Where else are you going to find such glorious hair?"

Rae Rae watched every flutter of my lilac mistake.

"Five," she said.

"Deal," I replied.

Twenty minutes later, I had a Dorothy Hamill bob cut and we had our weapons. She'd taken more than five inches, and I'd never had my head fondled quite like that, but since my goal was to come out of this with some sort of a hairdo, I let it slide.

The barrels of neutralizers slapped at my stomach as we hurried out of the shop.

"Keep them under your shirt at all times," Dad warned.

"I know." I wasn't about to lose these.

As it stood, I had two guns in my pants, the crystal pouches in my bra and a pair of cutters tucked in at my hips. I trusted Dad. Mostly. But I still wanted to hold all of the weapons.

He hadn't protested, which made me trust him a little more.

"Rush, but don't draw attention," he said. "We want to get across the city by nightfall."

"Which is in?"

"Two hours," he said, almost punching a Walk button before holding back. "Zatar is holding Rachmort at his compound on the north side."

"Compound? A little pretentious don't you think?"

"He's a demon. What do you expect?"

† † †

An hour and a half later, we reached the edge of the city. The air was different here, heavier and laced with fried food, ammonia and sulfur. I peered around a Chick-fil-A on the edge of civilization and saw Zatar's stronghold, about a hundred yards out in no-man's land. It was a monster, like Dracula's castle on crack.

Gray stone walls towered high into the sky. Red banners adorned with golden snakes fluttered from the walls. It was the first time since we'd been here that

I'd seen any color, other than my hair.

I counted at least seventeen turrets and only one way in—a black door flanked by a half dozen imps, slavering in formation. A half dozen more patrolled the skies, their batlike wings outlined against the coming darkness.

"How are we going to get in there?" I asked.

"I know a way," Dad said, settling in next to me.

My nerves tangled in my stomach. It had better be a very, very sneaky way.

"We want to attack at sundown," he explained, "when demons are their strongest."

It was possible my dad wasn't very good at this.

"We need to surprise them," he said, looking out at the castle. "And what better way then by letting them feel secure?"

Maybe he did have a point.

He nudged me. "Take a deep breath. Relax. We have a few minutes."

Oh sure. Let's whip out a game of Parcheesi. Or those ice cream cones.

"What's the plan?

"You are definitely my daughter."

"Why? I don't see how you have a plan."

"Oh, I do. Here we go," he said, excited and proud. "I sift us in—"

"What do you mean sift?"

"I can disappear in one place and re-appear in another. As long as the places are fairly close together. And in the same dimension. I'm an angel," he said, as if that explained everything.

"Gotcha." We let the 'fallen' part slide.

"Can demons sense you sifting?" I asked.

"Of course. That's why we throw out our light crystals and start shooting."

"Oh great."

"You have a better plan?" he asked.

"Unfortunately, no."

"We cut Rachmort out of his bonds, or if he's not attached to the wall, we take him lock, stock and barrel."

"And we sift out," I finished.

"Yes." He practically clapped.

"Where?"

"I have a place I use when I'm here—" he began.

No good. "Zatar will know about that."

"A secret place," he assured me. "Of course Zatar will track us in an instant. The demon dust should slow him down. That's where we count on Rachmort to give us a portal."

It made me nervous. "I don't know, Dad." A lot had to go right—even if Rachmort was alive and conscious.

"You have a better idea?" he asked.

"No."

I hated to admit it, but his plan was all we had. It was as simple as we could make it. Plus, if Dad was right about sifting and where to find Rachmort, we might be able to pull it off.

Unless we sifted into a room full of demons.

Focus.

I couldn't control that. The only thing I could do was trust Dad and fight like Hades. I leaned my head against the dingy gray wall.

Oh for my days as a preschool teacher when the little demons left school at noon.

I couldn't take my eyes off the castle. Suppose we did make it out of here in one piece... "What's Zatar going to do to you if he discovers you broke Rachmort out?"

He didn't answer. He just kept looking out over no-man's land.

"Dad?" I pushed.

"It won't be good."

"Now I know where I got my gift for understatement."

He turned to me. "You know what? I don't care. For the first time, I'm meeting Zatar head on. I need to do this, Lizzie."

"It's brave. And stupid."

"Kind of like you trying to be a demon slayer without any training."

"How did you know about that?"

"You're starting to get a reputation." He broke into a smile. "This is…" he began, searching for the words. "I was going to say hell, but it's not." He looked at me with such warmth that I melted a bit. "This is not how I would have ever chosen to get to know you, Lizzie. But right now, I can't think of anybody else I'd rather have with me."

Warmth crept into my belly. "Me too."

Sure, it wasn't a normal father-daughter relationship, but somehow it fit, although I could have done without the demon castle and purgatory.

He grew serious. "I never wanted to go, Lizzie. I wanted to raise you. I left because I didn't want you exposed to this world. You deserved better."

See, that's where he had it wrong. I hadn't wanted *better*. I'd just wanted to fit in.

"I'm glad I have you now," I said, looking out at the massive gray walls. I took a deep breath, feeling the weight of the neutralizers against my stomach.

"Here," I said, drawing out one of the guns. I didn't need to carry both of them anymore.

Dad grinned as he took it.

"Listen, can you sift me in and out from here?" I asked. Not that I wanted to break into Zatar's compound by myself, but… "If he's going to sense you or hurt you –"

"No chance." Dad tried to stuff the gun into the top of his pajama pants and when that didn't work, he gave up and held it low at his side. "Don't you see, Lizzie? I have to go in there. I haven't felt this hopeful in a long time. If we get Rachmort, we have a good shot at winning this."

"Brave and stupid."

"Like father, like daughter."

I couldn't help grinning. "In that case, I have some cutters for you," I said, sliding them out from my hip.

He hefted them before clipping them to his pants.

"And a crystal."

He shoved it in his pocket and held up his neutralizer. "Ready?" he asked, offering me his hand. I took it and he squeezed tight. "Let's go."

Chapter Eighteen

I'd expected sifting with a minor angel to be like flying. Or maybe like passing through a warm, inviting curtain of air. Instead it was like a big sneeze.

"Hold on," Dad cautioned.

No problem there. I clutched his hand and covered my weapons as the pressure built. I wasn't about to let my neutralizer or anything else fly out of my possession and into the abyss. Not this time.

"Brace yourself," Dad said, "Aaa…"

Boom!

We slammed to a knee-rattling stop inside a pitch black chamber. The smell of sulfur was enough to knock me sideways. Definitely a demon's lair.

My eyes watered and my nose tickled and I let out a sinus-rattling, "Aaa-cho!"

Dad gripped my hand tighter.

"I got it," I said, attempting to extricate myself. His fingers closed around mine in a vise grip.

What? Was he losing his nerve?

"Let go." I forced myself out of his hold.

No doubt Zatar knew we were here. He'd be barging in at any moment. I tossed my crystal to the floor, watching it shatter into brilliant blue spheres of light.

We were in a round chamber with gray stone walls

and a ceiling that stretched higher than the light afforded by the crystals. There was one door to my right, zero windows. It wasn't the best defensive position. If I had to guess, I'd say we were probably in one of the turrets.

Zebediah Rachmort sat tied to a heavy wooden chair. His white Einstein hair burst into an even bigger mess than usual. His hands bent at an unnatural angle behind the wide back of the chair and blood dried on his fingers and crusted around the chains at his wrists.

"Keep your back to the wall," I told Dad. I'd learned that one from Max.

I approached Rachmort carefully, aware this could be a trap.

"Who is it?" He struggled to turn. "Get away from me!"

My mentor wore a dirty gold waistcoat over a formerly white shirt and rumpled brown pants. His eyes were dull and glassy. I'd never seen him like this. Rachmort was the kind of guy who always looked like he was about to tell a joke. Of course I'd never seen Rachmort in the clutches of a demon.

"Hush, it's me," I said. His shoulders sagged in recognition. "Hold on. I'm going to see if you're wired." I ran my hands over him, looking for magical traps.

He strained to see me. "You have to get out of here. The demon wants you!"

"I know," I said, speaking low, purposefully calm. "Believe me, we won't be wasting any time."

He was clean.

I grabbed Rachmort around the arm. "Sift us, Dad. Now!"

Dad braced his hands against the gray stone, fear written on his face. "No," he shook his head. "Not yet. I need more strength."

"What?" He had to be kidding. That wasn't part of the plan. "How long?"

"A minute," he insisted, "at the most."

Yeah, well I didn't know if we had that long. I couldn't believe Dad didn't warn me about a sifting delay.

"At the most," I warned him.

I reached for the cutters at my hip. Maybe I could get us out of here. If I could get Rachmort unshackled, he could open up a portal.

"Lizzie," Rachmort said, struggling to see me, "this whole thing is a trap," he insisted.

"Yeah, I kind of figured that," I said, working my saw into the bands at his wrists. Maybe Zatar would get cocky and take his sweet time.

Or maybe he'd attack us any second.

"Did you know these cuffs are made of a titanium alloy only found in purgatory?" Rachmort asked, excited and a little breathless. The professor was back.

"Tell me later," I said, struggling. Dang. If these cutters were the sharpest around, I'd hate to see the dullest. Or maybe we were dealing with enchanted metal. Cripes. "If I get one hand loose, can you zip us out of here?" I asked.

"Yes," he nodded sharply.

Now where was my Dad? I spotted him against the wall.

"We need you over here."

Rachmort cleared his throat. "You do realize that I trained you so you could stay out of this place."

"Or survive it."

"He's here!" Rachmort shouted.

A second later, Zatar, Earl of Hades shimmered through the door. Showoff.

The photograph in Dad's book had been spot on. Zatar had the scaled body of a lizard and face of an angel. Silver and white wings of an angel sprouted from his leathery back.

He was flanked by six lesser beings on each side. They looked human, but I knew better.

Zatar gave me an intimate, smoky look like that of a lover. His wild golden hair fell across one eye and I almost forgot what he was.

Then he smiled, showing sharp bloody teeth. "Impeccably done."

I wasn't sure if he was referring to my sifting or Rachmort's job as bait. Either way, we weren't going to stick around to find out. Dad had frozen a few feet away. I ran straight for him, the neutralizer slapping at my belly. I grabbed Dad's hand, then snatched hold of Rachmort's arm, still chained to the chair.

"Now!" I said, bracing myself for my Dad to angel us the frick out of there. I hadn't even fired a shot. Who cared? We were leaving.

Why weren't we leaving?

"Dad?" I pleaded, panic rising.

His eyes were wild. "I can't sift. It's not working."

Wrong answer. "Make it work!"

His mouth gaped. "I can't."

H-e-double-hockey-sticks.

I couldn't fight Zatar. I'd barely made it out of a fight alive with a lesser demon and that was when I had my switch stars.

Zatar grinned like a school boy. "This is so much more fun than a dreg." He lowered his chin and shot green darts out of his eyes.

My dad screamed.

The demonic darts shimmered with an unearthly energy and streaked straight for my neck.

I reached deep down and put on the brakes, slowing the moment enough to get a good look. I'd seen these things once before—in my bathroom when I first learned about my powers.

Grandma had called them vox, part of a demon's energy. Zatar's vox shone like large, thick glow sticks. And they were sharp on the soul as broken glass.

I reached out and touched the closest one. It sizzled on the end of my fingertip. Hot, like touching a stove.

Sweet switch stars. This was going to hurt.

I winced as I grabbed the vox around the middle. Then I fired it lawn-dart-style at Zatar's head.

"Biiiiittttch!" The demon screamed as I fired another and another.

He threw one of his minions out in front of him. The vox smashed into its temple and it exploded into a million flecks of light.

Another blasted apart on the wall behind Zatar as he twisted to the side.

My hands seared with pain as I fired and fired, catching more minions, but not Zatar. The demon was too fast.

My arms sizzled from the energy in the air and every hair on my body stood at attention. My mouth tasted like sulfur and no doubt my hands had already begun to blister.

Zatar frowned. "Damned demon slayer."

I fought the urge to collapse. Okay. That was something. My body throbbed in protest, but I'd done it—I'd ticked off the demon.

It was a small victory for my sanity. I had to bury my fear, my hurt, my utter terror that this thing could not only kill me but trap my soul forever. Because if I thought on that too long, I'd be just as frozen as Dad.

"Your dregs didn't work either," I shouted over the buzzing in my head.

Two humanoid creatures lay dead at his feet.

Make that three. The last body teetered toward Zatar and he shoved it away. "You're the one," he said as his bodyguard fell in a lifeless, soulless heap. "Excellent."

He fired again, and this time the vox flew faster, blazing white at the tips.

This time, I couldn't slow them down.

Holy hell. I ducked the first one.

"Dad, watch out!" I hollered as the second nearly clipped him.

We couldn't keep doing this.

"Unchain me!" Rachmort demanded.

Oh sure. Why not? It's not like I was doing anything.

I caught the third one, searing my hand.

"Ow, ow, ow!" I aimed straight for Zatar's head. The remaining minions opened up with their own and I dove to the floor, knocking Rachmort's chair over with me as red vox sailed over our heads and burst into the wall behind us.

Rachmort grunted as he slammed into the floor. "Unchain me!"

"I'm," ignoring the searing pain in my hands, I dug for the neutralizer, "busy!" What I wouldn't give for a half dozen switch stars.

"I told you, she's mine!" Zatar shouted, shooting his vox and frying the demons on his left. They fell into a sizzling heap.

I used the momentary distraction to grab my cutters off the floor.

"Slice at a right angle," Rachmort ordered, head cocked around his shoulder.

"Do you ever stop teaching?" I asked, making my cuts clean and quick.

I got his left hand out and stuck the neutralizer in it.

He got off a half dozen shots. They bounced off Zatar. Two creatures to his right went down. But not Zatar.

Never Zatar.

Dad cowered against the wall.

"Shoot, Dad!"

Zatar let loose with a blaze of vox.

Rachmort threw up his hand. *"Caladai taniom abberaat!"*

A fiery silver portal sprang up between us and the demon. The vox slammed into it, blazing scarlet. I didn't care if the portal swallowed them or destroyed them or sent them to Santa Claus as a Christmas gift. We were leaving.

I dove for my dad and dragged him across the room. I could barely move him. It was as if he suddenly weighed five hundred pounds. His shoulder gave way with a sickening pop. I tried not to think about it as I yanked him toward safety.

"Caladai taniom abberaat!" Rachmort opened a second portal in the floor. His turned-over chair teetered on the edge and I tackled him, sending Rachmort through, still half tied, one arm wrapped around his neck and the other grabbing my Dad's hand. I didn't let go.

We fell headlong into the blazing hot abyss. I closed my eyes tight against the punishing winds. It was like being inside a tornado, but I didn't care. I'd never been so glad to get out of anywhere, no matter where this portal took us.

Chapter Nineteen

We hit the ground hard, rolling over mounds of earth and sandy soil until we smacked into a tree trunk. Dad flew one way, Rachmort skidded another and I got showered with dry pine needles.

I brought a throbbing hand up to my shoulder and then thought the better of it.

Everything hurt. Maybe I could just stay under this sad excuse for a tree. I didn't want to face what was out there.

I squeezed my eyes shut, then forced them open again. Rachmort might be injured. Dad, too. Then there was the issue of finding out exactly where we'd landed. The only thing I could tell so far was that it was night.

"Onward and upward," I groaned, scooting on my elbows until I could lurch to my feet. My hands were raw. They were already starting to blister.

The moon hung low, illuminating Rachmort as he lay in a heap of chair a short distance away. There were no other signs of civilization, only acres of scrub.

"I'm coming," I said, brushing pine needles away, forcing myself to block out the throbbing in my hands. I did a quick search of the ground around me. Cripes. I'd lost my neutralizer.

My dad sprawled between me and Rachmort. He

was starting to come around.

I tried to hold my head steady, hoping it would help the ringing in my ears. It didn't. "You okay?" I caught a whiff of the ammonia and sulfur of purgatory on him. No doubt I stunk too.

He winced as I helped him to his feet.

"I've been better," he groaned, holding his dislocated shoulder.

No kidding. At least both of us were upright. That was progress.

I made it over to Rachmort, realizing too late that I'd lost my cutters.

Rachmort lay on the ground, still bound to his chair, bracing himself with his free hand. I bent down to help steady him. "Are you okay?"

"Your cutters are in the Joshua tree."

"How do you—?" I began. "You know what? Forget it. I don't want to know.

I made a bee line for the Joshua tree. And there, at the base, I saw a pasty white butt, a silver ponytail and, "Oh my God," I spun away, covering my eyes.

"Hey, get your own—Oh wow, it's Lizzie!"

And that was Neal.

I didn't dare look again, even though I was pretty sure who was with the flower-powered menace.

Grandma chuckled. "It's the most natural thing in the world, Lizzie."

No it wasn't. Not when it was my grandmother, at the base of a tree, en flagrante.

"Can you stop making out?" We had problems here.

She didn't even have the decency to be embarrassed. "We weren't making out, we were making love."

"Too much information."

"Besides, you were the one who ran off. Looks like you did good. Hey, Rachmort!"

"Gertie!" The necromancer waved his free hand. "I was aiming for you. I figured you'd be somewhere fortified."

Oh please. "Get dressed," I barked. "And hand me those cutters."

"No wait!" I corrected myself as Neal began to stand up. "I'll get them myself." I reached into a high branch for the gleaming silver shears.

I still couldn't believe Grandma and Neal had been doing the horizontal pokey while we fought for our lives in purgatory.

Grandma had no business being out away from camp, especially with an aging hippie who couldn't keep his Birkenstocks to himself.

There were banshees on the loose for heaven's sake! Deadly cutters flying through the air! Although, frankly, I was more annoyed by Neal.

Not that I'd seen anything truly gruesome. It was dark. But the thought, the hint, the notion of Grandma doing *that* or anything leading up to it was a bit more than my brain could handle.

While Neal put his peace sign back in his pocket, I knelt beside my mentor and tried to focus on something I could control, like freeing him.

My hands shook with pain, but I held the cutters as steady as I could and sliced the last bond from Rachmort's wrist.

"How long do you think before Zatar tracks us?" I asked, helping him uncurl his wrist from the back of the chair.

Rachmort sagged to the ground, his white hair stark and bright against the brown soil. "Not long."

I got to work on the bands at his ankles.

Rachmort ran a dirty hand over his face and back into his hair. "How long have you been able to—" He winced as I nicked him with the cutters.

"Sorry."

"How long have you been able to handle a demon's vox?"

I cringed as his ankle bonds snapped and the kickback made my cutters vibrate against the burns on my hands. "It came with the powers." Grandma had locked me in my bathroom to undergo the change. I'd been mad and scared. "A few seconds after I turned into a demon slayer, a demon showed up on the back of my toilet bowl, spitting vox. I'd killed him with it."

Rachmort broke out in a smile and for the first time that night. He looked like his old self. "Splendid, Lizzie. Well done." He scooted away from the chair, his legs free.

Well it's not as if I had much of a choice. "How long have you been able to summon portals?"

He flicked his hand. "It's a common necromancer's trick," he said, massaging at his freed wrists. "I've never met a demon slayer who could touch vox, much less hold it," he said, barely containing his excitement. "And you threw it back!" He made a tossing motion. "Pow!"

"Yeah." He made it sound fun, when in reality it was downright terrifying. "You mean I'm not supposed to do that?"

He shook his head wildly. "No. It's completely baffling. Isn't that wonderful?"

I wasn't so sure. "Should I keep doing it?"

"Of course." He touched my arm, his expression more like a father's than I'd ever known. "You have gifts, Lizzie. It's your moral duty to use them well."

Grandma sauntered up to us, boots grinding against the sandy earth. "My turn to interrupt the love fest."

"Your shirt's on backward," I said.

She snorted. "Stop being picky. I had to do something while you were off saving the world." She straightened the silver rings on her fingers. "You said we had problems."

"Right." Rachmort scrambled to his feet, brushing the worst of the dirt from his brown trousers. "Zatar is going to be able to use that portal to track us."

"I don't know," I said, ignoring the pounding in my head as I stood. "I may have bought us some time. You see I had one of Grandma's jars left—"

"*You* stole my jars?"

"Borrowed," I corrected her. There was a difference. Maybe. "Anyhow, it broke and I felt Zatar fade."

"E-yah!" Grandma slapped me on the back. Grandma planed her silver ringed hands on her hips, coming as close as she ever had to beaming. "You unloaded an all purpose jar back there? That'll hold him back for three hours. Maybe four!"

"Then let's prepare," Rachmort said.

I nodded. "Okay, listen up."

Dad and I explained what happened in purgatory. Well, I did most of the explaining. Dad sat down against the Joshua tree. He'd gone pale and weak.

Grandma whistled under her breath. "How long did the demon have you?" she asked Rachmort.

He tugged at his goatee. "What month is it?"

She raised her brows. "March."

"Two months then." He blew out a breath.

Wow. He'd been taken almost the moment he'd left us in Greece.

He waved off our concern. "There's no time for that. Although I will thank you, Lizzie. And you, Xavier, for rescuing me. That was a fine piece of work. Most impressive." He winked. "Now." He clapped me on the shoulder. "The demon wants you dead, Lizzie. I heard him talking. He's made it his mission to eliminate the slayers."

Thanks for the reminder. "Roxie and I figured that out."

"Roxie?" He beamed with surprise. "She's alive?"

That's right. He didn't know. "I'm not the last demon slayer." To see his expression you would have thought it was Christmas morning, Easter and his birthday wrapped into one.

"There are five others," I told him, "including Roxie. They went into hiding."

"Brilliant!" He beamed. "I knew I trained them well."

Yeah, well training only got you so far. "We have a problem. Roxie's infected with a dreg. She's afraid she's going to pass it on to her sister."

"Yes, yes," he said. You could see the wheels turning in his mind. "We'll protect them. We'll make it our mission to stop the dregs and eliminate Zatar."

Dad started coughing. Hard.

"Are you all right?" He looked terrible. His eyes had gone glassy, his breathing was shallow and the cuts on his chest had begun to ooze.

"I'll take him back," Neal slipped an arm under Dad's uninjured shoulder. "We'll snap that joint back into place too. Come on, buddy." The Bohemian bane of my existence was actually quite gentle as he helped my dad back to his feet. Neal didn't even flinch at the blood or the smell. He gave Dad a reassuring smile. "We'll find you a comfortable spot on your very own bus."

"I'll come check on you," I called after them, grateful for once to have Neal around.

Grandma whistled under her breath. "That man has the finest ass."

And I was grateful no longer.

"Okay," I said to Grandma and Rachmort, "let's plan our attack here. We need to get rid of the dregs and get Zatar off our backs. Let's think of a way to do it."

I didn't know if I was strong enough to kill Zatar, but I was positive I didn't have a clue about how to eliminate a dreg.

"We can do what Evie did," Grandma said, as if it were the most natural thing in the world.

"How do you know what Evie did?" My Great Great Great Aunt Evie might have been one of the greatest demon slayers of all time, but she died in 1883

Grandma thwacked me on the arm. "Roxie came back here after you went to purgatory without her. She's pissed about that, by the way. But she brought with her that diary you found."

"So Evangeline was Evie."

I'd hoped, but I hadn't been able to take a long enough look at the book to be sure. Talk about knowledge. This could change everything. I wondered what my Dad had planned to do with Evie's diary—and how he came across the book in the first place.

"I was reading it when Neal suggested a walk."

Among other things.

"Lizzie, pay attention," Grandma ordered.

"I am paying attention," I snapped.

"Old people have sex," Grandma said.

Oh my god.

"Yes, they do!" Rachmort added.

"Please. Stop. Let's just talk about the diary."

Grandma huffed. "Exactly. I didn't memorize the details, but I know Evie could create a portal so specific to a demon that it stripped him of the magic things he had with him."

Wait. "I thought necromancers created portals."

"We do." He began polishing his glasses on his gold waistcoat. "In fact, it's much easier for someone like me to bridge the gaps between the worlds of the living and the dead. Part of the job, you could say." He held his glasses up to the moonlight. "But it's not impossible for you. Not at all. I tried to teach Evie portals. Years ago. Didn't know it took." He leaned close. "If you can re-create Evie's portal, you could banish Zatar and force him to release his dregs."

Hope blossomed. "I can do that? I could eliminate the dregs?"

"It sure sounds like it!" Rachmort exclaimed with no small amount of glee. He grew somber. "Of course, we'd have to catch them."

Great. Dregs on the loose. Provided I could even pull this off. I hoped Dimitri was ready. And still talking to me.

Rachmort put on his glasses and blinked a few times, testing them. "Your great aunt was a feisty one, always trying to improve on things. She exploded my hand-cranked Demon Duster. Kaboom! You should have seen it," he mused. "She sent my canoe to Hades… But I never knew she'd caught on." Rachmort clapped his hands, delighted. "Evie was special. Just like you."

"Ah, so now it's tradition." I kind of liked that. And it would be fun to create the kind of portal that could strip Zatar of those dregs and any other magic he happened to be holding.

"Where do you think we should send him?" I asked. "Personally, I'd prefer to impale him on one of the ice peaks of Hades."

"Excellent idea," Rachmort boomed. "Drag him deeper than you've ever gone."

How could I send him to a place I'd never even seen?

"This is starting to sound more and more impossible." My brain started to buzz, like it always did when I was thinking about the details upon details involved in pulling off an insurmountable task.

"Just remember the demon slayer truths, Lizzie!" Rachmort said.

Accept the Universe. Look to the Outside. Sacrifice Yourself.

I knew Rachmort was trying to be helpful, but truly, he was directing this. He wasn't the one who was going to stand toe-to-toe with a creature that wanted to kill him and try to use magic he'd never known existed until now, with oh wait—about three hours to prepare.

Hells bells. My head was starting to hurt. "You know what? While I'm at it, let's strip Zatar of his power and kill him too."

"No," Rachmort, "let's not innovate. We know this works. We have to count on what we know."

Oh, please. "I was joking."

Rachmort didn't get it. "This feels like old times," he said, rubbing his hands together. "I always enjoy spending time with demon slayers."

Glad one of us was having fun.

He caught my dirty look. "What? Will grumbling help us trap Zatar?"

No, but at least I understood it.

Grandma tapped her silver ringed fingers together. "Now, what about the dreg in Roxie?"

"Well," I considered, "what if I make a smaller portal? We could toss her across the field and pull the dreg out?"

"Yes, yes," Rachmort mumbled, tugging at his mustache.

"It'll be a test run," I said. And I needed all the practice I could get.

Rachmort nodded. "It will also help us determine what to do with a live dreg."

I crossed my arms over my chest. "As long as you

keep Max away from it."

"Dimitri can handle it," Grandma said. "He seemed to take care of the last dreg pretty well."

I nodded, my stomach flip flopping at the thought— Dimitri. He was going to kill me for running out on him like I had.

"Okay, so we use Evie's formula to create demon-sucking portals," Rachmort said. "Lizzie flings Zatar to hell and Dimitri helps us clean up the dregs."

"My dad also has something called demon dust."

Rachmort tapped his glasses against his chin. "Hmm…not much use outside of purgatory, but it might help keep Zatar in one spot. We'll have to see."

"Sounds like a plan," I said. "We'd better get moving." We had less than three hours.

"I'll go find Roxie," Rachmort offered.

Grandma grinned. "I'll convene the biker witches."

Rachmort leaned way too close into my personal space. "Leave it to Evie to think of something like this. She was always surprisingly practical. Just like you." He slapped me on the back and headed off.

"Wait," I called after him. "Do you know where you're going?"

"No worries," he called, "I can find Roxie."

"He's a pistol," Grandma said almost to herself. Then to me, "I'll drop you off at the cemetery."

"Excuse me?"

"To get Evie's main ingredient. You have to do it since you're the slayer."

"This better not take long." I cringed at what kind of an ingredient we'd find in a graveyard. "What am I looking for?"

"A single white rose mallow," Grandma instructed.

"Ah yes." I nodded. "What?"

"The soul flower," she explained, leading me farther into the scrub desert. "It blooms over graves that a contented spirit has recently visited. Believe me you'll know it when you see it."

"I didn't think ghosts in graveyards were content."

"These aren't ghosts. These are souls who watch over their loved ones, and us. The soul flower is simply a gesture to show they've checked up on us."

I didn't get it. "There's power in a gesture?"

"Of course there is, Lizzie."

If she didn't stop grinning, I was going to smack her.

"What if there aren't any of these flowers?" What if the souls were busy?

We needed a soul flower now. Preferably in the next five minutes.

Grandma tisked. "This is the Aquarius Ranch we're talking about. You can practically feel the love."

The most annoying thing about it was that Grandma was right. I knew she was talking about Neal. But it was true that the Aquarius Ranch held positive energy. I could feel the power and the influence of those who had lived and worked here, especially as we climbed up a low slope and stood on a small overlook at the edge of the mountain.

The moon was bright tonight, shining over the gravestones scattered across the scrubby field. Some were traditional upright tombstones. Other graves were marked with chunks of sandstone or painted rock. Twirling fish, peace signs and even a set of large red lips decorated the graves. It was a place of remembrance and celebration rather than mourning.

Someone had even carved a large totem, with fish and birds and topped by a blazing sun.

"The older, pioneer graves are on the far end," she said. "I don't think you'll make it that far, though. These hippies like to wander, but they always come back."

"Gotcha," I said, already looking for the white soul flower.

"I'll gather the rest of the ingredients. Rachmort will definitely handle Roxie. Let's meet back at the buses in an hour. If I need you sooner, I'll send up a red flare. Head straight this way," she pointed toward the direction Rachmort had headed, "and you'll be back at camp in five minutes."

"Sounds good," I said, moving on to another painted tomb rock.

So it all came down to this—my ancestor and her ability to discover new things *and* write them down. I vowed to keep adding chapters to the manual I'd begun.

"Thanks, Evie," I murmured. "If you could stick around to help with the actual portal, I'd be even more grateful."

I weaved in and out of the tombs, nudging the scrub brush with my Birkenstock sandal, hoping to find the elusive white flower.

It felt surreal to be in a place of positive energy and beauty when so recently I'd been in the gray world of purgatory. In a way, I was glad I'd been sucked down. It was one more world I'd beaten, one more thing I'd survived.

If I could handle myself against Zatar once, maybe I could do it again. Maybe I really could fling a portal at him that would send him to hell for eternity.

I knew I had to try.

Weaving in and out of the graves, I read the inscriptions, loving words about people who had lived good lives.

You saw the positive.

You loved us all.

And on a grave painted with rainbows. *You opened your heart.*

That last one stung. I wished I could be that way. I didn't want to be scared. But with all of the pain and suffering in our world—and in others—how could a person open their heart without getting it ripped out?

I bent down to caress a dried flower on the rainbow grave when I heard Dimitri behind me.

"Where the *hell* have you been?"

Chapter Twenty

Dimitri towered over me, more furious than I'd ever seen him. His shoulders shook and the edge of his jaw could split rocks. "Banshee got your tongue? You had to know I'd come looking for you." He ground out every word. "Now why the hell did you leave?"

Like he was one to talk. "I had things to do." He had to understand what was going on here. I couldn't wait around for Dimitri, not when griffin politics trumped getting my dad out of a bad situation. "Face it. We're going in two different directions right now."

His eyes flared. "That's your decision."

"What?" He couldn't be serious. "You think I have a choice in this?"

If I'd had my say, I'd be on a sunny beach in Greece with Dimitri. He'd be rubbing suntan oil on my back...and perhaps a few other places. But no. I was standing here in a hippie graveyard looking for a flower I'd never heard of in order to send demons to hell using a spell that we weren't even sure worked.

Which was just lovely because Zatar was on his way no matter what.

"This is bigger than us," I snapped. "In fact, I don't even know why I'm standing here talking to you when I have a flower to find."

Dimitri about fell over. "I'm worried sick about you

and you're out here looking for flowers?"

"I'm sorry. I didn't want to do this without you."
But now I couldn't seem to stop.

He sighed. "What do we need?"

A white soul flower."

"This had better be important," he said, scanning
the ground at his feet.

Yeah, I'd already looked there. "It is."

"Grandma again?"

"Something like that."

I kept my eyes on the ground as we walked through
the motley collection of graves. I didn't own my time.
We were on a countdown to a demon attack. Dimitri
was the leader of his griffin clan and he couldn't fritter
around either—tonight or any other night. The stakes
were huge and that meant we didn't have the kind of
choices other people did.

Dimitri moved so close to me we were practically
touching. He'd found another shirt. So now we were
both wearing a large black T-shirt, although I had to
admit he wore it a lot better. "I can't do this if you're
not going to let me be your partner."

"Why do you even want to be my partner? You
don't belong here."

I saw the hurt in his eyes, and I wanted to take it
back. But I couldn't. It was true.

Didn't he understand?

When I'd left him, I'd felt guilt down to my toes.
Now? Maybe it was for the best.

Yes, we had something extraordinary. I'd never met
anyone who could be so purely good and strong, or so
loyal. But that didn't mean he had to give up his life
for me. His tie to me was making him blind to the
differences between our two worlds.

He was here, in this graveyard, instead of taking
care of the family who needed him.

He was a griffin, the leader of his clan and he had to be that. He couldn't change or he wouldn't be Dimitri. He was endangering himself and them by lingering here.

I was a demon slayer. I couldn't back away from that, either. I wanted to be a slayer and a terrible, horrible, guilty part of me didn't want to change any part of my role—even for Dimitri.

I needed to be true to myself. I had a history now, a tradition. My Great Great Great Aunt was a legendary slayer and that was something to live up to.

For the first time in my life I knew who I was, and I couldn't give that up.

And thus, we were at a crossroads that neither of us wanted, neither of us planned. But we couldn't deny the reality of it.

Dimitri knew. I could see the fear behind his fury, and the hurt that had kept him from saying anything else.

"Help me find a white flower," I said, retreating farther into the cemetery. Grandma said I'd know it when I saw it.

We crunched through the scrub in silence. The graves were older back here. I saw the worn wooden tips of pioneer markers.

"Look," I said, working to keep my voice steady, "I know you're leaving."

We were fooling ourselves if we thought this was going to last, really last.

I saw the shock in his eyes and quietly broke his gaze. It was too painful to see him like this. So instead I focused on the bright painted tombstones of people who had already lived fully and loved deeply.

My gut churned. It wasn't always fun to be practical, to be able to recognize things for what they were. I wanted Dimitri with all my heart, but I could see the bare facts of the matter too.

As much as we don't want to admit it to ourselves, sometimes love just isn't enough.

I dropped my hands to my sides. "I love you, Dimitri." He had to see that. I needed him to understand. "I'm not going to let you destroy your family for me." His sisters deserved better. "I love them too much."

He closed the space between us, his anger gone. "I love them too. And I don't see why I have to choose."

"You can't have it both ways. You have to leave me." I could feel his heat as he stared down at me. Shards of moonlight fell hard on the angles of his face.

He was so beautiful, so perfect it almost hurt. "I know you have to move on."

People left. That was life. There was always a reason. I'd left my friends and my co-workers in Atlanta without a word, not a single goodbye, when I became a demon slayer. It was simply part of the price. My adoptive family dropped me to an every-other-Sunday obligation as soon as they realized I'd never turn into the perfect country-club daughter. My biological dad hadn't even stuck around to see me come into this world before he'd bolted. Even if I could save him, I had no idea what that meant for my dad and me. No matter how much they were supposed to love you or how much they *should* be there—everyone left eventually.

Dimitri touched my arm. "Look, I'm not your dad."

"Don't pull that b.s. psycho-babble on me. Like this is my dad's fault." He did the best he could, which admittedly stunk, but at least he belonged here. We could try to build something. Dimitri was committed elsewhere, whether he wanted to admit it or not.

His eyes blazed. "It *is* your dad's fault."

"How can you blame my poor sick father for your

issues with the griffins?"

"I told you, I'm handling it."

"Well, you're doing a super job."

Dimitri dropped his head. After a moment, he raised it, his eyes a blaze of green.

"I'm not blaming your father. I'm only saying you weren't like this until your dad showed up. You keep thinking I'm going to leave when to the best of my recollection, *you* took off on me."

Oh, so he should be the one who was mad. Okay, well maybe he did have a point. Still, one night away on a mission he couldn't join me on vs. griffins delivering armor at all hours of the day and night. "You're at war, for heaven's sake!"

"War?"

"You're the leader of your clan!"

He blinked. "No. Dyonne is the leader of our clan."

"You left poor Dyonne in charge?"

"She'd have your tonsils for breakfast if she heard you say that."

Okay, so maybe Dimitri's oldest sister was no shrinking violet, but, "She can't run the Helios clan." The other leaders would tear her up.

"Sexist much?"

"Of course not."

He shot me a superior look. "I don't know what assumptions you made while we were in Greece, but if you think I'm leader of our clan, you're dead wrong. In griffin society, power is passed down through the females. They hold our magic. They chart a clan's destiny. And they rule."

"Get out." It was almost too much to absorb. "They still need you, though." Even if it was just to have *somebody* to rule. Dimitri's clan had nearly died out. It was down to him and his two sisters.

"They need me to sort out their love lives," he

groused. The corners of his mouth tipped up. "You should see yourself right now."

Gaping, no doubt. "Explain, please."

"I'm the last of the Helios clan besides my sisters, right? So I'm the only one available to meet with suitors."

"Suitors?" I repeated. "As in boyfriends?"

"Yes. A formality—and a pain in the butt. I understand that after a lifetime under a demon's curse, my sisters are going to want to go out and have some fun. That is acceptable. But these potential mates are about to drive me off a cliff."

Off a cliff? Not too tragic for a griffin. He'd just shift and fly away.

"What? Are these guys not good enough?" Dimitri's sisters were smart and beautiful and independent—the whole package.

"Alexandro that you met earlier tonight? He breeds horses."

"Diana would love that."

"He paints their hooves and gives them horsey manicures."

"Diana would really love that."

Dimitri wasn't amused. "He and his brother Nicoli used to slip mermaids into the family pool. They hung out with the priests of Bacchus. And now they want to date my sisters?"

"What about the guy out in the desert?"

Dimitri sighed. "Kryptos is an admirer of Dyonne's. He's convinced he can win her over by replacing the family arsenal."

"Girls do like shiny things." Although if I saw Kryptos again, I might tell him to focus on jewelry.

"Do not let him hear you say that or I'll never get rid of him."

He stood tall, the moonlight playing off his

hardened features. "Griffin society is small. Unfortunately not so small that I don't have a battalion of horny goats following me." He sighed. "I suppose it has to be done."

"We're talking about dating, right?"

He nodded, hand to his head.

"I don't know. It sounds like fun to me." He needed to lighten up. "It's not like your sisters have to marry any of these guys," I said. "Right?"

"They will eventually," he said with such brotherly despair that I smiled despite myself.

"I think it's sweet that these guys are willing to travel halfway around the world to ask your permission." Especially when some human guys thought email was an appropriate way to ask a girl out.

"Yes, well, remember how Diana and Dyonne sucked up all that power form the altar in Greece?"

"I was there." A bit beat up at the time but present nonetheless.

He tucked a strand of hair behind my ear. "Power is very attractive to griffins."

No kidding.

The realization bloomed. "Wait, so you're saying your sisters are two of the hottest women going in the griffin world?"

"You are painfully correct."

I couldn't help smiling. Go Diana and Dyonne! They deserved it.

His fingers brushed my cheek and my insides went gooey. "Hmm…now if power is incredibly sexy to griffins," I began as he ran his fingers through my hair. "How do you feel about demon slayer power?"

His lips skimmed my ear. "Delicious. As is the particularly delectable demon slayer behind it."

I felt my toes curl. "You're just saying that because you want to get into my pants."

He tipped his head toward mine. "Is it working?"

"Maybe."

"I've known it from the beginning, Lizzie," he said, caressing my cheek. "You're powerful not because you've learned how to throw a switch star. It's because of what's in here." He touched the place above my heart. "What's inside of you, who you are."

"I could never lead a clan."

"But you led Roxie on a quest to find Zatar. You led Rachmort out of purgatory."

"Dad got me in there."

"It's okay to ask for help. That's what I've been trying to tell you."

"I don't know what's going to happen in a few hours." Nobody could help me create the portal to fling the dreg out of Roxie and if I couldn't save her, I'd be even more alone when Zatar showed up."

Dimitri burned with intensity. "You have more power than you know. And you can do this."

"I can't even keep my hair from turning purple."

The side of his mouth tugged into a wry grin. "Your new hair is hot."

Ha. "It's awful."

My heart sped up as pulled me toward him, slowly—deliberately. "It's such a turn-on."

Impossible.

His kiss drove straight through me. I gripped his shoulders, knowing exactly what this man meant to me. And how it would hurt to let him go. I tipped my mouth up to his again and again as his arms closed around me. When we came together like this, without trying to plan or worry or think about tomorrow, it made everything seem possible.

"Wait, stop," I pulled back. "We have to find the soul flower." I ducked out of his embrace, grabbing his hand. "Come on. It's a gift from a visiting spirit."

"Then the spirits need to give us a break," he said, running his fingers through my hair.

"I can't believe you actually like my violet hair," I said, bending to look at the base of a fallen wooden marker.

"Now that it's short, I can't keep my hands off it."

"I look like Frenchie from *Grease*," I protested.

"From Greece?" he asked, letting me go as far as I could stretch the space between us, and then drawing me close. "Do I know a Frenchie?"

I bent to search near another dry and crumbling wooden monument. "Forget it."

Two seconds later, I ended up back in his arms. I'd give the man points for persistence.

"You don't look like this Frenchie," he murmured. "You look like a wild woman." His mouth claimed mine in a hot, wet kiss. "And I would never," he nipped my lower lip, "never leave you."

"Dang. We gotta find a flower."

"Because...?" he said, nibbling my ear, knowing he was driving me crazy.

"Because then we have a few minutes alone."

Grandma said she'd send up a red flare when they needed me. In the meantime, I needed to gather my strength. Right?

"There's a flower," Dimitri pointed.

Holy moley. White flowers carpeted the hippie cemetery behind us. Their tiny white petals bloomed full and lush in the moonlight.

"Looks like hippies really do believe in free love," Dimitri said, leading me over to a small copse under a scraggly pine tree.

"I can't believe dead people are helping you get laid."

He nibbled my chin. "It's more than that and you know it." The space between us practically sizzled.

"Open yourself up to magic, Lizzie. You say you believe in it. Now let it touch you."

I snorted, not sure if I was touched or turned on.

Tears welled in the corners of my eyes. He wanted to be here with me, in this broken-down hippie commune with a demon on the way. He'd rather argue with me in a cemetery than sit on the veranda of his villa in Greece. And he'd helped me find the magic to bring me to him.

He loved me.

Dimitri pulled me down into the flowers with him. On top of him, legs straddling him, he caught me in a searing kiss. His hands slid down me, drove us together, rocked me against him. I poured all my love, my fear, my sheer desire for him into that kiss.

He made a low sound in his throat, raw and wild, as he rolled me under him. Dimitri never did anything halfway and I loved him for it.

And he loved me.

Not because we understood where this was going or how it would work, but because he needed me. I needed him.

Oh God, did I need him.

I reveled in the feel of his weight on me. He was hot and sleek as I stripped him, peeling the black T-shirt over his head, my mouth closing over his nipple, feeling him tense and shudder.

Breathing hard, he flicked open the button at the top of my leather pants and eased them down my hips. We were done sparring, finished pretending that we didn't know what we wanted.

We'd stripped away our excuses, gave up our defenses. There was only pure need and desire.

"Now," he said, driving into me. I looked into his eyes, the intensity in his expression raw and wild. Muscles tight, breath coming in pants, he drove into me over and over again. I wrapped my legs around him and urged him harder, deeper.

Yes. I threw my head back.

Ribbons of pleasure spiraled through me and I savored the sheer, rich pleasure of the moment, of being with this man. Of taking what I needed with no excuses, no regrets. No thought of what should be, reveling in what was real and good and *mine*.

Afterward, we cuddled under the weathered pine at the edge of the cemetery.

My head rested on his bare chest. We'd dressed again, but I'd asked him to forgo the shirt. Not that I needed another one. I just liked the skin-to-skin contact for as long as I could have it.

"You really think I can do this?" I asked, twirling the soul flower in my fingers. Grandma's signal should come at any time. When she sent up a red flare, my time with Dimitri here would be over.

He ran his knuckles across my collar bone, down my arm. "Yes, you can," he murmured into my hair, "I'm just waiting for the day when you expect it too."

I tipped my head up for a perfect kiss.

"Oh for the love of Pete," Grandma hollered, barreling across the field, kicking up a small dirt storm behind her.

Like she had room to talk.

"I sent up the flares ten minutes ago." Her eyes narrowed. "I don't even want to know why you didn't see fireworks going off." Her jaw dropped when she noticed the carpet of soul flowers covering the grounds. She shook it off. "Pick a flower. Any flower. Roxie's ready. Evie's ingredients are in place. We just need you."

I grabbed a handful, just to be sure.

CHAPTER TWENTY-ONE

The witches had been busy.

Grandma led us past the buses and back behind the cabin. Red lanterns blazed alongside torches set into the ground every few feet. An open field stretched at least fifty yards, ending in a hill filled with rusting hippie sculptures and scraggly clumps of grass. Torches scattered over the hillside as well, illuminating it in circles of light and valleys of shadow.

Frieda jogged toward us, holding her torch like it was the final lap of the Olympic relay. "You all set, Lizzie?"

Frankly, I had no idea. "I have the flower, I said, holding it out to her.

Plus about a dozen spares.

"I'll take that," Ant Eater plucked it out of my hand and stuffed it into a big, messy ball she was carrying.

"What is that?" I asked, trying to see. The gold-toothed witch hadn't bothered with light.

"Your hand looks like shit," she replied.

No kidding.

Chessie, the medical witch, rushed up to me.

"Don't tell me you know about vox burns." The woman had an incredible store of random knowledge, but this was pushing it.

"Doesn't matter what caused it," she said, opening

up a tube of something with her teeth. "It's how you treat it."

She slathered ointment onto my hands while the witch behind her cut bandages and tape.

"Listen up," Grandma said, turning me toward the field. "We have Roxie setting up over by the weed barrels."

So it was marijuana!

"You plug her with Evie's portal device. The same time you do it, you focus—really focus—use every thought you have to send her where you want her to go."

"Which is?""Here!" Frieda said, jogging out across the field. I had no

idea where she was going until she stopped over a large pile of mattresses and pillows. "We didn't want to put torches too close to the bedding," Frieda called, "but just aim."

"Okay," I said, fixing the spot in my mind. "So I wing Roxie into the pile of fluff. What do we do when the dreg comes flying out?" If we didn't have light, we wouldn't be able to see it or capture it.

"I do pretty good in the dark," Dimitri said, "I'll set up next to the landing zone."

Which meant I really couldn't miss.

I flexed my bandaged hands. They felt a lot better. "Thanks, Chessie."

"I'll stand by with torches," Frieda added. "I have a whole committee."

"I can't believe we don't have more flashlights," I mused. Until I lost it, I'd kept my Maglite with me at all times.

"Yeah, well we don't have time to go to the store," Grandma said.

"And," Neal piped up from somewhere behind me, "flashlight batteries aren't good for the planet,"

"Neither is a demon invasion," I shot back.

Grandma interrupted before I could show the hippie a close-up version of a switch star. "Just be glad we had time to throw together your portal recipe." She turned, "Now where is that portal recipe? Battina?"

The library witch shuffled up, her orange Kool-Aid hair pinned up in a loose bun. She held out a handkerchief-wrapped stink bomb.

"That smells like horse poop."

"It is horse poop," she said, unwrapping it into my injured hand.

"Urkle," I fought the nausea crawling up the back of my throat.

"Technically," Battina continued, "its manure mixed with herbs. Would you like to see your Great Aunt's recipe?"

Did she even need to ask me that?

Frieda held the light. I held the dung as I examined my Great Aunt's notes.

Evie's Best Portal Charm

Mix eight parts horse dung with one part mint

Yeah, well I didn't smell any mint. I could see it, though, threaded in the dung.

One part garlic strewn with salt

One Mugwort leaf

One soul flower

Mix well and apply straight over the heart. Keep back at least six feet as impact winds will be extreme. Remember to utter the words: Demons Out.

I like that. Nice and simple.

Demons out.

As for the rest of it?

"What's a Mugwort leaf?" I asked.

"Anti-demonic," Bettina shrugged. "I always carry them. Now add the soul flower."

I closed Evie's book and shoved it into the back of

my pants for safekeeping. Then I used my thumb to split a hole into the manure ball. Ant Eater handed back my flower. "Why horse dung, Evie?" I muttered to myself.

Bettina shrugged. "We could probably use modeling clay or some kind of epoxy these days, but why mess with the formula?"

Why indeed?

Because Battina didn't have to fling horse poop.

Well you could bet that if we survived tonight, I'd be developing my own recipe. I covered the flower with the muck, shaping it like a baseball. "Is everybody ready?"

We had less than two hours before Zatar showed up and we needed to know if this was going to work.

"There should be plenty of jars for you, Dimitri," Grandma said. "We put out two dozen. Six by the mattresses. The rest are scattered in the field, in case you need one on the fly. Here are two more to keep on you."

"We're only talking about one dreg, right?" I wanted to be clear here. Evie's portal would strip the dreg that had infected Roxie.

"Yeah. One dreg," Grandma said. "But it's good to have a backup plan, right?"

Oh my word. Was I actually having an impact on these people?

Dimitri planted a kiss on my head. I turned and gave him one on his shoulder before he trotted out to the pile of mattresses on the far end of the field.

I hadn't even asked him how he felt about battling a demonic dreg. We'd just assumed it was his role. It tugged at me, this whole idea of Dimitri, always stepping in. What did he really know about demonic dregs? He'd simply acted when I was in trouble. What he'd done out of love and desperation had suddenly become his job. I just hoped he was up to it.

And while I was wishing for things, I said a small prayer that this plan would actually work.

Roxie emerged from the cabin, wearing a mass of pillows and blankets. A woman with gray dreadlocks chased behind her, fluffing her padding. It had to be Neal's other flower-power buddy. I'd give them points for enthusiasm.

"So there you are." Roxie gave me the stink eye.

Yeah, well we needed less grumbling, more magic portaling. Although I supposed the other slayer deserved a break. She'd made it this far.

"Hold still while I banish you to the other side of the field." And get rid of that dreg.

"Hold up, Lizzie!" Dimitri called. He'd grabbed a torch and headed for the landing zone.

Sticks and dirt now topped the mattresses and pillows.

"Oh hey, Lizzie!" Pirate called as Flappy dragged an entire tree across the field. "I taught him to fetch!"

That would require Pirate having the upper body strength to throw a tree. But I didn't have time to explain it to my dog. Pirate had been much better at "keep" than he'd ever been at bringing things back.

"Take the sticks off the pile," Dimitri said, pulling some of the bigger ones off himself.

We needed to get moving here.

Pirate ran in circles around him. "But sticks are crunchy and soft. You can use sticks. It's like a nest."

"Pirate," I admonished as Dimitri pulled the last of the logs off the landing zone. He wouldn't be able to do much about the dirt. It clouded in puffs around him as he worked.

Roxie frowned. "You need to get a better handle on your animal."

If she only knew. "Hush up and let me throw horse

poop at you."

Hmm...perhaps this would be fun after all.

"Ready?" I asked the witches as Roxie moved into position over an "X" on the ground.

Dimitri gave me the thumbs up as Flappy and Pirate trundled into the woods, off on another adventure.

The witches backed away. The smart ones stayed behind me. This probably wasn't the time to tell anyone that I stunk at softball.

The bandages didn't help either—or the burns.

"One," I said, testing the weight of the portal charm.

"Two." I drew back to fire.

I focused hard on the pile of softness at the end of the field. Thoughts of Dimitri crept into my consciousness and I immediately shut them down. No. Think about the spot at the end of the field. The soft spot. The spot where Roxie must land. See it. Feel it. I could almost taste the dirt on those mattresses.

"Demons out!" I hit Roxie smack dab over the heart and she hurtled backward. Wind tore at my hair and the kickback sent me flying.

I landed on my butt in the dirt. Roxie hit halfway between me and the mattresses. She rolled sideways, in obvious pain as the dreg spun out into the night.

"Catch it!" I scrambled to my feet.

The dreg skipped sideways like a tiddly-wink. No telling what it could do to one of the witches—or to Roxie if it entered her a second time. I couldn't touch it.

Dimitri raced for the dreg, jar in hand. The plastic disk caught in midair as if on an invisible wind. It heaved and morphed into a flying insect.

Oh heck.

It dive bombed straight at Dimitri. He met it halfway, jar in hand as it zagged around the trap and burrowed into his neck.

He gave a hoarse cry.

I started running.

"Lizzie, no!" Grandma hollered, hot on my heels.

I couldn't touch it, but I had to grab it somehow. I couldn't let that *thing* take Dimitri.

He dropped to his knees. I watched in horror as Dimitri dug the creature out of his own flesh. Wide eyed and panting, fingers bloody, he mashed it into the jar and twisted the lid.

"Dimitri!" I fell to my knees next to him, examining his wound. It was raw and ugly. "Are dregs poisonous?" I asked Grandma. We knew what they did to demon slayers, but what would happen to a griffin or a witch?

Grandma tightened the lid on the dreg. It screeched and flung itself against the glass. "I don't know. I didn't see anything in Evie's diary about it."

"But you didn't read Evie's entire diary," I said, probing the wound.

"Ouch," Dimitri pushed my hands away. "I feel fine."

"No, you don't." His eyes looked glassy and he was still breathing hard.

I reached into my utility belt for a healing crystal. Closing it in both hands, I thought about his strength, his love and the devotion this man had for me. The clear stone glowed with pure light.

He closed his eyes, his jaw working as I touched the stone to the wound at his neck. It radiated with positive healing.

"How do you feel?" I asked, amazed as the raw wound began to heal.

"It's better," he said, wonder in his voice as his warm chocolate eyes opened and he touched his fingers to mine.

Roxie towered over us, holding her arm. "I'm fine,

by the way."

"Are you?" Grandma asked.

"No," she grumbled. "Lizzie broke my arm."

"Come here," I said, "I'll fix it." I had another crystal. Although I wasn't sure where the happy thoughts would come from.

"Don't touch me," she said, backing away.

Fine. "I was aiming for the cushions," I said, resisting the urge to apologize. I'd done my best. And it had worked. She was free of the dreg. She could try to be grateful, especially after what had happened to Dimitri.

I didn't know how he was going to defeat the multiple dregs that Zatar was sure to be carrying. Even if we could banish the demon to another dimension, were we doing the dark earl a favor, releasing all of his dregs at once?

"Help me up," Dimitri ordered, trying to stand.

"Sure," I said, taking one side, Grandma on the other. He was at least two-hundred-and-fifty-pounds of pure muscle. I knew. I'd made it my mission to explore as much of it as possible—as often as I could.

We helped Dimitri over to a picnic table by the main cabin. He slumped down onto a bench, not looking like anyone who could face a bunch of dregs in—oh, about an hour.

What were we going to do when Zatar got here?

"Huddle up," Grandma said, as she and the witches took seats and gathered in around us. She slammed the jar on the table, the dreg still battling with the glass sides. "I see one big problem."

"That this thing almost killed Dimitri?" I asked.

"No," she answered, torch light deepening the lines and shadows of her face, "you didn't get your fake Zatar to hell."

Sweat trickled down the back of my neck. "I

focused on the target area. I know I did." The only time my mind had wandered even slightly was to think of Dimitri and I certainly hadn't flung Roxie on top of him so I was pretty sure that was a moot point.

"Then why didn't I go far enough?" Roxie called from the end of the table as Frieda worked to splint her arm with a wooden board and several lengths of gauze.

"I don't know," I snapped. "What were *you* thinking?"

"About killing you," she spat.

"Perfect!" Neal clapped. "That's exactly what a demon would be thinking."

"Who invited him?" I demanded.

"Pipe down," Grandma ordered. "Everybody. Now listen. We know Lizzie didn't get enough power on her throw. It's probably because she throws like a girl."

"Hey—" I began. Oh frick. What was I saying? It was true. "You think that's the problem?" If so, I didn't know what we could do about it.

Grandma planted her elbows on the picnic table. "Evie's portal notes don't say you have to do the throwing by hand, so," she said, like a sergeant rallying the troops, "we build you a sling shot."

"You think I'd be better with a sling shot?" This is what I got for spending my childhood throwing tea parties for my stuffed animals. I had absolutely no outside skills.

I turned to Creely, the engineering witch. "Can you build a sling shot? One that *I* can use?"

She opened her mouth and closed it, nostrils flaring. "Goodbye," she said, rushing out of the circle.

"If you need help, the dragon can haul wood for you!" I called after her.

Heavens to Betsy. I was getting a sling shot.

Rachmort burst into the circle. "I've been testing the demon dust you and your father acquired in purgatory."

"And?" He was talking too slow.

"It's fake, laced with fillers. It won't hold a demon. The best it will do is slow him down."

"Okay, well then we'll sprinkle it around the target area." I needed all the help I could get. "Now what do we do about Dimitri?"

"Stop talking about me like I'm not here," he grunted through the pain. "I told you I'd do this."

Yes, well, wanting to do it and having the physical strength were two different things. I'd just demonstrated that myself.

But Dimitri was our only option. None of us could handle a dreg. Now he was going to get hit bad. I didn't know what to do about that.

"Come on," Grandma said, breaking up the meeting. "Zatar will likely be here within the hour. Frieda, go see if you can help Creely, even if that means keeping the rest of us out of her hair. Everybody else—we need more jars."

"Let's get you back to the bus," I said to Dimitri. At least he could rest up and recover there. "No need to be the hero right now." He'd be one soon enough.

"No," he said, wrapping his arms around his chest as if he were cold. A chill—or something worse— passed through his body and he cringed. "I have to stay close in case something happens."

I wanted to argue, but he was right. We needed him. "Okay, well sit tight. I'm going to double check the portal charms." Plus I could tell Dimitri didn't want to be babied, which was hard because there was nothing more I wanted to do than hold him close.

Men.

Out near the field, Bettina opened her cooler of portal charms and I inserted soul flowers into the center of each. We had six shots, which should be more than enough.

There would only be time for one.

Creely hunched in the middle of a circle of witches holding torches. She hammered a length of wood, barking orders to at least three more witches who were doing the same. It didn't look like a sling shot. It looked like a weapon.

More witches added torches at the edge of the field and sprinkled salt from large burlap bags. Normally, salt is used by witches to ward off evil. I didn't have the heart to tell them that those things wouldn't make a whit of difference to a demon like Zatar.

He was an Earl of Hades, demonic royalty for heaven's sake. I remembered the sheer power and evil he'd thrown at me—that was before he knew I could toss it back.

I watched as Neal helped my father past the cabin. It seemed Dad didn't want to miss this. Well, maybe it was for the best. This could very well be my final battle.

Chapter Twenty-Two

Neal deposited Dad at an empty picnic table before beating a hasty retreat. He'd found Dad a pair of baggy jeans and a green Bob Marley T-shirt.

I slipped onto the bench next to him, our backs to the table. "How are you doing?"

It was a loaded question. Anyone who took one look at him would know he was fading fast. His eyes were red and his body hunched. Shadows formed under his hollowed out cheeks and blood trickled from his nose. He clutched the wooden bench like he was about to fall off.

He was even worse than when I'd found him half-dead by the altar to Zatar.

Dad motioned me closer. "The demon is coming," he said in a garbled voice. The bench under him began to shudder.

"I know, Dad." I reached down and touched his bony shoulder. "Try not to talk."

The last thing we needed was a zombie picnic table.

I took his hands in mine. They were cold and shaking. "I will save you." He had to believe that. I needed to as well. "We *will* beat Zatar. We have a plan."

It was a shaky plan at best, but we'd do what we had to do. We didn't have a choice.

This was the dark time before the dawn, but the sun would rise. It must.

Dad nodded, tears in his eyes.

"It's time," he mouthed.

He was right. I could tell from the expression on Frieda's face as she jogged straight for us. "Break time's over, girlie," she said. "Creely needs you at the machine. Battina is unloading the portal charms and Roxie looks like she's the last pea on the plate."

I squinted at her. "I don't even know what that means."

She shrugged, white plastic earrings swaying. "Then follow me."

This was it. "Bye, Dad." I kissed him on the head before following Frieda out to the field.

On the way out, I saw Max and Roxie emerge from the cabin—laughing. The light from the door fell full on his face which held pure emotion.

It stopped me because I didn't think I'd ever seen Max genuinely happy. I didn't know he was capable.

No question about it, Roxie had powers that went beyond slaying demons.

Frieda nudged me. "Whatcha stopping for?"

"Nothing." She was right. We needed to keep moving. "We have ten minutes according to my watch." I wouldn't bother Frieda with the seconds.

Twenty-eight—in case you were wondering.

I rubbed at my eyes as a wave of exhaustion rolled over me. It was my body's reaction to stress, calm and now more stress. Either that or it was the fact that we were going on nearly twenty-four hours with no sleep. My watch read 4:36 a.m.

The witches lit so many torches it looked like daylight had already come to the field behind the main cabin. A steady wind whipped at the flames.

Dimitri, Max, Grandma and an entire gaggle of

witches stood to my right, positioning dreg jars and going over strategy. Another platoon of witches maintained the torches. Max and Roxie had their own pow-wow going farther back in the shadows.

I stopped short as we came up on Creely. She hitched up a red cowboy boot onto the bottom of her latest contraption. The witch never did things halfway, but this was impressive even for her.

The engineering witch gave me an ear-to-ear grin as she stood in front of a wooden creation the size of a mini van.

"I call this the Charm Flinger 3000," she announced, her green-streaked hair swirling about her face.

It looked like a medieval catapult but there were no wheels. She'd built it on the spot.

The throwing mechanism reminded me of a large spoon. Only this one was basically a blazing sun on a long colorful piece of wood.

"Where did you get that?" I asked, running my hand along it. I knew I'd seen it before. The memory of it tugged at a corner of my brain.

"Don't ask," she said, moving my hand from her precious piece of engineering.

Oh my word. She'd swiped the totem from the cemetery.

Then again, this was war.

"Simple to use," Creely said, beckoning me to the controls. She pulled a rag from the back of her brown leather pants and wiped her hands before she touched the machine. "Pull this lever," she said, giving a fake yank at the wooden stick, "and it releases the rope."

"Which fries the demon," I said. "Now how do I aim it?"

She shook her head. "You don't," she said, scratching her nose. "I didn't have time for a navigation system."

"Well then what good is a spell that misses?" I hated to break it to her, but we probably had one shot.

"Look, we're winging this," Creely explained in the understatement of the century. "The demon is going to show up because we're here. Then we just need to get him in place."

Get him in place? "Have you ever battled a demon?"

She glared at me. "You know I have. Now can it. This will work. Roxie needs to lure the demon to the spot I marked in orange," She pointed out ahead of us and I strained to see an orange beach towel spread over the grass.

"I hate to tell you, but your target can get blown away, or moved, or used to sop up a spill."

"It'll stick," Creely said. "Ant Eater used stakes. We don't have time for anything else. Then your friend Rachmort sprinkled demon dust to help stick Zatar to our spot."

I didn't like this. It was too complex. Simple plans seemed to work best in situations like this.

For example: my favorite—see a demon and then shoot a switch star at its head. Not a lot can go wrong there.

Okay, that's a lie. There were all kinds of things that could go South (and often had) but the basic plan was solid.

For the eight hundred and twelfth time, I wished I could kill Zatar myself and be done with Evie's formula. I didn't like trying to hit it with a charm that needed to be thrown perfectly for it to work. I didn't like having to rely on Creely or Roxie or a machine, or anything else for that matter. And I didn't like knowing that we had one shot at this—one—before the Earl of Hades was on top of us.

Creely slapped at my arm. "Stop stewing. We're going to pull this off."

Cripes. If I had my way, Creely and the rest of the witches wouldn't be anywhere near here when Zatar showed up. Of course this was not The Battle According to Lizzie.

Our choices were limited.

"Roxie knows about this?" I wasn't sure how I felt about using the other slayer as bait. Zatar was amazingly fast. I'd had seconds after he started shooting vox at me down in purgatory. What would happen to her if the demon opened fire?

"Roxie!" I called from across the field.

We didn't want to count on her catching vox like I had. According to Rachmort, it was a rare gift. He'd been her instructor. He'd know if she had it. Then again, he'd trained me too.

Roxie stumbled up next to me, wiping her brow with her good arm. Her platinum hair fell across her dazed eyes. "I don't feel right," she said, her voice scratchy.

"You just had a dreg pulled out of you," I reminded her. It had made me woozy too and I'd only had the thing under my skin for seconds. She'd had hers for nearly a day.

Which brought me back to my point. "Are you sure you're feeling up to this? Creely told me what you want to do." It was gutsy on a good day, much less now. "Maybe you should sit this one out." Max could watch over her. They'd be happy and I wouldn't have to worry about him eating any more dregs.

She looked at me like she had when she thought I was the scourge of the demon slaying world. "You've got to be kidding me. This Zatar is trying to kill me. He put something *inside* of me to make me want to murder my own sister. I'm going to smoke his ass."

Well, when she put it that way.

I nudged her. "Not unless I smoke him first."

That earned me a smile.

"Come on," I said, walking out to the field with her. I had to admit it was reassuring to have another slayer in the fight. Slayers naturally worked in pairs. Twins fought together, trained together, did everything really. It would have been nice to have that.

But what was I saying?

Roxie already had a twin. And what we were about to face was anything but nice.

"Here's your mark," I said, showing her the orange towel on the ground.

She rolled her eyes. "I know my mark. What I want to know is—oh hell."

"What?" I demanded. But I knew.

The earth rolled and shook as the demon emerged from the soil not five feet from where we stood. Zatar's golden hair tangled around the sharp lines and angles of his face as the dirt fell from him like water.

Die.

I drew my last switch star and fired, striking him in the forehead. He raised his face, the star's blades still churning, embedded down to the bone. A lover's grin tickled his lips.

He flicked it away like a gnat. My star smoked and fell from his body, leaving a bloody gash.

The silver and white wings of an angel sprang from the earth as he drove his lizard's body up.

Roxie fired a shot meant to decapitate him. It sliced straight into his neck at a deadly angle. Hope surged within me and then died.

He bled, but nothing more.

And I was out of stars. I felt the soul-crushingly empty holder on my belt as I made a mad dash for the portal charms.

"What the hell are you two doing?" Grandma bellowed.

What had I been doing? I'd been shooting at the thing while it was vulnerable. I'd been trying to kill it, chop its head off, do something besides watch it and wait for it to come out of the ground.

Yes, we established I couldn't kill it—not yet—not without gaining more powers and strength, but I had to try.

Zatar laughed. It sounded like bells to me.

Everyone else fell to the ground, clutching their ears.

Damn, damn, damn. We hadn't planned on that. We hadn't figured out anything. We had no idea what this demon could do.

Roxie had a belt full of Max's red stars. She was still at it, trying the Lizzie method of spending all your ammunition on something you can't kill. Then I saw what she was doing.

She fired again and again, luring Zatar to the impact zone.

The witches rose to their feet. Dimitri too. He and Max stood surrounded by witches with deflector spells, waiting on our signal. Rachmort held steady with them.

They would protect Dimitri as he captured the dregs, and Max as he'd most likely eat them. I'd have to kill Max if he turned.

I wouldn't expect Roxie to do that. Not after what I'd seen at the cabin.

Okay. Every muscle in my body tensed. Maybe we could get through this. "Hang on, Dimitri," I murmured to myself. And hang on Max.

Battina slammed a Charm Spell into the catapult, practically falling sideways as she did it.

"You okay?" I asked. She looked green. All of them

did.

"Damn it." Betty Two Sticks staggered up on my left, her gray crew cut caked with dust. "We spelled this thing to be invisible. That could go to hell if you draw him over here."

"You can barely stand and you're giving me a lecture?" I had to shoot. I couldn't be a demon slayer and not shoot. In fact, maybe it was good I had no weapons left because that's all I wanted to do now. Fire and fire and fire switch stars until I'd finally killed that scourge.

I had the demon in my sights. Just a little more to the left.

Come on, Roxie.

Battina sagged against the machine.

Roxie got him close enough and I shifted the entire catapult a foot forward.

"What the hell?" Battina demanded as I fired.

"Demons out!" I conjured up images of the deepest reaches of hell. Zatar and his dregs could rot there.

The charm spell shot straight at Zatar, hitting him smack in the chest.

It worked!

He screamed as the dregs poured out of him and a silver portal opened up behind him.

Wind swept over the field, carrying dust and debris as the portal I'd created consumed Zatar's earthly body. He shimmered at the edges, but the dregs flew straight out of him—toward us. There were dozens upon dozens—all deadly.

Why were they escaping? Why wasn't Zatar gone yet?

Dimitri sprang into action, but there were too many—even with the witches deflecting for him, they swarmed the tiny group and there was nothing I could do but watch.

The witch in front of him fell, screaming as a dreg burrowed into her. Holy hell.

"Dimitri!" I hollered. A dreg burrowed into his arm. Another landed on his neck as he slammed a jar closed on three of them. They were thick as a swarm of mosquitoes.

Rachmort opened glowing white portals in front and behind Dimitri, catching dregs.

But where would those portals take them?

Or take Dimitri if he fell too far forward or backward?

Maybe once Zatar was gone, they'd lose some of their power.

Zatar fought the suction of the portal, inching away from the silver light.

"What are we going to do if the portal doesn't work?" I demanded.

Battina shook her head and pointed to Roxie. She was running straight for Zatar.

"Get back," I ordered, abandoning my machine and tearing across the field. The portal was weakening. No matter how heroic she wanted to be, she couldn't go down with him.

I had to open up another one. Fat lot of good it would do. I had to do *something*.

"Now I've got you!" The demon lunged forward, seizing Roxie as the portal lost power and snapped closed behind him.

Dregs whipped around him as Zatar rose to his full height.

"Roxie!" Max flung himself at them, tackling Zatar.

Who in Hades tackles a demon?

Max drove a switch star into the demon, causing absolutely no damage beyond a paper cut.

H-e-double-hockey-sticks.

Zatar raised his hand to Max. I had to save them,

right then and there or I was going to have to watch them die.

"Run!" I screamed to them. Zatar zeroed in on me and fired a volley of vox. I dove sideways as Betty Two Sticks took the full brunt of the demon's fury. Her body incinerated as she fell to the ground dead.

I dashed back to the catapult, under a volley of vox. They slapped into the ground behind me, throwing up superheated soil and suffocating sulfur. The back of my throat burned and my eyes watered as I dove behind the machine.

Vox tore through the air, severing the main cord.

I about choked. I needed that cord! This demon could not escape. I could not fail.

Options flew through my mind as I gripped the wooden weapon. Belt? My utility belt was hard leather—no way to tie it up. Hair? I didn't have scissors—or much hair left.

Pirate and Flappy soared overhead. Damn it. I told him no riding the dragon.

At least they were off the ground.

The dregs were everywhere.

The ground rumbled as Rachmort's portal swallowed the dregs. There were too many. It was unstable. Rachmort fell.

"No!"

His face slackened with fear for a split second before he gathered his wits and calmed, falling backward into the abyss. Where had it taken him?

The witches threw spells, as more and more Red Skulls fell to the dregs. I watched in horror as at least two burrowed into Dimitri's arms.

Tears burned the back of my eyes.

Oh my god—Dimitri.

He lowered his head and shifted. Claws erupted from his hands and feet, and thick lion's fur raced up his arms. At least three more dregs tunneled into him as he shifted.

Why was he shifting?

Red, purple and blue feathers cascaded down his back and formed wings as bones snapped and his body expanded. Dimitri lifted his eagle's head and called out into the night.

He had no hands, only paws now. It was suicide. He couldn't catch them this way.

Then I saw the rippling under his skin.

The dregs! His skin flexed as it worked the poison out of him. The dregs crackled from his skin, broken to pieces. He shook them off like nettles.

Did he kill them?

Just then a half dozen griffins shot out of the dark. I recognized Kryptos with his gold and red jeweled necklace, and a pure blue griffin, probably the prince. They surrounded Dimitri and the witches, eating the dregs like candy.

Bad idea. Probably. Hell I didn't know anymore.

But at least Dimitri had survived. My handsome griffin shrieked like an eagle and stomped at the dregs on the ground.

I swallowed a lump in my throat. Okay, so no more dregs. And no more Rachmort.

Max dragged Roxie away from Zatar, but they wouldn't make it far.

Zatar laughed, firing vox straight into the griffins. They dodged his attack with lightening speed. For now. But it was only a matter of time.

He was toying with us. It hit me like a punch in the gut. Zatar knew he had us. He didn't think we could win.

The winds whipped around him, burning out torches and plunging parts of the battlefield into darkness.

Black settled over us like death.

We had to axe this demon. Now.

Before he decided to wipe every one of us from the face of the planet.

The ground shook as I barreled back to the catapult. It vibrated up and down.

"Stop it, stop it," I dove to the base of the catapult in a desperate measure to keep it in place. Zatar hadn't moved. He was still in range. If only I could fix the rope and load it again.

Simple. I needed something simple.

My old life as a preschool teacher had revolved around simple.

Then it hit me. "Pirate!" I hollered. At the same time, I took the zombie rope from the jar at my belt. He poked his end out of the jar. "You gotta help me." I told the quivering rope. "This will save Xavier, who sent you." And I'd sure appreciate it too.

"Please." I stuck him between two pieces of frayed cord. "Hold it together," I ordered.

He bobbed his head and twirled both of his ends around the main firing rope.

The earth rattled, and I fought desperately to steady the gun. I had to hold position. We couldn't lose our aim. We had one more shot at this. One. I strained to see the demon. We had no shot at all if Zatar so much as moved an inch.

Or if he realized we could beat him...

The demon practically dripped with satisfaction as he fired a volley of vox at the witches, scattering them.

"You think this is a game?" I grunted, dragging the oversized sling shot into position between Creely's hastily drawn lines.

Zombie rope twirled part of an end around to see me. "Eyes on the catapult," I told him.

Flappy cruised to a stop, his wings sending dirt flying into my face as Pirate leapt off. "Get behind me."

I loaded the anti-demonic cannonball. Would it be enough? It had to work. We weren't getting a second chance.

Hellfire. I was a demon slayer. I was part angel.

I laid both hands on the demon killer and willed my power into it. I focused my strength, my energy, my goodness. It radiated from my core, down my arms, into my fingertips until the cannon charge glowed with it.

It gleamed strong and white, a beacon of truth. A weapon that would set us free.

Brilliance flowed through me. It filled me up and made me whole. I'd never felt anything like it.

We needed to fire.

"Pirate," I hollered. I couldn't pull the lever on the gun. I didn't know what would happen if I let go of the cannon shot.

"Pirate, I need you to pull the lever," I pointed to the wooden handle. "Use your mouth. Get your teeth around it."

"Yes! It's rescue dog to the rescue." Pirate scrambled up the base of the firing mechanism and fell off as another shock rattled the earth.

"Go," I insisted, stomach sinking when I realized Pirate was too short.

"Flappy!" Pirate danced underneath our salvation. "Flappy, pull the lever!"

Flappy stared at him, tongue lolling.

"Pull Flappy!" I ordered as Pirate dashed behind the dragon and herded him toward the catapult. Flappy turned to face Pirate, his long spiked tail whooshing for the lever, threatening to flatten the cannon—and me.

He was too big, too close. He was going to wreck the entire thing.

"Sit, Flappy!" I hollered.
The dragon wound his bottom around.
"Sit!"
He thundered down onto the lever.

Chapter Twenty-Three

Wood crackled and split. Flappy's butt broke the lever and smashed half the catapult into the ground—but not before it released the portal charm.

"Demon out!" My voice came like a terrible thunder from the heavens. I heard my words and over that, my words commanding in a language I'd never heard. It shook the ground.

As Evie's grand invention hurtled through the air, I pictured the barren wastelands of hell. I fixed my mind on an icy place devoid of love, warmth or affection. A glacial prison in an apocalyptic underworld, where Zatar would be trapped in darkness, chained in despair, bound to that place for eternity.

The missile scored a direct hit to Zatar's heart.

The demon reared back, his lizard's body heaving as the glorious cannon shot launched him into the air. The backlash hit me with hurricane force. I tumbled backward into the dragon, my eyes forced shut by the dirt and debris.

Ice.

Hell.

Damnation.

I drilled the words into my mind, forced them into existence.

"Squark!" Flappy shielded me and I clung to his

scaly body, fighting to rivet my mind, my shock and my utter terror on sending the hell spawn back where he came from.

I saw him in my mind's eye, hurtling across the field and into a gleaming silver portal. I watched him falter, I relished the surprise and fear in his eyes as he fell backward, down, down, down off a sheer cliff, through entire dimensions into an icy vault.

He shattered onto the floor of it, breaking into a million shards.

I sealed him in. Melted it closed. Chained the vault and buried him alive so that no one—mortal or immortal—would ever be able to rouse Zatar again.

And when I was done, I lay against the dragon and simply breathed. There was nothing but the rise and fall of my chest, the air as it rasped dry against the back of my throat. I'd given everything I could and now I simply needed to be.

Until a dog licked the side of my face. "Lizzie!" And danced on my chest. "Lizzie?" Pirate's paws were like tiny pistons on my stomach. "Wake up, Lizzie. Did you see it?"

I reached for him, finding his knobby head before I'd even bothered to open my eyes.

Pirate stood over me, happier than if he'd scored a barrel full of bacon. "Flappy sat!"

"Yeah, buddy. I saw it." I tested my body as I rose to a sit. The air crackled with energy. I could taste the metallic tang. I brought shaking fingertips to my cheek. I truly was part angel.

"Flappy did a trick! You saw it?" He spun around as Dimitri reached down for me. "Did you see it?"

Dimitri, human again, grinned. Dirt smeared his face and chest, his hair stood out in spikes and he looked ready to fall over sideways. "It was amazing," he said, lifting me up, holding me against him.

I buried my face against Dimitri's warm chest. "Are you okay?"

He nuzzled against me. "As soon as Zatar fell through the portal, the dregs left my body," he murmured, as if he knew what I was thinking. "I could feel them dissolve."

"You might want to put some drawers on, buddy," Grandma said behind him.

Yes, well he had managed to find the orange towel we'd used as a demon target. It was wrapped around his very fine waist.

The rest of the griffins weren't so modest. "Did you see me?" Kryptos demanded. His olive skin glistened with perspiration, catching bits of sun as it rose over the horizon. "I destroyed many of your dregs. I am the most worthy."

I snuck a glance. I admit it. The man had assets.

"Dyonne would be lucky to have you court her," I told him.

He gave a small bow.

Turns out that was the wrong thing to say because then I had five more hot naked griffins crowding us.

"I caught seven in the air," Prince Thereos declared. "I am the most worthy!"

A griffin who reminded me a lot of Antonio Banderas pushed his way to the front. "Did you see me?"

Er, I wasn't sure I felt comfortable looking anymore. Yes, it was an embarrassment of riches, like being mobbed by Chippendales, but this was something for Dianna and Dyonne to sort out—I only had eyes for their brother.

Dimitri turned to the griffins. "You came when I called and fought admirably. Now I have one more request," he said, as the witches started wolf whistling. "Can you give me a minute?"

They backed off—for now. Knowing these guys, they were counting to sixty.

Dimitri turned to me, mouth quirked. "I just have one question for you."

"Yes?" I asked, perfectly content to run a finger down his chest.

His arms tightened around me. "How about that date?"

† † †

I left Dimitri with the griffins. It seemed they had much to discuss. I just hoped they'd take time out soon to find some clothes. Some of the witches were starting to take second, third and fourth glances.

Neal didn't even blink. "This is how it was in the old days. We don't need clothes to define us."

"Right-o." I patted him on the back and moved on, knowing there were some things I could never change, namely Grandma, Neal and anybody who had ever hopped on a Harley and decided to follow me anywhere.

"Lizzie," he called after me, purple sunglasses still on his head, "I found your dad asleep next to the picnic table."

Oh geez. "Is he okay?" I asked, trying to see.

"He's fine." Neal patted my arm. "I wanted to tell you I just helped him to his bus. It's the green one. You can't miss it."

"Thanks," I said, appreciation welling up inside me, bordering on affection. I stamped that last part down, even as I closed a hand over his. "I appreciate it. And everything, Neal."

He gave a small smile and a shrug.

Roxie lay on the ground, still coming around. She sat up on her good elbow, groggy.

"I've got you." Max knelt over her, embracing her as if she was the most precious thing he'd ever seen, which was another first for Max. She ran her fingers along his jaw.

"You saved me," she murmured, tears in her eyes. "Nobody saves a slayer."

Max drew her into his arms. "I like to do things differently."

He kissed her long and hard. I'd never known the hunter could embrace anything other than the idea of death.

She pulled away, her lips swollen. "I still hate you for what you did at the Tic-Tac Club."

"I know," Max thundered, moving in for more.

Okay. I turned my back on them. We'd consider her cured of the dreg. I let out a deep breath. That meant Zatar's awful tag-you're-it way of killing slayers was finally broken.

As for Max and Roxie? They'd have to figure out anything else on their own.

†††

Neal was wrong. Dad wasn't on the green bus. He stood next to it. He seemed twenty years younger than when I'd first seen him — his health restored, his shoulders squared. He was whole and healthy, grinning from ear to ear with life. I could tell right away he was cured.

"Dad!" I launched myself into his arms and he spun me around like I was a little girl again.

He winked and set me down. "You did it, Lizzie."

He showed me his hands. They were free of the demon's mark. He'd chosen the light.

"Did you see my angelic powers?" I asked, still not quite believing it.

"Like father, like daughter."

If I smiled any wider my face was going to break. "It was you too, Dad. We did this together."

He laughed and borrowed one from me, "A father-daughter kick-butt team."

Dad grew serious. "Thank you, Lizzie," he said, his eyes traveling over me as if he were trying to capture the memory. "I won't forget this."

"Are you kidding?" I was glad to help him. I'd found my father, that piece of me that had been missing my entire life. This was just the beginning. I had questions about him, his life, angels, you name it. I couldn't wait to get to know him. "You'll fit right in with the Red Skulls," I said, "not that you need to travel everywhere with us." He had a life. "Besides, New Jersey isn't that far." It was the same country. "You could visit." I could spend weekends in California. We had the fairy paths. Or Dimitri and I could make the journeys together—at griffin speed. It wouldn't be quite as fast, but we weren't in a hurry. I could savor this time, this life, with both Dimitri and my Dad.

We'd be one big, happy family.

Dad hovered on the edge of my emotional bubble. "The thing is, Lizzie," he said, choosing his words carefully, "I have a life."

Didn't I know it. "I can't wait to hear about your life. I've never known an angel."

"I'm not sure I want to be an angel," he said, heading back for the green bus, taking the steps two at a time. He emerged with a rainbow knapsack, already packed, courtesy of Neal, no doubt.

Wait. "How could you *not* want to be an angel?" It was his chance to do everything right. He could be the embodiment of love, order, all that was good and true and whole.

Dad hesitated in front of me. "I gave that up, Lizzie. It's not me." He gave the same look my equestrian trainer used to give me after practice: *Do I really have to tell you that you stink?* "Neither is being a dad."

Fear nibbled through me. "You can learn," I said with forced optimism.

He could do this. He couldn't think that he didn't need to be my dad. "I need a dad," I said, heart churning, insides mushing, afraid that by even suggesting he didn't need me that I'd somehow talk him into this idea that was cold and awful and wrong.

My mind swam as he backed away from me.

"I've come all this way," I said. "I've done everything right."

I deserved to have a dad.

"I'm sorry, Lizzie," he said, turning to leave. "I'm not dad material."

"But what about everything you said?" I asked, following him away from the buses, toward the lane, toward Neal's beat up VW bus.

He wouldn't even look at me.

"You said you wanted to get ice cream together. We were going to sit in a park. You said you wanted to get to know me and tell me about angels and life." I stumbled on my words and caught them and plowed forward. "You said you wanted me."

He lowered the driver's side visor and a set of keys fell onto the seat. "I was desperate Lizzie. I lied. It's how the world works."

I stood numb, watching him retrieve the keys. I'd saved his life and his soul.

"What happened with you and Zatar?" Why did he lie?

"Look," he said, jingling the keys, "Zatar needed to siphon some power. He paid me good. It was a living, right? But then he got greedy and I was in trouble."

"You sold your power?" Why would anyone sell a gift? Having power isn't easy. Responsibility is never easy. But it was who my dad and I were. What we were born to be.

"I don't want it. It's not me." He held the door open, regarding me as if I were a clueless child that wasted his time with silly questions and made up fairy tales. "You're smart, Lizzie. You'll do fine without me."

"I wanted a dad," I said, my voice so small I barely heard it.

He looked at me as emotionless as if this were a business meeting and I was an associate and I hadn't just followed him across the country and down into purgatory and out to Neal's bus. His mouth twitched with what might have been regret. "I don't want a daughter."

He slid into the VW, closed the door and drove out of my life.

I felt it most in my hands. They shook as tears flowed down my cheeks. I stood in a swirl of hurt and betrayal and soul-shattering loss.

He meant what he'd said.

My dad was gone.

CHAPTER TWENTY-FOUR

I didn't seek out Dimitri. Or Grandma. Or even Pirate. I didn't need anyone. Shock and hurt thundered through my body as I put one foot in front of the other—alone.

Slow and deliberate, I placed a shaking hand on the handrail of my red school bus, climbed the stairs and shivered my way to the soft bed in the back.

I clutched the pillows to my face, sobbing into them as if that would take the hurt away. And somehow in the midst of it, I fell asleep.

"Lizzie!" Pirate's toenails clattered down the aisle. "Lizzie?" The soft weight of him pulled at the covers as he landed next to me. A wet nose invaded the dull ache around my head. "You okay?" He swiped a warm tongue over my cheek. "I'm a dog. I can sense when you feel sad."

"Come here." I reached for Pirate as he tried to turn in his usual two circles before lying down. I caught him mid-turn, which always screwed him up. He twitched his back legs as I drug him up against me.

In the distance, I could hear the disco beat of "Celebration." That was a new one.

I buried my nose against Pirate's wiry back fur. The witches had earned their right to let loose.

He squirmed. "You know there's a party going on

out there."

"I know." I didn't feel like celebrating.

"I can help you," Pirate said, standing up so I was faced with a dog butt.

"You can't." I rolled away. My eyes itched. My head hurt from crying. Nobody could help me but my dad and I wasn't even sure I wanted someone like him in my life anyway.

"Your phone buddy can help you," Pirate said, his tags clanking as he jumped down onto the floor.

"Who?" I asked, rubbing my eyes. They were swollen to the size of tennis balls, no doubt.

Pirate blinked. "Someone's been calling you while you were sleeping."

Maybe it was my dad. Hope flickered, painful as it was. I fumbled in the back of my utility belt for my cell phone. I clicked on the screen.

Hillary Brown.

I clicked to the next call.

Hillary Brown.

In fact, it was like a parade of one Hillary Brown after another.

I clicked the button to return the call. What would it hurt? Maybe I should just tell her everything. Then I could go through all of the rejections at once.

Maybe it would hurt less that way.

I didn't know how it could hurt more.

"Hi, Mom." I heard my voice crack as she answered.

"Lizzie," she sounded surprised—and alarmed.

"What?" I asked, defenses at the ready.

"You called me mom." She responded with warmth, wonder and a bit of voice cracking herself. Being Hillary, she rallied. "I had a feeling you were having a hard time. Are you okay?"

I drew a shuddering breath. "A lot's been going on

lately. I'm fine. But—" how could I say it? "—you may need to brace yourself."

"Okay," she said, some of the crispness returning to her voice.

"You may not want to see me." She'd been watching over my old condo, planting bulbs, getting the newspaper. She'd been maintaining a life that wasn't mine anymore.

"Honey, no matter what, I always want to see you."

Tears flooded my eyes and dropped onto my pants leg. I was afraid to speak, or she'd know.

"Lizzie?" She paused. "Lizzie, come home."

"I'll try, Mom."

"I'll be waiting."

††††

I laid back and stared at the chipped paint on the ceiling of the bus. I was used to knowing what to do. I was the one who always had a plan. Now? I felt so lost.

Eventually, I forced myself to roll out of bed and join the ranks of the living.

I thunked down the front stairs of the bus, and saw Neal had been busy. He'd plastered the outside of my bus with messages scrawled in chalk. Heaven forbid he use paper—recycled or otherwise.

Wake up, sleepyhead!

Oh so Neal had seen me sleep.

Festival 2-nite!

That last word was worse than nails on a chalkboard.

Special events!

They'd better not involve weed.

No use stewing. Even I was getting tired of my mood. And Pirate had already wandered off somewhere, no doubt with Flappy. I grabbed the only clean thing I had left—the red wrap dress from the Ann Taylor outlet.

What the heck? It was a party.

I showered in an eye-searing yellow, orange, blue, purple, you-name-it paisley psychedelic contraption. It featured a hemp rope and pure (read: cold) rain water. I let my hair dry naturally while I swiped on some lip gloss, slinked on my new dress and headed for the party. I had to admit the dress made me feel better. It hugged my curves in the right places and as the lady in the dressing room said, 'red brings you luck in love,' I'd sure take that.

The Birkenstocks stayed on the bus as I picked my way barefoot past the prickly brush, keeping to the sandy soil. The late afternoon sun shone warm on my shoulders.

As I neared the cabin, I could see the witches and the griffins, along with Roxie and Max standing quietly in a circle. When I drew closer, I realized it was the memorial ceremony for Betty Two Sticks and Lazy Rita. The news lay heavy in my stomach. I hadn't realized Rita was gone.

I swallowed and kept walking. This was war. This was destruction on a fundamental level. I almost felt selfish in my misery when those two witches had lost so much more than I.

Dimitri and Frieda opened up for me as I eased into the circle. The power of the witches ebbed over the small clearing by the picnic tables as we said our final goodbye.

When it was over, Dimitri squeezed my hand. "I have a surprise for you."

"What?" I asked, taken back by his bemused expression.

He'd changed out of his orange towel, which was a shame. In fact, my hunk of a shape-shifting griffin now wore black dress pants and a dark blue shirt. They fit like they were made for him. And how he'd kept a crease for three thousand miles was beyond me.

"Eee," Frieda threw her arms around me.

I hugged her soft, bony frame. "Okay…what's up with you?"

When I'd extricated myself from the witch, Dimitri took my hand and led me toward the red cabin.

"What's going on?" I asked, tucking a lock of lavender hair behind my ear. I was still getting used to how short it felt.

He opened the door to the cabin. "It's time for our date."

Shocked, I looked up at my handsome griffin.

"Go on." He nudged me in the door.

Inside, the yellow-painted room was empty, save for a fold-out table covered with a white towel. Two chairs draped in hemp ribbon clustered around it and two wine glasses sat on top.

He'd even found a bottle of Santorini wine. Greek script curled around the blue label.

"A gift from the griffins?" I asked as Dimitri held out my chair.

"No." His eyes sparkled. "I've been saving this for a long time." His mouth quirked. "In fact, I bought it the first time I wanted to take you on a date."

"In New Jersey?"

"In Memphis. About a week after I met you."

"Aww…" Frieda simpered, digging into her white fringe purse. "Where's my camera?"

"Out," Dimitri walked over to the cabin door and closed it on a crowd of nosey witches.

I couldn't help grinning. "We're never going to get rid of them, you know."

Dimitri wet his lips, his movements stiff. "I don't want to."

He poured the wine into my glass. It was Nykteri, a Santorini white. A few drops sloshed onto the table, which was very un-Dimitri-like. His hand shook slightly as he poured his own glass. It tickled me to think he'd be nervous for a date, and it warmed me to know how much this meant to him as well.

He dropped into his seat. "To beginnings," he said, holding up his glass. We clinked our glasses and I savored the dry peachy notes of the wine.

"It's really good," I told him, noticing he hadn't even taken a sip.

His eyes found the floor before they found me again. "I was going to wait, but I have to do this now."

The door opened a crack. He ignored it. Or maybe he didn't notice. Dimitri knelt down on one knee and I really didn't want to believe what I thought was going to happen next.

My loyal, strong griffin knelt in front of us with an expression that nearly shattered me. "From the first time I met you, I knew you were special, but I never knew you'd come to mean everything to me. I understand our life isn't easy and it isn't always pretty, but I do know that I can't imagine my life without you in it. I would *never* leave you. You keep thinking I want land or power or all these other things when, Lizzie, all I've ever wanted is you."

Tears flooded my eyes and I looked at him and I knew that this was the purest, surest, most wonderful kind of love he could give. And it was more than I could have ever hoped to receive. I was overwhelmed and humbled and blessed.

His hand dug into his pocket and, shaking, drew out a perfect silver ring. "Lizzie, will you marry me?"

I swallowed, nodded and cried some more. "Yes," I whispered as he hugged me tight, "yes."

The biker witches cheered.

✝✝✝

That night, we sat around the campfire. Me cuddled with Dimitri. Max and Roxie, a deliberate yard apart. And Grandma with Neal. We'd deal with those two later. The rest of the Red Skulls were content to lounge around with forty-ouncers in paper bags. Recyclable, of course.

I held my hand out in front of me, letting my silver engagement ring sparkle in the light of the fire. Silver accents like sun rays set off a gorgeous diamond.

"It was my mother's," he said, his breath on my ear as we admired the way it shone. "I know she'd want you to have it."

I lowered my hand and turned back to him. "What about Dyonne and Diana?"

He traced his hands down my arm and back to the ring. "They wanted you to have it too."

"They knew?" I asked, surprised.

He kissed the soft spot at the back of my neck. "From the moment they met you."

I nudged against him. "I can't believe you proposed on the first date."

His voice betrayed a smile. "You're the one who said 'yes.'"

I did. And I'd meant it. I'd never stop saying 'yes' to this man.

Neal plopped down next to me. "Lookie here," he said, holding out a half-weaved wreath of poppies. "I can make you a wedding tiara."

"Oh you know, as lovely as your place is," I glanced out over the sagging hulk of his VW van, "I don't think I'm going to get married here."

Grandma slapped her thigh. "Of course not. This isn't your home."

"Home?" My stomach sank. Grandma had a point.

Hillary would want the country club.

Grandma held up her drink. "We could hold it at Big Nose Kate's. Get those beer can cozies with your names on it, nice and big."

"No, no no," Frieda butted in. "We need class." She spread her arms like a visionary. "Think taffeta!"

This wedding was going to kill me.

"And little stuffed doves," Frieda mused.

Maybe I should let them fight it out. Then I could have a hippie biker witch country club wedding, complete with griffin bridesmaids and a dragon pulling the wedding carriage.

Dimitri rubbed my arms. "Are you sure you know what you're getting yourself into?" he asked, the smile evident in his voice.

I snuggled against him, savoring his warmth and protection. Knowing my luck a demon invasion would break out during the vows. "I wouldn't have it any other way."

MY BIG FAT DEMON SLAYER WEDDING

BY ANGIE FOX

Lizzie Brown is about to have the destination wedding her dreams. But as this former preschool teacher knows, being a demon slayer makes everything more complicated. The vengeful Earl of Hell is still on her tail. And now it seems that one of the guests at the eccentric, seaside mansion is possessed and trying to kill her. Maybe she should just elope.

The groom, studly shape-shifting griffin Dimitri Kallinikos, vows to protect her at all costs. Yet even he is acting suspiciously. And minions of the devil are popping up everywhere. Now Lizzie must protect her socialite mother, her Greek in-laws and her grandmother's gang of biker witches—all of whom are convinced they know what's best for her, and her big day. As the wedding draws closer, Lizzie has to learn who is behind the attacks—and fast—or risk losing everyone she loves.

Coming July 1, 2013!

ABOUT THE AUTHOR

Angie Fox is the *New York Times* bestselling author of several books about vampires, werewolves and things that go bump in the night. She claims that researching her books can be just as much fun as writing them. In the name of fact-finding, Angie has ridden with Harley biker gangs, explored the tunnels underneath Hoover Dam and found an interesting recipe for Mamma Coalpot's Southern Skunk Surprise. (She's still working up the courage to try it).

Angie earned a Journalism degree from the University of Missouri-Columbia. She worked in television news and then in advertising before beginning her career as an author. Visit Angie at www.angiefox.com

32166185R00176

Made in the USA
Lexington, KY
10 May 2014